About

G000167943

As Professor of Philosophy at University College Dublin, Patrick Masterson enjoyed teaching both young full-time and mature part-time students. As president of both University College Dublin and, later, the European University Institute in Florence, he acquired broad, first-hand, and practical experience of issues that can convulse the tranquillity of the groves of academe!

Besides his many academic publications, *St Chinian University Comes of Age* is his second novel. He spends his time now between Dublin and a village close-by St Chinian in France.

PATRICK MASTERSON

ST CHINIAN UNIVERSITY COMES OF AGE

Vanguard Press

A CIP catalogue record for this title is
available from the British Library.

ISBN 978 1 80016 196 2

*Vanguard Press is an imprint of
Pegasus Elliot MacKenzie Publishers Ltd.*
www.pegasuspublishers.com

First Published in 2021

**Vanguard Press
Sheraton House Castle Park
Cambridge England**

Printed & Bound in Great Britain

Dedication

In memory of my beloved Frankie and for Rosemary, Laurence, Lucy, and Naomi.

This opening quatrain of W.B. Yeats' poem, *News for the Delphic Oracle*, anticipates perceptively the prevailing atmosphere at the University of St Chinian.

There all the golden codgers lay
There the silver dew
And the great waters sighed for love
And the wind sighed too.

The University of St Chinian and its personnel are all creatures of the imagination. Any similarity to living persons, however interesting, is fortuitous.

TABLE OF CONTENTS

CHAPTER ONE
Trouble Brewing

The February meeting of the Academic Council of the University of St Chinian was edging to a close in the comfortable, centrally heated council chamber. It had been, as usual, an unremarkable collective exercise in rubber-stamping routine decisions, and enjoying opinionated and, often, rather wicked interjections.

Its members, of course, like to portray the Council to the wider public as a judicious forum, where the communal wisdom of the assembled professors of the university selflessly illuminates and promotes its various noble academic objectives and aspirations. More realistically, they recognise that it is a somewhat inconvenient, but strategically necessary, gathering of academics (and a few token students) where members can keep an eye on each other and, if necessary, frustrate those ambitions of colleagues which might pose a threat to their own. It also functions as a theatre of light relief where notoriously incompatible personalities can wage their long running campaigns of academic guerrilla warfare.

This afternoon was no exception. The meeting had enjoyed a particularly satisfying vitriolic exchange between two well-known adversaries, Simone Blondel — professor of social administration, and Jacques Lamy — professor of political theory. The latter had denounced Simone as a crypto-communist agitator for her support of compulsory trade union membership for all academics. She returned the compliment by describing him as a capitalist lackey, pedalling obsolete liberal *laissez-faire* slogans, in his attempt to argue that 'Brexit' and 'Make America Great Again' indicated the international political shape of things to come.

In an attempt to lighten the atmosphere, the benign but decidedly eccentric professor of music, briefly suspended his characteristic *sotto voce* melodious humming. 'Perhaps,' he kindly suggested, 'dear Simone and Jacques might discuss their differences calmly over a friendly stroll on the beach at nearby Valras-Plage. And,' he added, smiling indulgently, 'maybe after your bracing seaside walk and with restored amity, you could perhaps enjoy a nice glass of lemonade together on the terrace of one of the jolly beachfront cafes.'

'No need for the lemonade,' replied Simone grimly. 'I'll have drowned him by then.'

This gleefully received remark tilted the verdict of the audience in her favour and the meeting proceeded, without further distraction or entertainment, to work its way tediously through the remaining items on the agenda. Finally, to general relief, the president, having dealt summarily with "Any Other Business", announced the date of the next meeting and declared today's one closed.

Afterwards, as usual, he invited his two chief advisers to join him in his office. These were Claire Macon, professor of psychology and vice-president for academic affairs, and Henri Campion, the university's secretary and bursar. It was at these "post-theatre" meetings, in the seclusion of his office, that serious issues were calmly addressed and thoughtfully advanced towards sensible solutions.

'Well,' said Guy, 'all things considered, that one went quite well. When matters might have got a bit difficult about the appointment of the new lecturer in migration policy, Social Science and Politics came predictably to the rescue by providing their welcome unscripted diversion. Let's hope that next month, should a similar difficulty arise, perhaps Economics and Marketing might likewise oblige by stepping into the sparring ring.'

The mutual contempt for each other of the very theoretically oriented Jacques Lamont, professor of microeconomics, and the down to earth, business-like Didier Ritz, professor of marketing, was legendary.

'However,' he continued, pouring each of them a robust measure of twelve-year-old Jameson "Redbreast" Irish whiskey, 'besides the usual concerns and lesser distractions which we have to discuss, there is one quite serious issue that we must consider very carefully and which I fear will preoccupy all of us in the months, and possibly the years, ahead. And that, as we know, is the issue which arises from the recently transformed age profile of our student population.'

His two colleagues smiled, recalling the brilliant initiative of the president, seven years previously, which had rescued the university from financial disaster. Because of the worldwide economic recession prevailing at the time, the annual grant to the university from the central government in Paris had been greatly reduced and students had begun to migrate to more academically renowned and scientifically focused locations. A creative response was urgently required to address the perilous situation.

The University of St Chinian had been established ten years after the Second World War. It is located in the beautiful Languedoc town of St Chinian, which is surrounded by wonderful vineyards producing the famous St Chinian wine. The town, nestling against a background of rolling hills and overlooking spectacular landscape, is just a half hour's downward journey to a relaxed uncrowded stretch of the Mediterranean.

The authorities in far-distant Paris had felt it expedient to address the notorious disenchantment and rebelliousness of the local Languedoc youth. In order to keep them off the streets and distract them from joining the Communist Party, it was deemed prudent to establish a small university where their youthful bucolic and, at times, aggressive energy could be contained for a few years in harmless educational and social

16

distraction. Hopefully, thereafter, their somewhat mellowed temperament could be seamlessly redirected to some commercially useful employment.

St Chinian was selected as an ideal place in which to locate the university to accomplish these bureaucratic desiderata. It was sufficiently beautiful to attract both staff and students, sufficiently remote not to be troublesome.

No expensive faculties such as medicine or engineering would be provided, or envisaged, for the fledgling university. Apart from its School of Oenology, Viticulture, and Agriculture, established in support of the local wine industry and local farmers, no role was planned for St Chinian's involvement in what were viewed by national government as the strategically important but costly disciplines of physical, biological, and engineering sciences. The university was established for political, rather than academic, motives. It would be an expedient but lesser jewel in the diadem of French intellectual life.

Nevertheless, notwithstanding its unpromising origin, St Chinian has developed its own distinctive, if modest, reputation for academic achievement and social responsibility. It did so in a cultivated, relaxed and tolerant atmosphere of "live and let live". The professors and lecturers are expected to take their teaching seriously. On the other hand, research is entirely optional and often resorted to only as a pretext for profitable external consultancy or for reproducing, under different titles, the same tired paper at desirable international conference locations.

The students also realize that some serious, but undemanding, attention to their studies is an unavoidable requirement of obtaining the coveted degree parchment which serves as a passport to employment in the local public, commercial, agricultural, and touristic establishments. They have ample free time and opportunity to indulge in the serious activities of hanging around, playing billiards, kicking football, listening to music, being misunderstood, cultivating exquisite expressions of existential anguish, fornicating, and appreciating various other forms of mind-enhancing delights.

A few years previously, the university had successfully outmanoeuvred most of the ominous recommendations of an externally imposed Quality Appraisal Committee and relaxed back into a state of inquisitive but undemanding academic equilibrium.

However, as the hard times of the turbulent 21st century unfolded, the university, with its characteristic profile of liberal arts, business studies, and social sciences, was again under scrutiny. It was deemed, from a national economic viewpoint, to be somewhat of an irrelevance and consequently its annual government grant was dramatically reduced. The number of young full-time students fell by 20% as many of the more ambitious ones, encouraged by their even more ambitious parents, migrated to the laboratories and experimental science programmes offered by Montpellier or Toulouse. They were heroically prepared to sacrifice their hitherto decidedly unscientific and leisurely social and interpersonal experimentation at St Chinian. They braced themselves for the more demanding experimental activity of the physical and biological sciences and the online revelations of advanced computer science and information technology.

Reflecting upon the challenge, and gravely worried, President Boulanger posed three questions to himself in writing on his notepad.

1) Who has the interest?

2) Who has the time?

And, most compelling if not most academic;

3) Who has the money to fund and enjoy what we have to offer?

The answer sprang off the page! The ideal supplementary supply of students for St Chinian in these perilous times would be people of leisure who had recently retired, or were about to retire, with generous pensions, or were in some comparably comfortable financial circumstance.

In several universities and colleges there had already been some minor altruistic experiments involving older people in what was tentatively called "The University of the Third Age". These experiments were usually peripheral activities and very subordinate offshoots of the main academic curriculum, which focused on the requirements of young, full-time students. The academic menu for "mature students" was offered only in the evening when the real students were otherwise engaged in very non-academic activities.

President Boulanger decided to bring these beautiful silvery and artificially golden-haired people of leisure centre stage at the University of St Chinian. It would become an internationally famous, if not quite renowned, university, catering explicitly for the eclectic and leisurely academic appetite of those who, though mature of years, were young at heart. As much attention would be devoted to the desires of these worthy and relatively affluent citizens as to the aspirations of impecunious and inexperienced callow youths. The University of St Chinian would be a wonderful example to the academic world of the harmonious scholarly cohabitation of zealous youth and experienced maturity.

The president's concept was adopted enthusiastically by the staff and, initially, also by the traditional young, full-time students who anticipated some collateral benefit from the university's enhanced financial circumstance. An energetic and very successful public relations exercise was launched to portray St Chinian as a welcoming academic paradise for people of mature years who wished to indulge, in a leisurely manner and in congenial circumstance, the improvement of what they were delighted to have had identified for them as their hitherto greatly underappreciated enquiring minds.

The initiative captured the imagination of the French nation. As elderly aspiring part-time scholars gravitated in huge numbers to St Chinian, the national press, radio and TV zoned in euphorically on the phenomenon and gave it even greater traction. Even sections of the international media became enthusiastically involved. They sent radio pundits and TV crews to explore this novel academic Nirvana. Their audiences were enthralled by the unconventional development and the seemingly endless stream of human-interest stories which it generated. The coverage had the effect of attracting a further cohort of international elderly swingers who hastened to participate in the exalted bliss of St Chinian's welcoming groves of academe. Even some international firms, wishing to encourage the early retirement of redundant staff, included scholarships for a year or even two at St Chinian in their carefully calculated retirement packages. This won them plaudits as enlightened employers rewarding their loyal staff with the opportunity of higher education, instead of the usual diatribes condemning them as hard-hearted downsizers.

Each succeeding year, the story became more fabulous and endearing and the number of older part-time students, now officially known as "mature students", participating in the activities of St Chinian continued to grow. There are now almost eight thousand mature students, whereas the cohort of young full-time students has shrunk to only four thousand.

'And that,' said Guy, 'is where our most pressing problem now presents itself. It is a somewhat unanticipated by-product of our own successful initiative. The development has given rise to a growing tension between the two categories of students. It looks as if it is going to escalate in the months ahead and turn into serious antagonism and open opposition between the two groups.

'The mature students,' he observed, 'are no longer satisfied to be welcomed simply as genuine but vaguely designated participants in the student life of the university. They want to redefine what it means to be a university student at St Chinian and to shape the profile and activities of the university chiefly to suit and reflect their mature requirements.

'On the other hand,' he continued, 'the initial welcome extended to the mature part-time students by the young full-time students has evaporated. Instead of being regarded with benign amusement as "eccentric old dears", they are now commonly described as mischievous old "golden codgers". They are now seen by the youngsters as a disruptive intrusion, usurping and undermining their own youthful status and standing as students.

'The young undergraduates cherish their student status as one traditionally recognized, tolerated, and indulged by the French public. They value the benevolent endorsement of this status as a characteristically high-spirited evolving stage of life of young people. They enjoy being valued as the future of the nation, entering upon a joyful learning experience and adventure which will lead them to a meaningful adult life. This "birth right" of being a student is now seen by the young at St Chinian as being deprived of its defining youthful, permissive quality. The meaning of "student" had been usurped by the pretentious claims and expectations of "old trouts", as one enraged young student activist recently described the "matures" in a letter to the student newspaper, *The St Chinian Trumpet*. He claimed that "they should be at home saying their prayers for a happy death".

'So, there we are,' said Guy. 'Faced with a problem arising from the remarkable success of our own decisions, a problem which will not go away. In fact, it will probably get worse. I think it is likely to come to an initial critical juncture with the campaigns for, and eventual outcome of, the upcoming election of the next president of the student union. He or she will have, in accordance with our statutes, significant authority in determining the profile, role, and activity of student life in the university for at least the next two years.

'Moreover,' he continued, 'as we know, the president of the student union is entitled to nominate five persons onto the twenty-eight-person governing body of the university. Given the difficulty of getting the academics that are on that body to agree about anything, the students can often play a decisive role in determining a decision on controversial issues. Admittedly, I usually have my own discreet powers of persuasion to reach the result I wish to achieve. However, the outcome of the forthcoming student election is likely to pose an added difficulty. It seems inevitable that the result will produce two sharply divided groups of students, one greatly empowered and one greatly disillusioned. It will also raise to a new level of intensity at the governing body formal discussion of the future profile of the university.

'Although it is more than two months away, I am reliably informed that the forthcoming election has already occasioned exploratory soundings and remote preparations by both categories of students. The political activists on each side are girding their loins, or at least tightening their Gucci belts, for an epic confrontation.'

'Yes, Guy, you are quite right,' said Claire. 'I have become painfully aware, because of complaints received, of this growing tension within the student body. In my thirty years at St Chinian, I have never noted such a highly charged atmosphere.'

'More disconcerting,' Guy added, 'is the rumour that members of the academic staff are beginning to align themselves with one or other group with a view to influencing in a decisive way the profile of the university and promote their own ambitions. Heretofore, we have managed to accommodate the presumption of each category of student that they are a valid and valuable embodiment of what it means to be a student of the University of St Chinian. But it is difficult to see how this balancing act can be maintained in view of the explicit and aggressive emergence of such very opposing conceptions.

'Over the next few weeks, I would like you both to keep your eyes and ears open to record any noteworthy developments in this matter. In particular, I would like to know of any involvement by the staff in the students deliberations. We can meet then and decide whether any anticipatory action on our part may be necessary or appropriate.'

His colleagues agreed that this was a sensible approach. They promised to do as requested and report back in due course. The three of them then briefly addressed the other matters which required their attention, finished their drinks, and headed to their respective homes, reflecting upon the issue which Guy had raised.

CHAPTER TWO
Madame Beausang

Dressed in blue jeans and a pink shirt, Lotti Beausang smiled down indulgently at the young man who lay asleep, stretched diagonally across the double bed. They had met at a party in the student club the previous evening and had engaged in animated discussion about the malaise of left-wing politics in France. The discussion continued over a bottle of wine in her apartment and terminated inconclusively in her bed, allegedly because it was raining heavily and he would have a very long walk home.

'Wake up, Sunshine,' she called. 'Time to take your shower and put on your clothes if you want to be in time for your economics lecture.'

He groaned awake, blinked, and returned her smile. 'What time is it?' he asked.

'Almost eight o'clock and you told me your lecture is at nine. I don't want to be responsible for distracting a young man from his university studies.'

'That was a lovely night,' he said, grabbing a towel and heading to the bathroom. 'Can we do it again please?'

'I think it best not,' she said. 'One unexpected happy encounter should be a sufficient delight for both of us — and you should be expending your considerable charm on girls of your own age. Let's just remain good friends.'

'I suppose you're right,' he said, 'but it won't be the same.'

'That's inevitable,' she laughed, 'when you consider that I'm more than twice your age.'

'But that's what helped to make it special,' he grinned.

When her youthful Don Juan had showered, dressed, demolished a coffee and two croissants, and kissed her *au revoir*, she poured herself another cup and sat down to review her situation and her plans. 'Well, my dear Lotti,' she mused to herself, 'hasn't your life changed, and certainly for the better, over the past few years.'

This was her third year of leisurely attendance as a mature student at the University of St Chinian. She had retired four years ago at the age of fifty after thirty-two years of employment with the same company which she had joined as a trainee clerk at the age of eighteen. The company published the local newspaper and a few magazines.

She spent her working life in the advertising department where her natural talent was soon recognized but never fully acknowledged. Eventually she advanced to the position of assistant director of the department.

To her irritation, she was never invited to become involved in the challenging external activity of selling advertising space. Her task was to arrange and oversee the internal organization and smooth operation of the department. This she did with admirable, some said ruthless, efficiency. Madame Charlotte Beausang, as she was known (she only became Lotti in St Chinian), was a figure to be reckoned with in the company. She was highly respected, even admired, but not greatly befriended.

Moreover, her single-minded devotion to her career adversely affected her social life. An only child, she lived with her elderly parents until they died. Although intelligent, good looking and amusing, she did not become involved in any permanent or long-lasting romantic relationship. Her activity in that domain, whether by choice or circumstance, was usually confined to occasional brief encounters, usually during her summer holidays in Nice.

When the company was bought by an international publishing house, she was happy to avail herself of a package which offered early retirement and a generous pension. She determined to apply her good fortune to a radical restructuring of her life. While pondering what form this might take, she read about the new initiative at the University of St Chinian and decided that it could provide an ideal opportunity to create a new *persona* for

Lotti Beausang. After a couple of exploratory visits, she decided that her intuition was correct. She sold her house and drove south to a comfortable, newly built apartment, which she rented on the outskirts of St Chinian. She decided that the new Lotti, reconstructed and re-advertised, would be, for the foreseeable future, a significant mature student at the University of St Chinian.

She became a popular member of the various student societies and clubs which she joined, and she participated whole-heartedly in their various pursuits. She also initiated a few new activities herself. Last summer she had organized a successful study cruise around the Mediterranean for seventy of the more adventurous mature students. The hectic preparation for this adventure involved serious retail excursions to Beziers and Montpellier to purchase appropriate nautical attire. Her handsomely proportioned body presented a pleasing appearance in flared white trousers, close-fitting navy and white striped T-shirt, and a jauntily placed sailor's cap.

Lectures on the cruise were provided by specially invited academics from the university. These, in some instances, were invited more for their pleasing appearance and convivial spirits than for their exceptional scholarly prowess.

Once at sea, even the more reserved mature students became surprisingly relaxed. With no solid ground under their feet, they deemed themselves to be released from conventional terrestrial constraints. They shed their inhibitions like their clothes and determined to enjoy a happy time on the ocean wave.

A nice bonus for the participants was the success of all but three of them in a perfunctory academic test conducted on the last day of the cruise. This maritime success provided them with another credit on their blossoming *curricula vitae.* Those who had failed to obtain this academic distinction were three gentlemen who had abandoned the official lecture course on "The Cultural History of the Mediterranean". They had jumped ship on its stopover at Agadir in Morocco and journeyed inland to Marrakesh, seduced by the prospect of its manifold temptations, of which they had been advised by a couple of members of the crew.

Lotti, herself, very much enjoyed her own participation in the relaxed quasi-academic cruise. A memorable feature of it had been an agreeable dalliance with a fellow mature student, recently retired from a long career as a weather forecaster with Toulouse TV. On the second day of the cruise, he had predicted to her that they would enjoy many prolonged sunny intervals together on their voyage. And such indeed had proved to be the case, particularly on those days when the sky was leaden and there was not much incentive to exercise on deck.

Today, however, other matters occupied her mind. A few of her politically active mature friends had asked her to join them later that morning to discuss the upcoming election of the president of the student union. From her knowledge of their concerns, and from some rumours she had heard, she had a shrewd idea of what they might have in mind. President Boulanger was not the only one who was aware of the political significance of the forthcoming election of a new president of the student union. She was curious to learn whether she was right about what she suspected they might be about to propose to her. Having tidied the apartment and gathered together some papers on which she was working, she threw on her duffel coat and drove to the Student Centre in good time for the meeting. On her way there she reflected upon the remarkable changes that had taken place at the University of St Chinian. 'A bit like the changes in my own life,' she said, smiling.

CHAPTER THREE
Mature Considerations

The University of St Chinian offers programmes in four different academic Schools. The most popular and best organized is The School of Viticulture, Oenology and Agriculture. There are always more applications to this School than places available. It caters specifically for the wishes of local vignerons and farmers to have their sons and daughters educated professionally in the basic requirements and current best practice for careers in agriculture and wine production.

Secondly, there is the School of Arts, Media and Communication. This is the school whose participants consider themselves the academic elite of the university. Besides providing programmes in the traditional liberal arts subjects, it manages the university's own radio and television stations. Their programmes are transmitted over a range of twenty-five kilometres and provide inhabitants of the region with much appreciated scandalous local gossip, light entertainment, and "phone-in" discussions.

Thirdly, there is the School of Economics, Business Studies, and Tourism. This is the school which offers an incongruous menu of abstract mathematically formulated economic speculation, business-like entrepreneurial activity, and practical courses on the promotion of local tourism. It is also one in which its business studies academics seek to dominate and promote their personally enriching financial initiatives. They are particularly active in providing expensive overseas undergraduate degree programmes in the Maghreb, a region comprising the traditionally French speaking countries of North Africa.

Finally, there is the School of Social and Political Science, and Migration and Mediterranean Studies. This is the school in which ideological and personal animosities flourish. It is also the one that is seeking to attract to the mainland French campus some of the affluent North African mature students whom the business studies academics claim to be their exclusive clientele.

The young full-time students of the university are each registered in a particular School to pursue a structured and largely predetermined undergraduate or postgraduate degree programme. However, by contrast, the mature students enjoy unconstrained freedom to indulge as they wish their intellectual curiosity and their flights of academic fancy. They can pick and choose topics ranging from the Archaeology of Athens to the Zoology of Zambia. However, unlike the young State-sponsored students, they have to pay a substantial annual registration fee and a fixed charge for each course in which they inscribe.

A few of the mature students, if they wish and are suitably qualified, may be admitted to a full-time structured degree programme like their younger counterparts. However, the vast majority of their mature colleagues despise them as deviants abandoning the radical academic freedom which is energetically proclaimed to be the true badge of a mature student. These free spirits usually enrol in no more than two, or, at most, three, courses annually, often selecting a most incongruous combination.

For the required participant fee, they may follow whatever courses, and whatever combination of courses, they choose to select from amongst those on offer in any of the schools. Whether or not they sit for examination in any of their chosen topics is entirely for themselves to decide. For each course in which they inscribe, they receive a richly embossed certificate confirming their participation, however desultory it may have been. They receive a further certificate for each examination passed successfully. When they depart, having been lavishly praised, clad in cap and gown, at an end-of-year ceremony, they have ample documentary evidence of their status as valued alumni of the University of St Chinian. The university, for its part, is grateful to receive their annual donations to its Academic and Social Development Foundation, and *post-mortem* affectionate remembrance in their wills.

Claude Ocler, a senior lecturer in tourism, has been appointed as assistant dean with special academic responsibility for mature students. An engaging and very popular feature of his devotion to his mission is his institution of what he has felicitously termed "The Bottom-Up Option". This is a provision which enables mature students to propose the establishment of a one-off course of academic lectures on any topic whatsoever. The main requirement is that at least fifteen of them are prepared to sign up for it and defray the cost of a lecturer and a modest university overhead. Any proposed programme has to be approved by a specially convened academic committee but this is usually just a *pro forma* exercise.

The mature students wholeheartedly welcomed this initiative, and various exotic academic agendas have been brought into transitory existence, many of them of a practical or therapeutic nature.

There are mature students, tax inspectors or chiropodists in a previous existence, who harbour secret ambitions to exhibit their remarkable culinary skills on television programs such as *Come Dine with Me*. They gladly commission and pay for progressively more specialized cookery courses on Spanish, Italian, Greek, and Caribbean cuisine. These are usually organized in consultation with the Department of Tourism in the School of Economics, Business Studies, and Tourism. This department's degree programme in hotel management includes a modest range of cookery courses. These are conducted as a hands-on training exercise, for prospective hotel managers, in a hotel owned by the university and which the Department of Tourism, itself, manages. In addition to these standard courses for the young, full-time degree students, mature men and women are happy, having paid for more exotic experiences, to don an apron in the hotel kitchen and devote themselves to the gentle art of enabling apples to crumble or soufflés to rise. One idealistic group of "matures", who funded a Bottom-Up course on cookery for vegans, is seeking to require the university restaurant to devote one day every week to an exclusively vegan menu.

To his astonishment and confusion, Antoine Chevalier, the doddery professor of Latin, whose undergraduate student numbers had evaporated, suddenly found himself the subject of a dramatic renaissance. It originated from the request of a number of silver and golden codgers for an introductory course on Cicero's *De Senectute*. His course on this famous text on old age soon assumed the status of a political rallying call rather than an academic exercise and, by popular demand, had to be repeated every two months.

To poor Chevalier's consternation, the class would erupt into whoops of triumphant delight when he provided translations such as, "Clearly rashness is a feature of exuberant youth whereas discretion is characteristic of maturity" (temeritas est videlicet florentis aetatis, prudentia senescentis), or, "You will find that the mightiest governments have been weakened by the young, but sustained and revived by the elderly" (Maximas res publicas ad adulecentibus labefactatas, a sensibus suitemates et restitutes reperietis).

For these selective lovers of Latin, a dumbed-down examination paper was devised which was popularly known as "Baby Latin". Junior academic staff, who supplemented their modest salaries by supervising university examinations, eagerly sought to supervise this exam. They whiled away the three-hour exam period, happily competing in a most politically incorrect contest to choose the year's "Miss Baby Latin".

Another particularly popular "Bottom-Up" option, but for a different reason, is the course on Colloquial English, which could earn a candidate two credits, although not many of the participants took the exam. The main attraction of the course was that it corresponded appropriately to the requirements of the European, mainly French, elderly free spirits who wished to seduce the good looking American, Australian, and Canadian "golden codgers" of both sexes who had been attracted to the university. The conversation at lectures discussed how to formulate pithy phrases such as, "Would you like to come for a drive in my vintage Lagonda?", or, "I think your eyes are like pools of the Mediterranean", or, "As my English is not very good, I would like to have intercourse with you to improve it". One aspiring Lothario couldn't understand the puzzled look on the face of a comely

Australian swinger when he offered to help her to alight onto a bus.

The corresponding courses in "Colloquial French" provided overseas mature students with comparable access to "Les Liaisons dangereuses". They gladly honed their powers of seduction by their introduction to the idiom of courtly love in French, gladly acknowledging it to be the most romantic of Romance languages!

These French and overseas heroes and heroines of the third age were equally committed to more esoteric courses on mindfulness, yoga, and enlightenment. They made commendable progress in these studies by their dedicated devotion to complicated techniques of meditation, accessible only through the study of Buddhism and Sufism.

The satisfaction of such exalted intellectual desires often involves employing an external temporary visiting lecturer to deliver the course. As these are birds of passage, the arrangement usually works very well, and such transient, part-time lecturers, happy with a little unscheduled remuneration, lend an exotic ever-changing dimension of unpredictability to the academic mix on offer to mature students.

Inevitably, there is the occasional embarrassing incident. A particularly piquant one occurred a couple of years ago when a group of mature students in a yoga programme, unable to get their heads around a specific injunction to concentrate on the sound of one hand clapping, decided that they needed to deepen their acquaintance with the appropriate background literature. This, they were advised, would involve acquiring some familiarity with certain venerable oriental Buddhist manuscripts about techniques of meditation originating from Tibet. Taking the matter seriously, they requested and financed an introductory course in Tibetan. A search was immediately initiated for a suitably qualified lecturer.

Eventually, an Irishman living in the close-by village of Puisserguier, and glorying in the name of Matt Shay Dunne, which had a pleasingly oriental ring to it, applied for the post. Fortunately, he appeared to be very well qualified. 'I believe,' he confided to the interview committee, 'that providence has prepared me for this particular appointment. You will note on my CV how I have spent several years of missionary work in Tibet itself.'

He was eagerly employed to provide the course, which, by popular demand, had to be repeated several times. It was increasingly acknowledged to be an absolute requirement for progress on the path of Zen. Matt devoted himself to his task with dedication, enthusiasm, and panache. He was very popular and became fondly known as "The Irishman from Tibet". He warmly encouraged his eager students to persevere in their enthusiasm for yoga enlightenment. Indeed, it was even rumoured that, occasionally, after an official two-hour seminar on pronouncing Tibetan phrases, he would invite a particularly promising female student back to his home for extracurricular initiation into some long-lost unconventional Tibetan yoga positions.

Unfortunately, and inconveniently, and notwithstanding his stylish presentation, Matt Shay Dunne knew no Tibetan. Instead, he taught his students Irish, for which they showed a gratifying aptitude. Some, as they sat cross-legged on their yoga mats, were even able to provide a credible rendering of a number of Irish ballads. Thankfully, they were not young enough to cause any international incident, which might have been occasioned by a subsequent inauspicious diplomatic posting.

Another group of politically ambitious "matures" wished to relive the glorious Paris student movement of May 1968, which they had missed out on because they were either too young or were at work earning a living. They attempted to occupy the university's administration building but were easily ejected because, to their disgust, the young, full-time students, anxious not to miss lectures, would not join them. To boost their revolutionary aspirations, they tried to invite Daniel Cohn-Bendit to deliver a series of lectures on "Red, Green, and Anarchy". He thanked them graciously but declined, allegedly because of prior engagements.

Logic was another popular subject with those mature students who considered themselves to be of above average intelligence. They persuaded the professor of logic, a short-sighted amiable elderly gentleman, to provide a specially designed course for them, entitled Introduction to Logic. About sixty signed and paid up for the course. The group included butchers, hairdressers, postmen, accountants and even a retired medical missionary nun, who for her golden jubilee had been granted a year off to attend some part-time courses at St Chinian.

They were delighted with the early lectures. They came to greatly appreciate their own superior intelligence as the professor helped them to apprehend the validity of syllogistic arguments such as; "All men are mortal, Socrates is a man, therefore Socrates is mortal". Or, "No cats have beards, Socrates has a beard, therefore Socrates is not a cat".

However, as he sought to lead them forward to deeper considerations, their interest flagged. When, chuckling to himself, he started explaining "the logic of material implication", they lost interest. They were not impressed when he enthusiastically assured them that, 'Material implication involves a logically valid rule which allows a conditional statement to be replaced by a disjunction in which the antecedent is negated.' They thought he must be losing the plot when from this he claimed excitedly that, logically, 'If the moon is not made of green cheese, then St Chinian is in France,' is a valid argument. They were convinced that he had definitely lost it when he subsequently subsequent claimed that, logically, 'If St Chinian is not in France, then the moon is made of green cheese,' is also a valid argument.

No longer enthralled, they began surreptitiously to consult their smartphones or to read the sports page of their newspapers. However, they could not be sure how short-sighted the professor really was and were disconcerted when he seemed to be trying to peer at them. One of them in the back row had the bright idea to half-open a small black umbrella and pass it along onto the next row. When it reached the fourth row the professor, who had been peering uncertainly, threw down his notes and said, 'Sister, will you please sit down.' They knew now that, until he got a bit more interesting, they were safe to pursue their own interests, at least in the back four rows.

Another programme popular with mature students was the specially designed short course on Greek mythology. They could easily identify imaginatively with its heroic and divine personalities. One enthusiastic participant, a tall, thin, retired bank manager from nearby Beziers, claimed that it helped him to understand his passionate involvement with several robust older women of ample physical proportions. His therapist, herself a reinvented midwife, had suggested that this attraction was a transferred substitute Oedipus complex. As both his parents were even leaner than himself, he had no Oedipus-like wish to murder his father in order to sleep with his mother. 'Your current amorous proclivities are,' she kindly explained, 'simply a delayed and enjoyable transferred fulfilment of that desire.'

In general, the mature students were very well satisfied with their newly discovered leisurely lifestyle. Some of them are on their third year of academic pursuits, usually following two or, at most, three courses. They tend to seek some entirely new experience each year; sometimes determined more by the appeal of the lecturer than the topic itself. They are also well pleased by the novelty and range of social distractions made available by their recently enabled student status.

These broad-minded lovers of *à la carte* university life, are determined to consolidate their conception of what this life is all about. They consider it too much fun, after the tedium of more than thirty years of routine employment, to be impeded from exploring its many enticing possibilities. If safeguarding this newfound liberation involves certain political initiatives with regard to electing the president of the student union, so be it. They would not be found wanting in promoting this noble idea.

CHAPTER FOUR
Nomination No. 1

Half an hour before Lotti's arrival to the meeting, arranged for eleven o'clock, the four mature students, three men and one woman, who had invited her to join them, met together to review the proposal they intended to put to her. They were all in their third year at St Chinian, enjoying a leisurely and varied life of part-time studies, social engagement, and political activism.

The self-appointed leader of the group was Louis Dupre a retired gay police detective inspector. Another member was Paul Moulin, the weather man from Toulouse who had been Lotti's intimate companion on last year's memorable Mediterranean cruise. Although Lotti was well known and appreciated as a handsome, stylish, and popular figure around the campus, it was he who had adverted the group to her considerable talents and her ability and determination to achieve whatever she sought to accomplish. The other two, Luc and Marie Dupront, an amiable couple in an exultantly self-proclaimed open marriage, had recently semi-retired. They had sold the beauty salon, which they had successfully operated together for many years, and where they had devoted themselves to the challenging task of gilding the somewhat aesthetically challenged lilies in the nearby city of Narbonne. They were interested in exploring more adventurous ways in which they might deploy their exotic skills in St Chinian.

What united the group was their desire to enjoy many more years of academic insouciance and delight at the University of St Chinian. They intended to take the necessary steps to safeguard and expand its various resources to satisfy their seemingly insatiable thirst for cultural, social and humanistic fulfilment — all rather broadly understood. After careful consideration and discreet enquiries, they had agreed that Lotti Beausang was eminently qualified to play a crucial role in this enterprise.

When she arrived punctually at eleven o'clock, they welcomed her warmly and invited her to take a seat at the table around which they were assembled. Emeritus Detective Inspector Louis Dupre, exercising the role of chairman, addressed her directly. 'Dear Lotti,' he said, beaming, 'thank you for joining us this Saturday morning on which I'm sure you have many other interesting ways of diverting yourself. I think you know us all quite well. However, more important is that we all know you well and hold you in such high regard.

'The reason why the four of us have been meeting together over the past few weeks is that we are worried that the wonderful initiative which has made the University of St Chinian a famous academic centre for students such as ourselves may be in danger. We fear that there are hostile forces at work, wishing to marginalize our significance and restore St Chinian to being just like any other university. They would undermine our glorious achievement and seek to return the university to the state being just another dull degree printing factory for the benefit of gormless youths and simpering wenches.

'We want,' he continued, 'to safeguard, consolidate, and expand our remarkable achievement. Our aim is to ensure formal recognition that the basic mission of St Chinian is to exist and to flourish, primarily and avowedly, as a university of the third age. We want it to be one devoted to enabling and celebrating the liberal, unfettered, personal and academic expression of our mature years. Our unwavering dedication to this objective will, of course, with our characteristic generosity of spirit also benignly tolerate, but in a subsidiary role, a limited cohort of youthful immature academic novices earnestly and unimaginatively dedicated to full-time studies.

'A crucial stage in this undertaking,' he emphasized, obviously pleased with his own eloquence, 'will be the election in six weeks, at the beginning of May, of a new president of the student union. It is essential, in our view, that the person elected to this office at this perilous juncture be somebody committed to our authentic conception of the essential and unique nature of student life at St Chinian. It is equally essential that this person has the ability and determination to succeed in promoting the success of this undertaking.

'Having considered the matter very carefully,' he declared, his voice assuming a timbre of grave solemnity, 'it is our unanimous and informed conviction, dear Lotti, that you are the person most eminently qualified to fulfil, as we envisage it, this role of president of the student union. Consequently, it is our great pleasure to invite you to accept our offer to nominate you as a candidate for this office. It is our earnest hope and desire that you will accept this invitation and we pledge our wholehearted support in the strenuous campaign which it will certainly involve.'

Louis' oration was accompanied by "hear, hear" and polite applause from the other three members of the group. They looked expectantly at Lotti who appeared composed and appreciative.

'Dear Louis, dear friends,' she said, smiling, 'what an inspiring vision you have for our beloved University of St Chinian, a vision which I wholeheartedly share. I am truly honoured by the invitation which you have offered me. I won't waste your time by claiming that it comes as a complete surprise. It is widely known that you were preparing to contest the upcoming election on behalf of the mature students. The only issue was whom might you select as your preferred candidate. When I received your invitation to this meeting, I won't pretend that I had no idea what you might propose. I am realistic, or vain, enough to believe that I would be an excellent candidate to project the vision which inspires us. Consequently, I thank you for your confidence and I willingly accept your invitation.'

The four of them crowded round, embracing her and exclaiming, 'we're on our way.' In anticipation of the rigors of the campaign, the Dupronts offered to provide her with a complimentary course of beauty treatment; an offer which didn't seem to impress her. Inspector Dupre's assurance of all necessary security throughout her campaign seemed more to her liking.

'Of course,' she said, 'before we enter upon our initial planning it is important to be clear on a couple of points about which I'm sure we are in total agreement. I will rely greatly upon your valued advice and practical support. I will consult you attentively about formulating and publicizing my election manifesto. However, it must be understood from the outset that I speak for myself and am not just your mouthpiece, however much I share your convictions. Also, if successful in the election, I am sure you will agree that, when I appoint members to fill posts on various committees to work with me in promoting our vision, I am not committed in advance to any particular appointments. Although I will, of course, give careful consideration to those who share my views and have been supportive of my campaign, I will propose only those I consider most suitable for the various posts.

'And now,' she said, by way of conclusion and to deflect any comment, 'perhaps we should begin to discuss our plans over lunch in the student restaurant to which it is my pleasure to invite you. Our presence there together will doubtless provoke some comment. However, it is better to be seen chatting openly together in public than to be surprised, and presumed to be conspiring, in a corner of some secluded restaurant.'

The "gang of four" had been left in no doubt that their chosen one had her own ideas and aims and had no intention of being their puppet. Any disappointment about this was more than offset by their appreciation that, in selecting Lotti Beausang, they had chosen somebody who would be a formidable candidate in the upcoming election. They would have no difficulty in securing the further six names necessary to achieve the ten signatures required for a valid nomination.

She was right, also, about the interest that their lunch together would occasion. Some younger students seated near them in the restaurant, aware of their reputation as prominent and influential figures amongst the body of mature students, could hardly eat their hamburgers, staring and speculating about the group's animated discussion. Their indigestion would have been even greater had they heard Lotti articulate her ideas about how to present the voters with a conception of St Chinian as a university devoted specifically and primarily to the requirements of mature students. Younger, full-time students would, of course, continue to be welcomed as an integral and vivacious complement to mature insight. However, they would

49

have to understand their minority role on the great canvas of academic life at St Chinian. They would have to appreciate their good fortune in having the opportunity to pursue their studies in a university where the many dimensions of the remarkable talents of students of the "*troisième âge*" were promoted and set the tone.

CHAPTER FIVE
Nomination No. 2

The following Wednesday, ten days before nominations for the office of student president would have to be officially registered, a lively meeting was taking place in the bar of the Student Centre. It was a meeting of young, full-time students who were leaders or actively involved members of various university student societies and clubs. Mature students who featured on some of the committees of these clubs and societies had not been invited. The purpose of the meeting was to nominate a full-time undergraduate student for the office of president — a responsibility which had assumed particular significance in view of the now widely publicized news of the nomination the previous week of Lotti Beausang.

The early phase of the meeting was characterized by opportunistic or light hearted contributions about the qualities most desirable in a student president.

'I think that our new student president should be a good listener,' declared the auditor of the Music Society.

'She should be able to last the pace for ten rounds,' affirmed the captain of the Ladies Boxing Club.

'The president must be able to see both sides of an argument,' countered the auditor of the Debating Society.

The captain of the Swimming Club opined that the president should be able to swim against the tide!

Finally, these preliminary suggestions were brought to an abrupt close by a fiery intervention from Jeanne Mandel, a tall intense young woman with flashing green eyes and swirling red hair. She was chairperson of the university's National Front student society. 'Fellow students,' she exclaimed, 'for God's sake, let us get serious. We are in a dangerous situation and our concerted action is required to address it. The only thing that matters in the forthcoming election is that we elect somebody who will firmly reassert the traditional values and rights of genuine French students. We must demolish the absurd pretensions of the crowd of old codgers who have invaded our beloved university and are scheming to transform it to their own desires.'

Then, unable to conceal her political commitment she added, 'If "Marine" Le Pen, with her pure undiluted French values, were president of this country we would not even be having this dreadful discussion about how to maintain the genuine ethos of our university.'

Her perfectly timed outburst was greeted with loud and enthusiastic applause. Thereafter the discussion concentrated upon the issue of selecting the most suitable nominee as president. Jeanne Mandel rejected the suggestion that she might be the appropriate candidate to oppose Lotti Beausang. 'We need somebody with broader appeal,' she said. 'I am too closely identified with my work for the National Front, to which I devote most of my free time publicly and unreservedly. We need somebody with wide appeal who is generally liked and admired but also wholeheartedly in agreement with our view about what it means to be a student instead of playing at being one.'

Eventually, after several possible candidates had been suggested, considered, and rejected for various reasons, a young second year student tentatively made a proposal which won instant and delighted approval. 'I would like to propose,' he declared, 'that we nominate Yves Leroy to be the new president of our student union.'

Once proposed, this seemed such an obvious choice that everyone was surprised that it had taken the adulation of this young student to identify him. And this is how, with unanimous approval, Yves Leroy — the talented captain who had led the university's rugby team to glorious victory in the regional inter-university competition for the coveted De Gaulle Cup — came to be nominated as the full-time students' candidate for the office of president of the student union. A small group of students was delegated to invite him to accept the nomination and to report back the next evening.

Yves is the twenty-four-year-old only son of a prosperous sixth generation *vigneron,* who cultivates an extensive and profitable vineyard in the local Corbières region. When he left school, aged eighteen, with his *baccalaureate,* his father indicated that he expected him to acquire the skills of an expert *vigneron* and eventually succeed him in managing and developing the family vineyard. Yves accepted the indicated career path but negotiated an arrangement with his father.

'Before I do what you suggest,' he said, 'I would like to take a few years out to travel and enjoy the sort of worldly experience which my life in our vineyard spraying grapes in unlikely to afford.'

His father agreed on condition that, upon his return from his global peregrinations, he would attend the local University of Saint Chinian to study for a degree in viticulture and oenology which would qualify him to manage the family vineyard in a professional and profitable manner.

It was in this roundabout way that Yves became a full-time student of St Chinian at the age of twenty-two, a few years older than most first-year students. He was effortlessly popular and his striking looks and air of worldly sophistication endeared him particularly to a number of discerning female students. He seemed like a godsend, providing much needed distraction from the onerous requirements of German grammar, Plato's *Republic*, Keynesian economics, or the amateurish advances of eager eighteen-year-old suitors who were still on a steep romantic learning curve!

At university, he resumed his earlier passion for rugby football and within a few months had achieved a widely acclaimed reputation as an outstanding out- half. The following year he was elected captain of St Chinian's senior rugby team. He justified this confidence by leading them to victory, for the first time, in the regional inter-university rugby competition for the De Gaulle cup. Unfortunately, a few minutes before the end of the final game of the competition, he was robustly tackled while speeding with the ball for what looked like an assured try. From the impact of the tackle, he suffered a badly broken ankle. This injury prevented his active participation in the sport during the current season. However, he remained the team's staunchest supporter, assisted with its training, and hoped to return next year to active engagement.

This rugby mishap had the unanticipated happy outcome of affording him enough free time to accept the proposed nomination as candidate for the office of president of the student union and to devote himself wholeheartedly to an energetic campaign. The following day he accepted gracefully with conviction and enthusiasm. He pledged to devote the same energy to this political objective as he had to leading the rugby team to victory.

The various captains and chairpersons of the student clubs and societies were delighted with their selection and his enthusiastic acceptance of the challenge. He was a very popular choice. The young, full-time students believed they had identified a worthy contender to meet the challenge and devious machinations of the mature part-timers. He was assured of their fully committed support which he gratefully acknowledged.

A group of his female admirers, led by Marie Regis, the beautiful blonde captain of the women's tennis team, organized a sub-committee devoted exclusively to anticipating and counteracting the special feminist appeal which Lotti Beausang might have for female voters. The driving forces on his main committee were Jeanne Mandel, the National Front activist, Jacques Delon, the young undergraduate who had initially suggested his nomination, Marie Regis, the tennis star, Henri Herrera, a serious postgraduate student of economics, and Andre Leon, a bright student of public relations and media. Andre believed that his professional academic interests would be of significant value to the campaign and would be required in order to temper the ideological exhortations of the fiery Jeanne Mandel.

The evening of his acceptance of the nomination developed into a celebratory and exuberant party in the Student Centre. As the beer flowed, the exuberance bubbled in direct proportion. Eventually, before suggestions got totally out of hand about how the outrageously depicted aspirations of the mature students might be countered by even more outrageously indecent responses, the party was brought to a timely end by the midnight closing hour. The happy crowd dispersed, some to continue celebrating in their student apartments, others to more intimately interpersonal discourse, and just a few to their virtuous couches in anticipation of early morning lectures.

CHAPTER SIX
The Die is Cast

The last Wednesday in March was the date on which all nominations for the office of president of the student union had to be lodged with Henri Campion, the university's secretary-bursar. It was widely presumed that, as heretofore, there would be just two high profile candidates.

Secretary Campion had posted in various buildings large posters stating clearly the date for nominations and the requirement of ten nominators. The posters also indicated that voting would open at nine thirty a.m., close at seven p.m., on Sunday May 1st. The count would proceed on Monday May 2nd. He had discussed these arrangements with President Boulanger and Academic Vice-President Claire Macon. He also informed them confidentially of an interesting development which was likely to occur and obtained their agreement about how to deal with it.

In smaller print, the posters also mentioned that, whereas the vote of each full-time student was accorded a value of two points, that of each part-time student was accorded a value of only one point. When this allocation was initiated by formal decision of the university's governing body seven years ago, it was agreed unanimously. Indeed, it was seen as a generous recognition of the importance which the university intended to accord to the new part-time students it wished to welcome. This recognition would acknowledge them as genuine students of the university and not just visitors. They would be accorded the status of valued students of the university though not, of course, in exactly the same sense or to the same extent as full-time students.

Now, however, what had been originally crafted as a generous recognition of the status and contribution of part-time students was fiercely opposed by these part-timers as a disgraceful discriminatory treatment of them as second-class students. It was also rejected by them as blatant "ageism"; a cowardly discrimination motivated by jealousy of the superior wisdom and academic freedom of people of mature years. The retort that it was a decision based on the distinction between full-time and part-time, not between young and mature was dismissed as mere verbal obfuscation.

Irrespective of how the distinction was interpreted, it gave rise to an interesting electoral situation. If students voted broadly according to their age, it would be very difficult to predict the outcome of the ballot. The eight thousand mature students would balance the four thousand young full-timers. Any swing voters would be crucial to the outcome.

At four p.m., Lotti Beausang arrived with her required ten nominators. They lodged the appropriate documentation to the sustained and admiring applause of a small group of mature students who had gathered to witness the ceremony. Lotti greeted them warmly and encouraged them to spread the word of her nomination amongst their friends.

About a half an hour later, the sound of music was heard and a brass band led the procession of Yves Leroy's nominators and supporters. Secretary Campion duly recorded the nomination. When the formalities were concluded, Yves thanked his supporters who, aided by the band, burst into enthusiastic song, chanting the anthem of the rugby team. 'St Chinian lads will cross the line, St Chinian forever, rah, rah, rah.'

The unprepared group of mature students was musically outflanked. But, realizing the popular attraction of musical commitment, they sought bravely to respond with an enthusiastic but rather unconvincing rendering of *La Marseillaise.*

At a quarter to seven, fifteen minutes before closing time for lodging nominations, a large white van skidded to a halt in front of Secretary Campion's office and ten students tumbled out. The one in front, clutching the nomination paper they had all signed, declared they had come to nominate Alex Denton and handed the paper to Secretary Campion. The secretary examined the document carefully. Then he solemnly declared, 'I announce to all here present that Alex Denton is validly nominated as a candidate for the office of president of the student union.'

Initially, the announcement was greeted with a stunned silence. There had never been more than two candidates for the office of president. Nobody had any idea who Alex Denton might be. A cacophony of voices erupted.

'Alex who?'

'Who the hell?'

'What's all this about?'

'Where did this come from?'

'Is Alex a man or a woman?'

'Is s/he full-time or part-time, mature or undergraduate?'

Answers were demanded of the nominators. They, in turn, provided no further illumination or detailed information. Their leader, Thomas Mansion, who had presented the nomination paper to Secretary Campion, is a serious PhD student, writing a thesis on "The Past, Present, and Future of the Eurozone". He waved his hands down to silence the uproar and conveyed a brief message.

'Alex Denton,' he said, 'is a brilliant, but also a modest, person, a person with a message but with no interest in the cult of personality. She or he has therefore decided to retain his or her anonymity. Tomorrow his or her election message will be made public. It will be brief, to the point, and remain the same until the vote at the end of next month. On Alex's explicit instruction, I have nothing further to add and I bid you good day.'

Sandra Ricoeur, a clever third year student in the School of Arts Media and Communication, and editor of *The St Chinian Trumpet,* walked up to Secretary Campion. 'Surely, Secretary,' she proclaimed, 'my readers have a right to know the precise identity of the candidates for whom they are invited to cast their vote as president of our student union, and surely you, as returning officer, have a duty to disclose this information?'

Secretary Campion looked quizzically at her and, smiling indulgently, replied, 'A candidate, provided he or she is validly nominated, is entitled to preserve his or her anonymity. Surely you, as an editor of our subsidised but regretfully often fake-news student newspaper, must appreciate the importance of maintaining the anonymity of one's sources, if so requested.'

'That is a complete *non sequitur,*' she replied tartly, 'and I will pursue my concentrated journalistic investigation until I have confirmed to my own satisfaction, and for the benefit of my readers, the identity of this mysterious candidate.' But Secretary Campion's smile just broadened.

The supporters of Lotti Beausang and Yves Leroy were left dumbfounded. They didn't know what to say or think. They wondered who this last-minute candidate could be or why he or she had been nominated. They could find no intelligible responses to these puzzling questions. There had never been more than two candidates for the position of president — usually one of outdoor athletic celebrity and the other usually of more sheltered literary disposition. But a third candidate, and one who claimed anonymity, was too much to conjure with.

Eventually, their spirits were somewhat restored when they began to surmise and to agree that this latest nomination must be simply a silly distraction, a massive practical joke. However, neither Lotti nor Yves were as readily reassured and each continued to wonder what might be behind this latest development. They each began to think that the other must be somehow involved but couldn't make out with what intention or to what end. The crowd began to disperse, each group in different directions, to ponder the situation and prepare for what promised to be a very lively campaign.

Later that evening, Henri Campion reported to Guy Boulanger and Claire Macon that the nominations, including the surprise one of Alex Denton, had occurred as he had previously advised them was likely.

'I could hardly keep a straight face,' he declared, 'When Sandra Ricoeur, the editor of the *St Chinian Trumpet,* insisted that, in the interest of transparency, I should reveal the identity of the mysterious Alex Denton. She gave a most convincing warning that, in her respect for journalistic integrity, she would not rest until she had ascertained for her readers the identity of this surprise nomination. I was sorely tempted to inform the puzzled audience that the surprise candidate was none other than Sandra Ricoeur herself. However, as I had promised her, and as agreed with you, I insisted that the candidate's identity should, as requested, remain anonymous.'

'Well,' said Guy, 'watching how her campaign unfolds will probably be the only amusing feature of this election campaign. We must respect the assurance we gave her. Her nomination may yet turn out to be a blessing in disguise.'

CHAPTER SEVEN
'Academic' Interest

The students, whether full-time or part-time, were not the only members of the University of St Chinian community who took a lively interest in the upcoming election of the president of the student union. Members of staff were keenly aware that the outcome could have a significant and possibly decisive impact on the profile and operation of the university.

Many of these staff, without losing much sleep about the issue, favoured a traditional view of the university as characteristically a forum for the higher education, at undergraduate and postgraduate level, of young, full-time students. They accepted and appreciated the presence of a cohort of part-time students of mature years who lent a rather exotic dimension to routine academic activities — not to mention a welcome salary supplement, and the prospect of an occasional agreeable extracurricular encounter. However, they would deem this to be just a pleasant distraction from the main task of guiding bright young students to a successful degree and subsequent career. A radical reorientation of the profile of the university, which would accord primary importance to the requirements of the part-time mature students, would not be generally viewed by the more conservative academic staff as a welcome development.

However, a significant number of academics viewed the prospect of such a reorientation as offering an interesting opportunity to advance their own views, aims, and ambitions. They were determined to play their part in ensuring its success. Included amongst these, though for decidedly different reasons, are two senior and very energetic professors. One is Didier Ritz, professor of marketing and dean of the School of Economics, Business Studies and Tourism. The other is Simone Blondel, professor of social administration in the School of Sociology, Politics, Migration and Mediterranean Studies.

Didier Ritz, a graduate of INSEAD, the prestigious French Business School, likes to convey the impression of a no-nonsense, business-like, man-of the-world academic. His lectures on marketing emphasize how he "has walked the walk and not just talked the talk". They are laced with references to the captains of industry who have sought his advice and how appreciative they are of the benign effect it has on the sale of their merchandise and services.

It is generally agreed that the most impressive evidence of his professional marketing skill is the brilliance and assurance with which he marketed himself. He is the living, self-assured, practical confirmation of the validity of the theoretical suggestions, affirmations, and directives propounded in his lectures on marketing. His main ambition is to extend this impressive marketing of himself into the office of president of the University of St Chinian in two years' time when, it is widely speculated, the present incumbent might not seek re-election. It is rumoured that Guy Boulanger is interested in a well-remunerated but undemanding position in the European Union bureaucracy in Brussels. And even if Guy does seek a further term, Didier Ritz is determined to challenge him for the post. He frequently reminds himself that, 'This university needs, even if it has not merited, the benefit of my remarkable ability and leadership.'

He reckons that the campaigns for the election of the president of the student union would provide him with valuable information about social and political trends at St Chinian, which might be useful to his own campaign in a couple of years. More directly, he intends to support publicly the agenda of one of the candidates and thereby seek to influence the outcome of the election to his own advantage.

Having estimated that the mature students were more likely to carry the vote he has decided to support Lotti Beausang's campaign and to become an ardent advocate of a radically new kind of university, one primarily concerned with meeting the aspirations and desires of mature students. In so doing, he could pretend that he was only pursuing an objective which President

Boulanger had initiated several years ago but which he had failed to carry through to its logical conclusion.

He realized there was a risk in directly confronting the President again. Three years previously he had done so when he publicly supported the chairman of an external quality appraisal committee who wished to transform the whole university into a business school, operating simply as a business. President Boulanger had seen that challenge off, and Didier Ritz had to pretend that he recognized the error of his ways and was now a reformed supporter of the president. He could now pretend that his support for the mature students' candidate is simply a faithful commitment to what the president must surely want even if he had not said so. He reckoned that this hypocritical posturing was worth the risk of not deceiving Guy Boulanger about his real objective. If his predictions about the outcome of the election are verified, being recognized as having played a prominent role in the election of the successful candidate would significantly enhance his own presidential aspirations.

He also believed that, with the success of Lotti Beausang's campaign, the climate in the university would be amenable to a specific commercial project which he hoped to initiate and which could further favour his own presidential aspirations. He had in mind the idea of forming a profitable company, funded by some of the more affluent mature students as shareholders. It would provide, with himself as a key player, a very expensive consultancy service, promoting throughout Europe and further afield the conception of the university as essentially an activity of the "third age". It would assist other universities, using St Chinian as a model, to develop their profile as a "third age" institution. The University of St Chinian as a dedicated and inspirational university of the "third age" would become one of the great marketing sensations of the century.

Another professor, tending to support the mature students' campaign, but from a very different perspective, is Professor Simone Blondel, professor of social administration. She is a convinced Marxist, determined to play her part in establishing the dictatorship of the proletariat, which will accomplish the withering away of the state and usher in a communist era of sweetness and light and champagne and caviar for all. Her problem is that she finds the contemporary, full-time undergraduate students of St Chinian, who should be her fiery disciples, completely indifferent and even hostile to her revolutionary zeal. They seemed quite happy to attend their lectures and then to knock out as good a time as possible in congenial downtown capitalist St Chinian — rather than engaging in heroic class warfare. A few years of carefree fun, combined with the modicum of study necessary for the university degree, appeared to be the height and breadth of their aspirations.

Disgusted by such ideological mystification of the young undergraduates, Simone is determined to concentrate her crusading enthusiasm on the mature students. Having been forced into servile work directly from school by a corrupt capitalist system, and having missed the opportunity of participating in the heroic student movements of the previous century, they would be easily convinced of their alienated condition. Now they will have the opportunity, under her guidance and fortified by comfortable pensions, to avail themselves of inspirational Marxist terminology to interpret the exploited world of their experience. Lotti Beausang, crowned with the electoral success facilitated by Simone's support, would blossom into a secular Joan of Arc, a republican Marxist French Marianne. The "third age" University of St Chinian would become an internationally renowned centre of Marxist renaissance.

Another sociologist, Dr Thomas Van Velsen, a handsome Dutch lecturer on the history of sociology, is also determined to support the mature students' candidate. In his ample spare time, he has become the founder, and self-anointed chairman for life, of The St Chinian Community of Latter-Day Albigensians. This is a group of like-minded people devoted to reviving the medieval Cathar religious movement that had been popular in the Languedoc region, but which was condemned as heretical and persecuted in the thirteenth and fourteenth centuries by church and state. Its animating idea was that the world was created and governed by two opposing principles, God and Satan, one a good principle and the other an evil principle. The purpose of one's life was to strive, by means of an ascetic process of self-discovery, to liberate oneself from the clutches of the evil principle and gradually become a Perfect. Having merited this illustrious state of being a Perfect through one's virtuous activity, one could be initiated to it by receiving the sacrament known as the *consolamentum* ("consolation"). Thomas Van Velsen was convinced, and had convinced others, that he had already attained this happy state of being a Perfect and had a divine mission to lead others to it.

Nevertheless, his interpretation of what this involved would have seemed very strange, indeed completely unorthodox, to a traditional devout medieval Cathar. For he deflected the salvific ascetic process of self-discovery into a dedicated programme of experimental promiscuity, orchestrated generously by himself and fellow Perfects. This enabled adventurous young novices to be led joyfully along a primrose path to perfection, anticipating in various preparatory encounters their eventual totally blissful consolation. The nature and conscientious observation of the *consolamentum* had also to be redefined. In orthodox Cathar belief, it had involved total abstinence from sexual activity and from the consumption of meat of any kind — which is why most believers had postponed reception of the sacrament until their deathbed! The reformed version being promoted in the University of St

Chinian had a much more enjoyable initiation ceremony and a much more appetizing code of conduct!

However, the Perfect Dr Van Velsen had encountered some disconcerting reactions to his dedicated service, some of which almost cost him his job. These were chiefly in the form of encounters with furious and indignant mothers of the eager young seekers of perfection. In one case, the mother of a particularly infatuated young student of political economy and Spanish had threatened to report him to the university authorities. Fortunately for him, his compelling eloquence came to his rescue. ('Abandon your worldly pursuits, your distorted moral evaluations, and experience the embrace of love.'). The mother is now herself a mature student and an eager disciple, well on the way to becoming a Perfect.

In view of such hazards, Thomas has decided that his missionary activity would be safer in a university operating according to norms more appropriate to the personal independence, and non-accountable carefree pursuit of perfection available to mature students. He would use his unconventional influence to support the election of Lotti Beausang as an icon of contemporary "Latter Day" Cathar fervour.

However, it is unlikely that a majority of academics will favour this mature student preference being advocated by some colleagues with personal agendas. Certainly, Jacques Lamy, the professor of political theory (and a great admirer of Margaret Thatcher's dictum, "There's no such thing as society") will, as a matter of principle, be opposed to any project supported by Simone Blondel.

The small department of migration and Mediterranean studies has declared itself to be all at sea and unable to make up its mind about what sort of university it would like.

It seems certain, however, that the prestigious School of Viticulture, Oenology and Agriculture will remain steadfast in its conviction that its defining objective is the professional formation of local young *vignerons* and farmers, rather than welcoming elderly city dwellers to try their hand at pruning a vine.

Undoubtedly, the occasional outings of mature students to the school's six-hundred-hectare estate, and their bibulous participation in streamlined short courses on wine appreciation, are enjoyed by all as an amusing distraction. However, their imitation of pre-revolutionary aristocrats playing at being milkmaids at the palace of Versailles is no substitute for the youthful energy, physical strength, and dedication required of trainee wine producers and farmers. The support of the School of Viticulture, Oenology and Agriculture will be decidedly with the candidate in support of young, full-time students.

The area in which divided opinion is most likely to be encountered is, as always, the School of Arts, Media and Communication. The Arts department of the School is by far the largest in the university and includes most of the subjects which may be studied for a traditional Bachelor of Arts degree. It is the department which attracts most mature students. They can select, from a great variety of courses of lectures, any combination which takes their fancy. Unlike the young, full-time students, they can, if they so wish, avoid any of those courses which might involve some demanding but unexciting application of their mature minds to matters of grammatical complexity, detailed historical analysis, or mathematical exactitude.

Courses of lectures from the extensive range offered by art history are greatly favoured. One retired pharmacist has put together a nice combination of, "The Golden Line in Greek Architecture", "Masterpieces in Silver of the Renaissance", and the humorously titled, "Monet is Called but Rothko is Chosen". From a wider selection of topics, another mature scholar, an elderly unmarried lady, until recently a post office official and part-time church sacristan from Lille, selected as her intellectual menu, "The Sexual Mores of Ancient Greece and Rome", "The Mystical Writings of Saint John of the Cross", and, "How to Choose a Good Bordeaux".

The lecturers in the arts department are usually delighted with the respectful admiration accorded them by the mature students, who find them refreshingly remote from the competitive cut and thrust of the commercial or public life from which they themselves have thankfully recently retired. Not being familiar with the even more incendiary nature of academic politics, they imagine their lecturers to be simple, unworldly, even saintly shepherds of truth and beauty. The same lecturers are happy to bask in this long overdue recognition. It differs so greatly from the scornful, unenlightened, and perceptively humorous descriptions of them by the cheerfully unimpressed young, full-time students. These, unlike their appreciative elders, disrespectfully view the pearls which are cast before them more as an unavoidable means to a degree than as priceless ends in themselves. It is virtually certain that most of academics of the arts department of the School of Arts, Media and Communication will exercise whatever influence they can in support of the mature student option.

Those academics of the communications department of the school, concerned with advertising and public relations, are more likely to support the conception of the university as primarily a forum for the education of the young. They view such disciplines as best suited to engaging the febrile imaginations of turbulent young minds. They see them as requiring fresh, innovative, and often outrageous ideas which they believe to be quite beyond the capacity of the disillusioned and disenchanted mindset of more senior citizens. Moreover, they are also somewhat apprehensive that many of these mature students may have been, in their previous existence, practitioners of these dark arts and might have a keener practical knowledge of what is required than their own bland academic nostrums may convey. They will certainly wish to support the youthful, full-time student option.

This preference will be endorsed by their colleagues in information technology. This area of the communications division of the school has, in recent years, been transformed and exhilarated by the arrival of Antonio Santoro a young Italian technologist with academic aspirations. He transferred to the university from a job with a major computer company. He is now the school's lecturer in ludology, i.e., the design of computer games. He has been very innovative and successful in attracting huge grants for his laboratory and pedagogic activity from various commercial enterprises. His lectures and practical illustrations are enormously popular with young students, many of whom are dedicated and even addicted to playing computer games. However, those students graced with greater maturity show no interest in what they considered to be a waste of time. The support of the ludologists will certainly be with the option for the young.

The media department of the school is the one in which the students, young and old, show most passionate interest and where one finds the greatest diversity of views about the future course of the university. This diversity finds vehement expression amongst both the academic staff and the students. The media department's proclaimed range of professional expertise includes film studies, television, radio, print journalism and social media. The mature students are as passionate as the young "wannabe" media personalities about pursuing courses in these various areas.

However, for the upcoming election, the main focus of interest is on the university's own radio and television station which is controlled and managed by the media department. The station broadcasts both radio and television programmes not only inside the university but also to the wider local community within a range of twenty-five kilometres. During the day, the media department performs its professional function by training students how to broadcast local news and university cultural events under the careful editorial direction and surveillance of the academics responsible for the various productions. The station's ringing slogan echoes around the Languedoc; "St Chinian Radio and TV tells it all as it's known to be".

However, from eight p.m. in the evening until eight a.m. in the morning, the station is made available for operation exclusively by the students themselves. This enlightened policy is intended to enable them to exercise their virtuosity and creativity by devising, presenting, and accepting responsibility for their own programmes. The mature students have been at least as keen as the young, full-timers to avail themselves of this wonderful facility.

The younger producers like to play loud music, cover university sporting events, and comment humorously on local affairs. As experienced students of Tinder and Grindr, they have developed their own very popular and much availed of online dating service called "Finder". It has done much to stimulate local interaction between town and gown.

The "matures", as the senior part-timers are derisively known, are more interested in trying their hand at producing foodie *"Come Dine with Me"* TV programmes, radio chat shows, and quizzes. However, they are not averse to availing themselves occasionally of the resource afforded by "Finder". Indeed, one of the mature students has suggested that the name of this student online dating service should be changed from "Finder" to "Ponder" to convey an appropriate sense of scholarly pursuit!

Intense interest in obtaining access to the station's television facility was already being expressed by supporters of the two publicly identified candidates, Lotti Beausang and Yves Leroy. However, Secretary Campion, the official returning officer for the election, had summonsed Lotti and Yves to a meeting in his office at five o'clock on the afternoon after the nominations, to lay down ground rules for use of the university's station for election purposes. He considered it important to ensure that there would be equity in the access to this popular and influential resource. How to accommodate the anonymous Alex Denton within this objective might pose a problem. People wondered would s/he express some interest, or simply abstain from any involvement?

CHAPTER EIGHT
Opening Salvoes

The day after the nominations for president of the student union were lodged, the candidates' campaigns got under way. Central committees and various subcommittees composed of eager supporters were established to pursue different aspects of the election programmes of both Lotti Beausang and Jean Leroy. They both did walkabouts, allegedly seeking to ascertain the wishes of individual voters but, in truth, just attempting to make themselves better known to them.

They each promised that, in the light of these kerbside consultations and advice, they would have a comprehensive election programme available in a few days. These, voters were assured, would incorporate their suggestions. In fact, in each case, such programme documents, were already in final draft form and almost ready to be dispatched to the printer.

The question that exercised everybody was the whereabouts and identity of Alex Denton, yesterday's mysterious last minute third nomination for president. The nomination had created a whirlwind of curiosity and astonishment. Everyone wanted more information about him or her. The nominators had promised that s/he would indeed deliver a clear election message today.

A careful survey of class lists, conducted by supporters of each of the other candidates disclosed no Alex Denton. A bright student raised the possibility that Alex Denton might be a clever pseudonym for somebody with the same initials, namely, A.D. Another, a student of data analysis, suggested that this might be too simple a solution and that A.D. might be just a further clue to the real initials of the candidate, namely, B.C. Did either set of initials, "B.C." or "A.D." provide reliable access to the identity of the real Alex Denton? The searchers returned feverishly to another exploration of class lists.

The result of this research proved to be of little worth. It produced only two names. However, excitement mounted throughout the morning as various outlandish rumours spread about the names that had been discovered. One such rumour declared that Alex Denton is a pseudonym for none other than Andre Dupuy, a young Belgian priest, who is on temporary leave from his parish in Ghent and is inscribed as a full-time student at the university, studying for a Master's degree in public relations. The rumour included the information that a key feature of his election manifesto would be the promotion of same sex marriage but only for heterosexuals. It was further rumoured that his bishop is worried that this brilliant theological refinement could be going a bit too far and might end up pleasing nobody.

The students were looking forward to hearing him debate with the other suspected Alex Denton, namely, Beatrice Coton. Beatrice is a fifty-two-year-old librarian who is inscribed as a mature part-time student in courses on "French Hedonism", and "The Philosophy of Soren Kierkegaard". 'I am much taken,' she confided, 'with Kierkegaard's claim that "truth is subjectivity". It makes life so much more interesting and unpredictable.'

Twice divorced, she is vehemently opposed to marriage of any kind. It was confidently asserted that she is the real Alex Denton and that she would be running a campaign centred upon an insistence that marriage is an outdated institution and that the university has an obligation to confirm this thesis experimentally by sponsoring an extensive programme of free love. Even Thomas Van Velsen's Community of Latter-Day Albigensians was not liberal enough for her. One wit suggested that she might be persuaded to explore another approach to conjugal engagement, namely, to marry herself and see how the experiment worked out.

The likelihood of either B.C. or A.D. providing the solution to the real identity of Alex Denton was argued enthusiastically throughout the morning. But, by lunchtime, there was no sign of her or his election message which had been promised by the nominators.

The lively discussion and eager anticipation gradually dissipated. The students gathered in the main square began to believe, somewhat reluctantly, that the whole last-minute dramatic nomination had in fact, as previously surmised, been just a massive practical joke orchestrated by a group of pranksters with little else to do. A few were even wondering was it too late to nominate both Dupuy and Coton for election, if only for the pleasure of hearing them debate with one another.

However, at three o'clock in the afternoon, the same large white van that had brought the ten nominators the previous day swerved into the square and shuddered to a halt with loud military marching music blaring from its open windows. The ten occupants tumbled out, each bearing a large bundle of leaflets.

Thomas Mansion, who had presented Alex Denton's nomination and was now registered as his or her official election agent, used a megaphone to address the students who remained in the square. 'Fellow students,' he declared, 'I told you yesterday that our dear friend, Alex Denton, would deliver to you today his or her election message as a candidate for the office of president of the student union. Faithful to his or her word, s/he has commissioned us, his or her nominators and ardent supporters, to deliver this message to you today, which we will now gladly distribute to everyone who wishes to receive it. We urge you most earnestly to vote for Alex as president.' His associates clapped and cheered loudly and started to distribute the leaflets, which were eagerly seized by the curious audience.

The message, printed on plain white sheets, was simple but disconcertingly brief and uninformative. In large black letters it proclaimed simply, "ALEX DENTON SAYS NO — VOTE FOR ALEX".

As the students gazed at the leaflet, they didn't know what to make of it. Some began to laugh, others sought further elucidation. 'What the hell does it mean?' they asked the unresponsive election agent, Thomas Mansion.

'I have nothing to add to, or about, the message,' he said. 'But I am authorized by Alex to inform you that s/he will address you personally here in this square at nine fifteen a.m. on May 1st, just before voting officially commences.'

As the students tried to absorb this meagre announcement, they remained completely mystified. 'What in the name of God,' they asked, 'is he or she up to? Is s/he just having a big laugh at our expense?' Others, more reflectively, pointed out that the promise that s/he would personally address them before voting commenced would certainly help to clear matters up. At least they would know who Alex Denton is and whether s/he is a man or a woman, a young, full-timer or a mature, part-timer. One thing which was certain was that there would be an impressive gathering of curious students in the square at nine fifteen on May 1st. In the meantime, Sandra Ricoeur promised to keep them informed in the *St Chinian Trumpet* about the progress of her research into the identity of Alex.

At five o'clock, Lotti Beausang and Yves Leroy presented themselves, as requested, at the office of Secretary Campion, the official returning officer for the election. They were eager to know what official television exposure might be available to them.

'I know,' the secretary declared 'how interested you both must be in securing as much exposure as possible on the university's television station to promote your respective campaigns. You are well aware that it has a large student following and that your performance on it will undoubtedly influence the decision of undecided voters.

'However,' he continued, 'as returning officer, I have a responsibility to see that there is equal treatment of candidates in their access to this influential resource. As you know, this access is limited to the evening programmes, which students themselves present. I have decided, in the interest of equity, to confine access to this popular platform to the Friday evening before the Sunday election. On that occasion, you will be invited to participate in a debate with each other. This debate will extend over two and a half hours, in the presence of a live audience. Holding the debate on the Friday will enable the electorate to devote the following day, Saturday, to calm reflection and informed discussion about the outcome of the debate before casting their vote the following day. You will each be afforded an uninterrupted half hour to present your election programme. During the final ninety minutes you will each have an opportunity to challenge the other's presentation. This stage of the debate will also be open to the live audience. They will be able to pose their remarks and questions directly to each of you. The debate will be chaired by Professor Claire Macon, the vice president for academic affairs.'

When Lotti and Yves realized that the secretary was determined that this would be the extent of their television exposure, they thanked him and were about to depart when it occurred to Lotti to remark, 'I presume that the publicity-shy Alex Denton has no interest in these television proceedings?'

Secretary Campion smiled. 'Oh, indeed, he or she has. S/he informed me through his or her election agent that s/he would be happy to go along with whatever is decided, provided s/he is afforded adequate exposure. S/he does not wish to participate personally in any debate. However, as a token of his or her goodwill towards the exercise, s/he has offered, as his or her contribution, to exhibit some simple uncontroversial visual effects as an appropriate background to it. Whereas this appears a little odd it does not seem entirely unreasonable and, having taken legal advice, I have agreed to his or her request. Consequently, throughout your debate, Alex Denton will be permitted to post, in support of his or her campaign, whatever background visual effects he or she wishes to display.'

The secretary stood up shook hands with each of them and, as he led them to the door, remarked, 'I wish you both every success with your campaigns, which I am sure will be of great interest to your fellow students and, indeed, to myself. As I must now prepare for another meeting, I wish you both a very good evening.'

Lotti and Yves left the secretary's office somewhat nonplussed. Each of them was thinking silently, *This Alex Denton, whoever s/he is, is becoming a right pain in the neck — a ridiculous distraction from the real business.*

'Look, Lotti,' said Yves, 'I know some of our supporters might disapprove but before we go back to our discussions with them would you care to have a drink with me? I could certainly do with one after that revelation about the invisible Denton.' He had been observing her closely in recent days and, to his surprise, began to find himself liking her very much.

Similarly, Lotti had come to appreciate, almost despite herself, that Yves was a genuinely nice person and, although determined to oppose him fiercely in the forthcoming election, found herself attracted as much by his open manner as by his striking good looks. 'I would love to,' she said. 'I think we both need a drink but on condition that we totally avoid the topic of the election.'

'Agreed absolutely,' he said and suggested that instead of setting tongues clacking at the Student Centre, they go to a quiet bar in the town. There they had not just one but two drinks and managed to learn a lot about each other while carefully avoiding any reference to the election.

She spoke of her rather sheltered background as an only child of elderly parents and of her determination to fashion a more interesting and engaging life for herself after her early retirement from a life sentence in an uninspiring job. He described his adventures during his extensive travel around the world for three years before coming to the university. 'I'm a bit apprehensive,' he admitted, 'about my agreement to return, after my studies, to a life just minding a vineyard.'

'And I'm wondering,' she said, 'where all my new interests will lead.' They laughed at their contrasting situations, she, trying to create a new life, he, wondering about going back to an old one.

An hour later, they returned to their respective bases to update their supporters about the meeting with Secretary Campion. They had both greatly enjoyed their brief interlude together and each had expressed a hope to see more of the other after the election.

The following day, the weekend edition of *The St Chinian Trumpet* was published. It contained an article by the editor, Sandra Ricoeur, remarking that the usually uneventful election for president of the student union had been greatly enlivened by the nomination of the mysterious Alex Denton.

I welcome this nomination, she wrote. *It provokes voters to think beyond the simple alternatives proposed* by the other two candidates. *Perhaps the enigmatic slogan, "Alex Says No — Vote for Alex", contains a profound message. The anonymity of the candidate is disconcerting but may be intentionally so, in order to concentrate attention on the message. Maybe we are being offered a brilliant inversion of Marshall McLuhan's dictum, "the medium is the message".* Chuckling to herself, she pledged, *I will continue my intensive investigative research to discover for my readers Alex's real identity.*

CHAPTER NINE
Interim Discussion

Ten days later, Guy Boulanger's two principal advisers, Claire Macon and Henri Campion, came at the end of a busy working day to his office for one of their regular meetings. Pushing aside the papers he was working on, he welcomed and seated them. Remarking virtuously that it was well after six o'clock, he poured each of them, and himself also, a measure of his Jameson twelve-year-old whiskey to lubricate their discussion.

'We have some important matters to consider,' he remarked, 'but I suppose we should begin with this upcoming election of the president of the student union. Although it is essentially a student matter, which normally would not feature highly on our agenda, we know that, in this instance, the outcome may have a significant influence on the profile and future development of the university. Have either of you formed any opinion about how it might turn out or learnt anything of which we should be aware?'

'Well,' said Claire, 'it has certainly provoked more interest than any other student election I can recall in all my years at St Chinian. It has caught the students' imagination and there have already been a number of heated discussions and a deepening division of opinion about the appropriate future for the university. Lotti Beausang and Yves Leroy are two strong candidates and each has accumulated a large and enthusiastic body of supporters. Denton remains an unknown figure to the voters. So far, he or she is considered a bit of a joke and is not being taken too seriously. However, Sandra Ricoeur is determined to change that situation.

'In my opinion,' she continued, 'although a part-time student's vote is worth only half that of a full-timer, if Beausang can maintain the interest and enthusiasm she has generated among mature students, she can win this election. Her electoral machine got into operation earlier than Leroy's and seems to be more dynamic. Many of the young, full-time students seem not to be taking the challenge she poses seriously enough.'

'You might be right,' said Henri. 'But if she does succeed, it will certainly create a rum situation for us. Needless to say, as returning officer for the election, I am careful not to express an opinion. But I agree with you that Leroy's team would need to be more focused and dynamic. However, it is still relatively early in the campaign and there is plenty of time for the picture to change. Speaking of pictures, I imagine the television performances two days before the election will be of particular importance and may even decide the outcome.

'I don't know how to evaluate the impact of the Denton candidature,' he continued. 'It has certainly generated considerable interest or at least curiosity, involving, as it does, an insistence on maintaining the candidate's anonymity. Our journalist friend, Sandra, is playing a clever game, stimulating her readers' interest about the merits of the unpretentious Alex. It will be interesting to see how they react when they discover that she and Alex are one and the same.'

'Have you anything to report, Claire, on the views of our academic colleagues about the election?' Guy asked.

'Well, it has certainly aroused their interest. And those of them who are more politically alert realize that it could have a significant impact on the future development of the university. Needless to say, there are clear indications from the usual suspects who take the exalted view that what is most important about any election is how it might facilitate their own wishes, aims and ambitions.

'Didier Ritz has made it known that he supports the programme of the mature students. He sees it as a wonderful opportunity to market a new conception of a genuine university and, incidentally, to market himself as an exceptional academic visionary.'

'Simone Blondel in sociology also seems to favour the campaign of the elders. She is convinced that their enthusiasm has greater revolutionary potential than the lethargy of the young students, whom she dismisses as more interested in promoting social media on their smartphones than spreading social revolution throughout the local vineyards. Jacques Lamy in political science can be relied upon to adopt exactly the opposite point of view to any espoused by Simone Blondel.

'Jocelyn Breton, head of media, in her typical state of agitated indecision, is trying, as usual, to ensure that she will be on the winning side. So far, she has confined her enigmatic utterances to affirming that she can see considerable merits in the views of all the candidates, including those of Alex Danton about whom she has no information whatsoever. Appealing to her characteristic mantra, she has encouraged all three candidates to "up their game".

'I think,' Claire added, 'that we will have a lively academic council meeting next week as the actual election draws nearer. There are bound to be some interesting and entertaining declarations of support for the various campaigns.'

'Indeed,' said Guy, 'and undoubtedly a few heroic self-sacrificing proclamations about the future development of the university; intended for wider dissemination throughout the student body. Let's just keep an eye on events as they unfold.

'However,' he continued, 'there is another related matter to which we must devote some attention. As you know, I have been keeping in touch over the past couple of years with our financially most successful student,

Jean Martin. His mother was a French actress from nearby Narbonne. She met his father, Jake, who owned a couple of nightclubs in Louisiana, when she was on tour there. She had a double act in a traveling vaudeville show. Early in the show, she performed as a scantily clad exotic dancer. A little later, she reappeared as a magician's assistant who sprang to her feet from a coffin, very much alive, having been sawn in half by Marcel the Magician, and holding on each arm a pair of magically produced turtle doves. Jake Martin was smitten. She abandoned the traveling show and continued dancing in his nightclubs. They married shortly afterwards and miraculously Jean appeared four months later. She reckoned that "Jean" would be a more distinguished name than Jake Junior and she personally ensured that he could speak French as well as English.

'He visited us in St Chinian for a year, on a junior year abroad programme in the mid-1970s, when the university was only about twenty years old. The records indicate that, although it would be a generous exaggeration to describe his academic achievements as modest, he made a significant contribution to the social life of the university. In fact, he devoted most of his time to organizing dances, parties, picnics and musical extravaganzas. He also participated enthusiastically in the productions of the drama society. He modelled himself on George Harrison and was known to his fellow students as "Le Beatle Martin".'

'He certainly created quite an impression,' remarked Claire. 'When I was appointed to St Chinian, years later, I heard colleagues still talking about the escapades of the American student with the funny French accent. I got the impression that he was very popular.'

'What little spare time he had from his social engagements,' added Guy, 'he devoted to a passing but intense romantic involvement with one of the drama society's leading ladies. She was a wealthy *vigneron*'s beautiful daughter who was studying public relations at the university. Throughout her brief liaison with Jean, she demonstrated an even greater aptitude for private relations.

'He returned to the United States with very happy memories of his "year in Languedoc". Upon graduation, with an unpretentious degree from an equally unpretentious college in Louisiana, he joined the family business where he put his University of St Chinian experience to good use. He devoted his social talents and enthusiasm to the entertainment industry and is now the sole owner of a nationwide chain of nightclubs, music halls, and restaurants, extending from Boston to Las Vegas. In America he is now affectionately known as Johnnie "the Music-Man" Martin and is reputedly a billionaire!

'When I visited him in New Orleans last summer, he expressed his delight at the international publicity which his French *alma mater* has received for its innovative development as a university harmoniously combining the academic requirements of both young undergraduates and mature students of the "third age".

'More significantly, in the light of our discussion over cocktails at the poolside of one of his hotels, I encouraged him to celebrate his appreciation of this happy evolution of his *alma mater*. He responded with a promise of by far the largest donation which the university, indeed any French university, has ever received from an alumnus. He proposes to donate a gift of thirty million dollars to the university. This will be used to fund additional student residences to be shared communally by younger and older students, a new state of the art Student Centre, incorporating a nightclub and restaurant, and a new theatre for performances by the student drama society of which he had been such a dedicated member during his own student days. Still commercially astute, he intends that the new student restaurant, modelled on those he owns in America, will be the prototype for a new chain of them throughout Europe.'

Claire and Henri were astonished at the scale of the proposed gift. 'It will certainly make a big difference to our campus,' exclaimed Henri appreciatively. He was the one, in his role as bursar, to whom people turned to find money for their various projects. For a change, it would be a pleasure to receive cash instead of having to try to provide it.

'Nevertheless,' said Guy, 'we will have to deal with a rather awkward coincidence, namely, his scheduled arrival on his visit to the university just ten days before the student election when the canvassing will be at full volume. On this short visit he intends to make a "surprise" announcement of the donation at a press conference before flying back to New York.

'He is unaware that the two categories of students, whom he imagines to co-exist in a state of beatific harmony, are currently at each other's throats in advance of the election which occurs soon after his arrival. It will be up to us to try to ensure that he remains in this state of blissful ignorance until he is safely on his flight home. We must protect our beloved alumnus from being distracted by the current electoral turbulence. I will need your advice and help in keeping him otherwise engaged.'

Claire and Henri assured him that they were fully available to help in any way he wished. He asked Henri to meet Jean on his arrival at the airport and to escort him and his secretary, who would be traveling with him, to the opulent suite which had been reserved for them in Château Les Carrasses, in nearby Capestang. He himself would bring the visitors to dinner, on the evening of their arrival, at "Le Table", an excellent restaurant recently opened by a Belgian consortium in nearby Assignan.

He requested Claire to escort the visitors, the day following their arrival, on a carefully orchestrated tour of some of the university facilities, including the library, the media centre, and the extensive estate which accommodates the School of Oenology, Viticulture and Agriculture's vineyard and farm — located safely some fifteen kilometres away, near the village of Berlou.

'Your scintillating company,' he said smiling, 'and a leisurely lunch there, attentively refreshed by scholarly samplings of recent vintages, should provide adequate distraction from any concern with the minutiae of student election campaigns.'

He advised them that he had arranged with the student drama society to stage a special performance for the visitors that evening. Henri and Claire were surprised to hear this and wondered, in the current circumstance, whether it was a wise suggestion. Might not the students seek to present a performance exploiting the explosive atmosphere of the current campaigning? Guy reassured them enigmatically that he had discussed the performance with the leaders of the drama society and that he was confident that it would meet with their approval.

Claire and Henri looked at each other, wondering what Guy had arranged. He always seemed to be a few steps ahead in any difficult situation. Smiling, he told them not to worry because he had every confidence that the drama students would provide a delightful performance. All they could do was laugh. After discussing the candidates for the vacant professorship in Italian, which would be on the agenda of the next meeting of the academic council, and some other less pressing matters, he thanked them for their support and advice and wished them a pleasant evening.

A little later, the auditor of the drama society came to his office, as invited. He brought Guy up to date on the progress of the rehearsals for the theatrical performance which they had discussed together a few weeks ago, and which the American visitors would attend. Guy thanked him for the update, happy at the way things were shaping.

CHAPTER TEN
Preparations

Both Lotti Beausang and Yves Leroy issued manifestoes and a programme of social and cultural events for the final two weeks of the campaign. Alex Denton retained strict anonymity. His or her nominators had posted many notices stating simply in stark black letters the now well-recognized slogan: "ALEX DENTON SAYS NO — VOTE FOR ALEX". However, they reaffirmed that he or she would indeed personally address a public gathering shortly before voting commenced on Sunday May 1st.

Lotti's election committee had been particularly industrious. Posters appeared everywhere portraying her as an inspiring combination of Joan of Arc and the revolutionary Marianne. Her handsome face gazed forth resolutely and wisely wherever students congregated or moved around. And beneath her blonde mane, blowing in the breeze, a firm declaration: "ST CHINIAN COMES OF AGE: A MATURE UNIVERSITY FOR MATURE STUDENTS".

Her election committee was more experienced, affluent, and professional than those of her two competitors. One enthusiastic member, a fundraiser for a major charity in a previous existence, had effectively exercised her well-polished skills of appealing and shaming. She had accumulated a very satisfactory campaign fund. Another member, a political activist, who had worked as an event organizer for the Republican Party, gave valuable advice on how best to dispense this campaign fund. It involved the provision of well-advertised free snacks, drinks, fountain pens, and baseball caps (proclaiming "KEEP LOTTI AHEAD" or "KEEP LOTTI IN MIND") at the various promotional talks and supporting events.

Louis Dupre, the retired detective and chairman of her election committee, also put his professional skills to effective use. He spent evenings in bars frequented by students and engaged them in discussion about the upcoming election. On one such occasion, he convinced a young student of history and politics that the university would be a much more interesting place if mature students had greater influence.

When the young man learnt that Louis had been a detective, he confided that when he obtained his degree he would love to train as a detective himself. 'Well,' said Louis, buying another round of drinks, 'perhaps you could do a little bit of detective work for me and I could judge how good you would be at it. You told me that you know some of the members of Yves Leroy's election committee. Why don't you try to discover some information for me about their plans?' Two pints later the aspiring detective agreed.

When they met again in the same pub a week later, the student had some disconcerting news for Louis. 'The committee,' he reported, 'has decided that their campaign should sponsor a range of social and sports events at which young, full-time students would excel and at which mature, part-timers would be at an embarrassing disadvantage, even if they could be persuaded to participate.

'These events,' he explained, 'would be represented, both subliminally and explicitly, as activities intrinsic to the nature of a genuine university in pursuit of its more than academic role of developing the character and personality of its students.'

They would be events which clearly favoured a predominantly youthful student ethos, events in which robust activities are resolutely promoted as intrinsic to the effective exercise of genuine university life. How could a university dominated by students of the *"troisième âge"* meet the character-building requirements of the rugby field, the boxing ring, the rowing regatta, the tennis court, or even the rigours of a three-day pop music festival? By their valiant display of youthful competitive vigour and *joie de vivre,* the young, full-timers would give effective witness to the authentic idea of a university. They would embody John Henry Newman's "Idea of a University"; one in which the presence of a phalanx of mature "troisième âgers" would be, at best, merely an entertaining and exotic addendum.

The events would be staged, for the most part, in the week leading up to the election. This was the week of the mid-term break, during which students could apply themselves energetically to whatever non-academic diversion took their fancy.

Louis thanked the young man and, having bought him several more pints, advised him to keep up the good work, and assured him that he would make an excellent detective.

The information provided was received in the Lotti Beausang camp with expressions of outrage and indignation. Serious and heated discussion ensued. Some of her supporters were in favour of ignoring the proposed events as peripheral distractions from the real issue of their vocation to accomplish the historical destiny of the University of St Chinian. This was the vocation to be the first and exemplary realization of the University of the Future, namely, a university devoted primarily to meeting the intellectual requirements and indulging the social proclivities of free-spirited mature students.

Others encouraged acceptance of the challenge which the proposed events presented. They would hoist the youngsters on their own petard by determined participation in all of these events and victory in most of them. However, it soon became obvious that this proposal, however emotionally uplifting and inspiring, had rather selective appeal. A few who fancied their tennis or kayaking skills were willing to compete. But there were very few foolhardy mature volunteers eager to expose their cherished if somewhat creaky physical attributes to the vicissitudes of the boxing ring or the impact of a robust rugby tackle.

Eventually, after several other unconvincing suggestions were impetuously advanced and summarily dismissed, an alternative strategy emerged which was enthusiastically adopted. It was agreed that Lotti's supporters, as advocates of "St Chinian, the exemplar university of the troisième âge", should stage their own programme of events in which mature students were likely to excel and in which any younger students, foolish enough to compete, would be ignominiously outclassed.

Various competitive events for the programme were imaginatively proposed. Luc and Marie Dupront, previously the proprietors and professional operators of the Beauty Restored Parlour in nearby Narbonne, immediately volunteered to challenge a team of young, full-timers to a beauty treatment contest. 'Let us see,' said Luc, 'which of us can provide the most transformative beauty treatment to a number of aesthetically challenged subjects selected by each team for treatment by the other.'

'Yes,' echoed his wife, Marie, 'between us we have nearly eighty years of hands-on and, indeed, fists-clenched experience of erasing facial wrinkles and dissolving or reallocating abdominal spare tires. The youngsters won't have a chance!'

'But they might land you with a few pretty challenging cases to treat from amongst us,' laughed Lotti.

Cooking, ballroom dancing, choral singing, table tennis, billiards, and, possibly, hill walking, were also suggested as activities in which "the matures" could compete comfortably. However, *pétanque* was the proposal which generated most excited approval and three teams promptly volunteered themselves for competitive engagement.

'*Pétanque,*' one proponent explained, 'otherwise known as *boules,* is a well-known and hugely popular game in France — almost a national sport. It is played by millions of people, mainly in the later stage of their life. It can be played by individual contestants or competing teams. For those few of you who may not be familiar with it,' she continued, 'the game involves pitching large hollow metal balls towards a smaller wooden one, known as a jack or "*cochonnet*" (piglet). The objective is to see who, by adroit pitching, and cunning displacement of the opponent's ball, can get closest to the jack. Although not very physically demanding, it lends itself to the most insidious and sly manoeuvres which can be perfected only over a long life of dissimulation and deceit. A young undergraduate would be an innocent abroad amongst seasoned practitioners of the game like ourselves.'

An attractive feature of the inclusion of the game in the proposed programme of events is that it corresponds admirably to a controversial feature of Lotti Beausang's election manifesto. This is the demand that one of the university's three football pitches be converted into two state of the art *pétanque* parks. This proposal has enraged members of the university's rugby and soccer clubs and elicited bloodcurdling threats of vicious reprisals if any attempt is made to implement it.

Meanwhile, Yves Leroy's election team has been equally industrious in planning and promoting their campaign. Besides the preparation of the proposed programme of sporting and social events, posters abound, showing him diving to score a try in an inter-university rugby match, or in poised display of his splendid physique at the edge of the university's swimming pool. Slogans exhorting "Let's Try with Leroy", "Score with Leroy" and "Make a Splash with Leroy" compete everywhere with the posters adulating the virtues of the beautiful Lotti Beausang and the enigmatic utterances posted on behalf of the mysterious Alex Denton.

The Yves Leroy election team published, with great exuberance, their challenge to competitive participation in various sports events such as rugby, boxing, soccer, tennis and rowing. They relished the prospect of the consternation it would provoke in the other camp. They were confounded to discover that the programme had already been covertly obtained by Louis Dupre for the Beausang camp, which simultaneously announced its own alternative programme.

However, the announcement of one event took both official teams by surprise. The informal group of admiring young women who eagerly supported Yves election had arranged a public lecture to be delivered by a renowned health expert on the advantages and academic merits of breastfeeding by comparison with powdered milk. It was intended as a subtle reminder of the sort of topic which would naturally be of interest to genuine university women students, namely, those of childbearing age, but which would be pointedly irrelevant, to older, postmenstrual part-timers playing at being students! It was yet another indication of the highly charged election atmosphere which would be played out during the following couple of weeks.

CHAPTER ELEVEN
April Academic Council

President Guy Boulanger rapped the table to attract the attention of the assembled professors and to open the April meeting of the academic council of the University of St Chinian. As it was the only time each month that they were all assembled together, it usually took about five minutes to distract them from greeting one another or confidentially soliciting support for some pet project.

Guy promptly signed the minutes of the March meeting, and headed straight into the various items of the rather extensive agenda. The first hour was taken up dealing with routine matters. Examination dates were agreed. Temporary and part-time lecturers were appointed. New candidates for PhD studies were approved, as were the external examiners proposed for PhD students submitting their theses. The opening hours for the Library and Information Centre during the summer period evoked some debate but were left to the discretion of Claire Macon, vice president for academic affairs, to decide after discussion with students and library staff.

Approval of a sponsored lecture on "The Importance of Cathar Mysticism to Contemporary

Languedoc Identity" was briefly delayed when a recently appointed German professor of accountancy objected that it might be seen as an attempt to promote religion in a secular university. Dr Thomas Van Velsen, the Dutch self-proclaimed authority on contemporary Catharism, instantly quashed this objection. 'I would remind academic council,' he proclaimed, 'that I am the chairman of the university's Community of Latter Day Albigensians and I can assure you that we have given a wholly secular reinterpretation to Cathar thought. Our Cathar way of overcoming the evil spirit and attaining the status of a Perfect has nothing to do with prayer, fasting, and sexual discretion — quite the opposite in fact. You would be surprised at the nature of our mystical raptures.'

He sat down with the satisfied smile of one certain that he has already attained the status of a Perfect and was dutifully pursuing a self-appointed mission of leading some of the more attractive and enthusiastic students, both young and mature, along a path to perfection largely of his own invention. It is one which would have astounded the pious self-denying Cathars of previous times who had been burned alive in their thousands for fidelity to their very different theological beliefs and ascetical practices.

President Boulanger moved on to the next item on the agenda. It was a request by Jacques De Bon, professor of European history at St Chinian, who had been appointed in the late 1970s, that a disciplinary committee be established to consider a charge of plagiarism against a third-year student, Madeline Inglis. 'This young lady,' he explained indignantly, 'for reasons or unreason best known to herself, chose to follow a course on Australian history instead of what I can, in all humility, confidently describe as my own remarkable and insightful course on European history. She subsequently had the nerve, in order to obtain an additional credit, to take the examination on my course which she had not attended. This was in addition to the examination on the Australian history course which she had attended. She met the examination requirement of my course by writing the required two essays on the content of the course which I had delivered, in twenty carefully crafted lectures, to an attentive and delightful audience of devoted and appreciative students.

'You can imagine my amazement and distress when, upon examining the young lady's two essays closely, I discerned that they were entirely composed, word for word, of paragraphs from my lectures. These must have been copied from the notes of other students who had studiously followed and conscientiously recorded my illuminating and original verbal presentation of the subject. I think that this must be deemed an open and shut case of plagiarism of my work, even if executed at one remove through recourse to the notes or essays of other dutiful students who had faithfully recorded my words. I respectfully suggest that this academic council institute a disciplinary committee to consider this grave charge.' He sat down with a pained self-righteous expression on his face.

'Does anyone wish to comment?' the president asked.

One of the student representatives entitled to attend the council meetings as an observer raised his hand. 'I was aware that this matter would be considered at this meeting,' he said, 'and, having made some discreet enquiries, I can assure the council that there is no case to answer for a charge of plagiarism. The learned professor seems to believe that because Madeline reproduced exactly his own spoken words without having been present, as other students were, to hear them uttered from his own lips, that, therefore, she was technically guilty of plagiarism. The charge is that, because she had not been present at his lectures, she had illegally reproduced his words as though they were her own, having accessed them by purloining them from the notes of students who had dutifully attended and legitimately recorded them.

'The actual provenance of Madeline's essays,' he continued, 'is much simpler. Professor De Bon is well known to students for repeating the same three-year cycle of lectures for the past twenty years. A couple of enterprising students, aware of this unswerving dedication to academic stability and consistency, and in order to help fund a fun weekend in Paris with their girlfriends, published privately last summer for sale to fellow students, his famous cycle of lectures on

European history for the next three years. Consequently, since Madeline knew, "prophetically" she might well claim, what he was going to say in his lectures before he actually did so, there can be no case of plagiarism for her to answer. Indeed, the student union has advised her that if she is able to establish that she had written her two essays on professor De Bon's course before he delivered it last term, she might well have a case to claim that it is he who has plagiarized her work. However, being a tolerant and good-natured young woman, she has decided not to pursue this course of action.'

As he sat down there were many barely concealed chuckles and smiles. Poor De Bon was not very popular. He was known to be prone to ludicrous expressions of self-importance and to exhibit tiresome manifestations of creeping infallibility. This amusing disclosure should keep him quiet for a while. The few who did not appear to appreciate the joke may not have been sympathizing with De Bon. More likely, they were wondering might their own academic offerings be liable to comparable pre-delivery publishing initiatives.

President Boulanger moved expeditiously to the next item on the agenda and the council resumed its routine rubber-stamping of inconsequential recommendations until a new item engaged their attention about half an hour later. It was the recommended new appointment to the vacant professorship of Italian.

This professorship had been a hotly contested post. Not only were there several shortlisted external candidates but also a popular internal local candidate, Dr Louise Mouton, who had been declared qualified but placed second by the assessors on their list of recommendations. The person recommended was Dr Antonio Frescobaldi, senior lecturer at the University of Fiesole.

The professor of sociology, Simone Blondel, indicated that she wished to address this issue. 'I have studied these applications carefully,' she exclaimed. 'Undoubtedly, Dr Frescobaldi has an impressive list of publications. However, being considerably younger, he has much less teaching experience than our own dear Louise. Moreover, whereas it is hardly difficult for an Italian to publish a lot of stuff in Italian, for a Frenchwoman to have published anything in that foreign language is surely a greater achievement.

'I have also,' she continued, 'been confidentially advised that Dr Frescobaldi is a committed capitalist and dedicated supporter of Silvio Berlusconi whom he regards as an Italian Trump before Trump.

'Finally, however, and most importantly,' she declared solemnly, 'I must once again raise the gender issue. In view of my well-known involvement in our equality studies programme, and bearing in mind this university's deplorable under-representation of women professors, I demand that we appoint our esteemed senior lecturer, Dr Louise Mouton, to the vacant professorship of Italian.'

This outburst provoked a lively and predictable reaction. Simone's well-known adversary, professor of political science, Jacques Lamy, dismissed her contribution as another flagrant example of her disregard for academic standards. Others supported her concern for gender equity and recognition of local talent.

Before the debate got out of hand, President Boulanger called the meeting to order. He pointed out that the discussion might have been labouring under a serious misapprehension. He disclosed that it was Professor "Antonio" Frescobaldi's somewhat eccentric but understandable practice to keep the domains of public, professional life and private, domestic life completely separate. 'And this,' he explained, 'is why, professionally, as author of her many distinguished publications, she presents herself as the widely read academic Antonio Frescobaldi. However, privately and domestically, she is Melanie Gucci, beloved wife of Marco Gucci and devoted mother of young twin daughters.'

This information was greeted with amusement and delight and the Frescobaldi appointment was enthusiastically approved, all participants in the debate convinced they had somehow contributed significantly to the outcome. However, Simone Blondel's satisfaction was tinged with a suspicion that she had made a bit of a fool of herself.

The next item on the agenda to arouse the council members from their dogmatic slumbers was a motion from Didier Ritz, professor of marketing, who stated that, 'This council must discuss, as a matter of urgency, the future orientation of the University of St Chinian.'

President Boulanger, well aware of Ritz's ulterior motive, had initially been inclined to disallow the motion. However, on reflection, he decided it would be better to allow him to air his publicity-seeking initiative rather than enable him to posture as a silenced martyr. Therefore, he called on Ritz to make his point but to do so briefly. Ritz, who considered himself the leader of the not very loyal opposition of the Boulanger administration, and eager to replace it with himself as president when the opportunity would arise in a couple of years, rose ponderously to his feet.

'Several years ago,' he proclaimed, 'I supported, and would even claim to have in some measure inspired, our president's initiative to welcome mature students of the *troisième âge* to our beautiful university. This initiative has been a remarkable success, for which, because of my professional marketing advice, I can claim some credit. As we all know, the university now enjoys the company of twice as many mature, part-time students as young, immature undergraduates. However, the logical outcome of this initiative has not been followed through.

'And what is that logical outcome you may ask? Stated quite simply, it is that the University of St Chinian should officially revise its profile and organization to acknowledge and proclaim itself to be formally and primarily a university dedicated to the intellectual and social requirements of students of the *troisième âge.* I hereby publicly declare my commitment to this conception of our beloved university and pledge myself to promoting its accomplishment. I am pleased to say that already there is a grass roots movement in this direction. It is rooted in the current campaign by many mature students to achieve the presidency of the student union for Madame Lotti Beausang. She is campaigning heroically for the conception of the university which I have indicated. I wholeheartedly support her campaign and, if she is elected, I will be glad to offer her my professional marketing advice.' He sat down to a mixed reception of suppressed laughter, indignation, head-nodding or shaking, indecision, and fence-sitting.

Marc Tavel, professor of viticulture, begged to disagree. Insofar as he was concerned, the university is there to educate young students — in his case to educate young vignerons. The troisième âgers might be helpful in consuming the vineyard's end product but, in his opinion, this was a decidedly subsidiary university role.

Other participants rowed in on one side or other, generating more heat than light. Simone Blondel expressed her opinion that the mature students were commendably more disposed to a revolutionary transformation of the university which, in her view, could be a decisive stage in the realization of a communist society. Marie Latour, professor of animal husbandry and poultry, found young, full-time students more able and more disposed to helping out around the farm. They were particularly co-operative in the piggery, which was her pride and joy. It was there, as she told anyone who would listen, that she pursued her lifelong ambition to generate, by experimental cross breeding, a characteristically St Chinian pig to be hailed as *Porcus Chinianus*. She found the mature students, both men and women, disinclined to slosh around in the piggery mud in their Valentino slacks and Gucci shoes.

Before the discussion became offensively adversarial, President Boulanger intervened sharply and terminated the debate. He thanked members for their contributions but advised that discussion of the matter should be deferred to a later date when it could be discussed dispassionately. 'The academic council,' he said, 'should not be embroiled in the vicissitudes of student politics. It might be interpreted,' he warned, 'as an attempt to influence the outcome of their election.'

This was, as Claire Macon appreciated, a pointed criticism of Didier Ritz for raising the matter at this time. However, Ritz himself was quite satisfied with the discussion. He had raised the matter precisely to influence the student election and intended to make sure that Lotti Beausang was made well aware of his intervention on her behalf. She would be an important ally in a couple of years when he himself intended to campaign strenuously to become president of the University of St Chinian.

The meeting arrived, finally, at the last formal item on the agenda. It was headed simply "Confidential notification of an imminent endowment". Council members were intrigued and keen to know what it meant. They wondered might it be just another endowed lecture funded perhaps by the local *Office du Tourisme au Saint Chinian,* or another weekend conference on "Safeguarding Our Students' Moral Standards", funded by *The Concerned Mothers of the Languedoc.* However, the president proceeded to deliver the good news.

'Our financially most successful student, Jean Martin,' he informed them, 'who pursued his brief period of studies here at St Chinian very happily, if without notable academic distinction in 1977, is an American citizen and now a billionaire who will revisit his *alma mater* tomorrow for a couple of days. He is delighted by the initiative of the university in promoting the harmonious coexistence of young undergraduates and older mature students, which I described to him at a meeting which I had with him in New Orleans some months ago.

'To express his appreciation of this development, he will announce, on Saturday morning, a gift of thirty million dollars, equivalent to twenty-five million euro, to provide for new student residences, a new Student

Centre, and a new student theatre. This announcement will take place at a meeting in our Aula Maxima at eleven a.m. He has also offered, although this will not feature in the official announcement, to install a state of the art American-style cocktail bar in the academic staff common room. You are all cordially invited to attend this meeting and to greet our munificent *alumnus* at a reception which will follow the announcement. Although by then he will have announced his endowment, I would urge you in your conversation with him to emphasize the positive and complementary aspects of student togetherness at St Chinian.'

The council members were astonished and delighted by the president's disclosure. A good attendance at the meeting was assured — not only because of the accompanying reception that in the circumstances would have to be decidedly hospitable — but also to get to see this remarkable product of the University of St Chinian's educational prowess, and perhaps learn a bit more about the proposed new cocktail bar!

Didier Ritz was already wondering what more financial support might be solicited to further his own plans for the development of St Chinian's business school. 'Splendid news, dear President,' he declared, 'I'm sure our distinguished graduate with such entrepreneurial prowess would be most interested in our cutting-edge business programmes. I would be delighted to invite him to my home for dinner and to detail for him our exciting plans.' The idea of a munificently endowed Jean Martin chair in international marketing and a new state-of-the-art business school was already beginning to blossom in his ambitious mind. If Boulanger could land thirty million dollars, surely Didier Ritz could do the business for twice as much!

'That is very decent of you, Didier,' replied Guy. 'However, I fear our dear alumnus's schedule is fully booked for the whole duration of his brief visit on this occasion. I'm sure, however, you'll get a chance to have a word with him at the reception after his announcement, although he will have to leave that gathering rather early to catch his private plane, which is scheduled for departure that afternoon, to bring him back to New York.' Privately, Guy made a mental note that he would have to ensure that Didier did not monopolize Jean Martin at the reception in his honour.

Having thanked the members for their attention and enthusiastic reception of the news of the endowment, he passed smoothly over "Any Other Business" and brought the meeting to a close, reminding them that the next meeting would be on Wednesday, May 24th, three weeks after the student election.

As the participants dispersed, Guy quietly asked Marc Tavel, the professor of viticulture, to come to his office for a few minutes.

When they arrived there, having noted that it was almost seven p.m., he offered him a glass of his treasured Jameson twelve-year-old. 'It will be a welcome change from all that wine you have to sample in the line of duty,' he said, smiling. He went on to explain that he had asked Claire Macon to bring Jean Martin on a visit to the University's School of Viticulture and Oenology and Agriculture, at nearby Berlou, around midday on Friday. 'As he is in the entertainment business, it is probably the area of the university in which he will have a professional interest. I would be grateful if you would show him around and offer him a light lunch and a tasting of a few of your better wines. It would be good also if he could see a few of the mature students working harmoniously alongside the younger students who constitute the majority of your student body.'

'No problem, Guy,' replied Marc, sipping his whiskey appreciatively. 'I'll be glad to show him around and to offer him lunch. Who knows, I may learn a thing or two from him myself about how to run the business side of the school. I'll ask Marie Latour, head of animal husbandry and poultry, to join us for lunch. She is good company though I doubt that our guest will share her passion for breeding pedigree pigs!' He remained for a further ten minutes, discussing matters of interest to the school. Having finished his drink, he congratulated Guy again on the remarkable financial endowment, and departed.

Guy remained working on papers for another hour until his wife, Lucy, collected him and they returned home for dinner where university affairs gave way to the more serious preoccupations of their teenage children, Guy Junior and Anne. Guy Junior was in the intimidating final year of secondary school and studying for the BAC. He hoped to study medicine at Montpellier, the oldest medical school in France. Anne-Marie, a couple of years younger, was hoping to go on an exchange visit to a family in Dublin during the summer to improve her spoken English. Listening to their chatter, Guy welcomed the distraction from university matters.

CHAPTER TWELVE
Campaign Planning

News of Jean Martin's proposed endowment spread like wildfire throughout the student body. It was greeted almost unanimously with enthusiasm and appreciation. Predictably, however, a couple of small groups opposed the gift. One band of anarchists, more dedicated to fiery declarations than practical action, spent several unproductive hours discussing ways in which Jean might be kidnapped and held to ransom. Another small group of committed Marxists argued that it presented a wonderful opportunity to strike a revolutionary blow at the heart of capitalism by refusing the endowment. They claimed that it obviously represented dirty money obtained by the exploitation of notoriously badly paid proletarian victims. It was the congealed blood money of those unfortunates, many of them students, who laboured for endless unsociable hours in the decadent American entertainment and hospitality industry as bartenders, musicians, kitchen staff, waiters, and bouncers. It should be publicly rejected as representing a typical capitalist ploy to buy respectability at the expense of the downtrodden masses.

When this demand received no support whatsoever from the general body of students, they modified their revolutionary proposal. They demanded that, at least, the new Student Centre, which would be built with funds from the endowment, be officially named Kim Jong-un House in honour of the heroic North Korean communist leader. This demand was received on all sides as an excellent joke but it did provoke reflection amongst the election campaign committees about an appropriate name for the new Student Centre. Yves Leroy's team favoured various pop stars and sports heroes. However, one of his keen supporters, Jeanne Mandel, who was also chairperson of the St Chinian University student branch of the National Front, suggested "The Marine le Pen Centre". The attention of Lotti Beausang's supporters hovered over names such as De Gaulle, Saint-Laurent, Édith Piaf, and Maurice Chevalier.

Initially, each group considered how they might exploit Jean Martin's visit to further their candidate's case. But it soon became obvious that this would be a dangerous path to pursue. For it was evident that the motivation of the endowment was Jean Martin's optimistic belief that the University of St Chinian was a beacon of light for the academic world. He was convinced that it demonstrated how the same institution could foster, in an astonishing spirit of harmony and mutual affection, the academic and social requirements of both young and more mature students. It was tacitly agreed by the competing groups that the boxing gloves should be temporarily discarded, in public at least, until the endowment was in the bag and the benevolent but gullible Martin was safely *en route* home to his castle or tower on Fifth Avenue.

However, none of this prudent discretion interfered with feverish planning and preparations by both sides for the final decisive week of the campaign. Each side had challenged the other to compete in the range of events in which they expected to succeed and thereby promote their vision of the university. After much argument, both sides finally agreed upon which competitions should be scheduled to take place.

The "matures" agreed to tennis on condition that it include table tennis. Likewise, they agreed to include rowing and hill-climbing if cake-baking and ballroom dancing were also accepted. They resolutely opposed all forms of football but eventually agreed to a mixed six-a-side touch rugby contest in exchange for the inclusion of bridge. The "youngers" agreed to *pétanque* in exchange for basketball. There was general agreement to accept chess, and poker. And neither side could resist the challenge of Luc and Marie Dupront's proposal for a beauty treatment competition.

A surprise development was the announcement by Thomas Mansion, Alex Denton's campaign manager, that although s/he would not be participating in any of the physically demanding competitions, s/he would, in a generous spirit of goodwill and camaraderie, participate in the chess competition. This disclosure generated great interest. Did it mean that Alex was going to reveal his or her identity some days before the promised revelation on the morning of the election? The electorate seemed destined to enjoy an entertaining week ahead.

Meanwhile, Lotti Beausang entertained her own committee with an account of her meeting earlier that evening with Professor Didier Ritz. He had contacted her immediately after the meeting of the academic council to ensure that she received his own account, rather than some second-hand version, of his inspiring and unambiguous support for her vision and campaign.

'He assured me,' she recounted, 'that he was in complete accord with my aim to reorient the organization of the university to operate as an academic and social resource serving the requirements and desires of financially comfortable, part-time, mature students. He told me that I could publicly declare his wholehearted support for this vision, and he promised to assist me in developing a sensational marketing strategy to bring it to triumphant realization. Needless to say, I did not discuss with him how I might square his support with the equally encouraging assurance of support by Simone Blondel, who views the mature students as the long-awaited apostles of the dictatorship of the proletariat, who would engineer another great French socialist revolution.'

Diplomatically, she did not divulge to her committee that Didier had also intimated that when, with her support, he was elected next president of the University of St Chinian, he might return the compliment. In order to complete the implementation of her programme, he would probably resign after four years, leaving the way clear for her to become the first mature student president of a university!

Yves Leroy's election committee was equally eager and industrious in preparing for the final decisive week of the campaign. Meetings were arranged to provide career guidance for prospective young graduates, who were pointedly reminded that the university existed chiefly for the benefit of those who had their whole life ahead of them.

Yves was also able to report that he had received a contribution of one hundred euro towards his campaign expenses from the Concerned Mothers of St Chinian. 'They told me,' he laughed, 'they were concerned that if the mature students got control of the university, their innocent young sons would be distracted from their studies and cradle-snatched by a coven of unprincipled and scheming brazen old hussies.

'They also told me...' he added, 'that the contribution would have been larger had there not been a number of so-called concerned mothers who were actively considering becoming mature students themselves and that some others would have no objection to having their daughter courted and even married by some of the better off mature gentlemen.'

The self-appointed subcommittee of admiring female supporters of Yves Leroy was also busy arranging Facebook and Twitter discussions. They were also preparing for their sponsored public lecture, "Keep Abreast of the Times — No Formula Our Formula", which was widely advertised by posters depicting delectable young women clasping joyful anticipatory babies to their bosom.

Meanwhile, the most concentrated attention was devoted by both campaigns to preparing the arguments which each candidate would present to a live audience during the television debate two evenings before the election. On each side, considerable ingenuity was also devoted to formulating particularly offensive "spontaneous" comments and questions to be directed by designated members of the audience to the candidate who was not of their choice. This debate and discussion would be eagerly followed, not just by those actually attending but throughout the cafés and bars and student lodgings within the twenty-five-kilometre range of the TV programme.

The lively encounters at various levels between the competing candidates and their supporters during the coming week promised to be a source of great interest, entertainment, and controversy. However, for the next two days, by agreement, a deceptive calm would prevail to safeguard the anticipated munificent endowment by Jean Martin, whose arrival was scheduled for the following afternoon.

CHAPTER THIRTEEN
Visitors from America

Thursday dawned a bright, beautiful and sunlit late spring day. The cloudless blue sky appeared to be complicit in welcoming home to the University of St Chinian it's recently rediscovered and esteemed son, Jean Martin.

Henri Campion was waiting to greet him at Béziers airport, about forty kilometres from St Chinian. Guy had informed him that Jean would arrive with his secretary and that his flight was due at four thirty. Arriving at the airport at four p.m., Henri was disconcerted not to see any airline flight from New York scheduled on the electronic noticeboard. However, upon enquiry, he was informed that a private plane was expected shortly.

At four thirty precisely, a beautiful silver Gulfstream G550 private jet glided to an impeccably smooth landing and taxied to a halt in front of the arrival hall. A door opened, steps were lowered automatically, and two people alighted. One was a stocky, grey-haired man, undoubtedly Jean Martin himself. The other was a strikingly beautiful, dark-haired, young woman in her late twenties, presumably Monsieur Martin's personal secretary. 'My goodness,' remarked Henri to himself, 'if that young lady is as efficient and computer-wise as she is beautiful, Jean Martin is a lucky man.'

He greeted them outside passport control, introduced himself and told them that President Boulanger, who would be collecting them later to bring them to dinner, had asked him to bring them to the beautiful two-bedroom suite which had been discreetly reserved for them at Château Les Carrasses.

Jean thanked him and introduced his companion. 'This is Molly O'Brien,' he declared. 'A remarkable young New Yorker of Irish descent. I call her the Secretary General of my United Affairs because she takes care of everything for me. I don't know what I would do without her.' This was an accurate evaluation of the situation. Jean, who had survived three divorces, had recently decided henceforth to elude the expensive distractions of matrimony and to combine business and romantic distraction in the company of Molly O'Brien. As she found him interesting, amusing, and admirably indulgent, Molly herself was entirely happy, for the present, to go along with this harmonious arrangement. Privately, she retained, on her personal agenda, the interesting possibility of reincarnating in due course as Madame Martin IV.

When their expensive luggage had been loaded into the boot of Henri's Renault Estate, he drove them to the beautiful Château Les Carasses, located about twenty kilometres from the university, near the village of Capestang on the Canal du Midi. Situated in extensive grounds, the famous old estate had been recently restored and developed into twenty-five luxurious apartments to cater attentively to the recreational requirements of a wealthy international *clientele*. Monsieur Martin felt quite at home there. Later that evening, he and Molly enjoyed a culinary experience, featuring seaweed *bouillon* and roast boar, to which Guy invited them in the exclusive *Le Table* restaurant, which had recently been established in nearby Assignan. Jean had come a long way from his student days in a bedsit at St Chinian above a *Café des Arts,* where he drank beer and ate "burger and *frites* ".

The following morning, Claire Macon arrived with a university limousine to collect a greatly refreshed Jean and Molly after they had consumed the *café et croissants* which had been discreetly delivered to their apartment. The experienced waiter, noting that one of the bedrooms was unoccupied, had discreetly left the two trays together on the table in the reception room of the apartment!

'A pleasure to meet you both,' Claire said, smiling. 'I hope you had a good night's rest and are ready for an interesting programme today. First, I would like to show you the Library and Information Centre. Afterwards we will visit the media department in the School of Arts, Media and Communication. It has grown significantly in size and importance since you were a student here. Then we will drive into the country to visit the School of Viticulture, Oenology and Agriculture, with which you would not have been very familiar given the more centralized location of your own academic and social pursuits. Later, after you have been left back to your apartment to rest for a couple of hours, you will be brought to a theatrical performance, produced specially in your honour by students of the university's drama society in which you yourself participated so eagerly and with distinction.'

'That sounds just fine,' said Jean enthusiastically.

Their first port of call was the Library and Information Service, situated in a large modern building, constructed a couple of years after Jean's departure. They were greeted by the director of the centre, Monique Dubray, who was head of computer services, and Jacques Rulent, who was chief librarian. The superficially cordial relationship between the two was maintained artificially as they each sought to engage the visitors' attention, emphasizing the crucial importance of their own particular responsibility.

Several years previously, in the wake of the traumatizing external quality appraisal of the university, a recommendation was implemented to combine into a single Library and Information Centre the two separate operations of the library and the computer service. This had involved exhaustive trade union negotiation and generated serious personal animosities between the two groups of staff.

Although claiming to be concerned only with the large picture, the particular issue of who should be the overall director of the new Centre exercised, almost to the exclusion of every other consideration, the close attention of both Monique Dubray and Jacques Rulent. The matter was referred for arbitration to President Boulanger. He, with Solomon-like wisdom, advised them that they should alternate the directorship between them every three years and that, if they could not agree with this proposal, he would advertise the post publicly and they could apply for it with any other external applicants.

In view of this decision, they quickly agreed to alternate the responsibility as proposed. However, this happy solution gave rise to further acrimony about which of them should be the director for the first three years. Extended arguments and further intense trade union mediation unfolded. Eventually, the proposal by a young librarian that they should decide by the toss of a coin was accepted. As the young man spun the coin in the air, Monsieur Rulent called "heads" and thereby became the first director. Madame Dubray, who had to wait three years to become the current director, is still firmly convinced that a two-headed coin was employed.

Oblivious to the strained personal relations of his two hosts, Jean Martin proclaimed himself greatly impressed by his tour of the Centre. He marvelled at some students casually taking down several books from readily accessible shelves. He noted others downloading catalogue information from university computers, while still others, cups of coffee at hand, worked simply from their own personal computers.

Although never a serious patron of the library himself, he could appreciate the extent of the change from his own time. There were no library computers then and the books themselves, carefully assembled and catalogued on index cards, were jealously guarded and made briefly and individually available only on presentation of a documented request. The whole operation was meticulously conducted under the watchful supervision of the university's first librarian, Mademoiselle Rachel Chastide, known disrespectfully but affectionately as Hop-Along Chastity.

At the media department, in a building close by, they were welcomed by the deputy head, Luc Simonart. He explained that the department head, Professor Jocelyn Breton, was unable to greet them as she was abroad participating in a conference in Berlin on the academic heritage of Marshall McLuhan. He had directed her PhD thesis in Toronto University. When pressed by her colleagues to elucidate what she meant by her frequent unexplained exhortations to them to "up their game" she would simply reply enigmatically that "the medium is the message".

She also liked refusing to deny an entirely groundless rumour that she had enjoyed a torrid affair with her thesis director in Toronto. It invested her otherwise uninspiring persona with an implausible aura of sensual depths. Her more unsympathetic colleagues suggested it might explain how she ever managed to obtain a PhD.

Jean was equally impressed by the developments in the media department. It differed greatly from his time when the department only provided a rather boring course of lectures on "Principles of Responsible Journalism" and had begun to experiment with a campus radio station. It was now quite at ease, providing a local television service and pontificating about social media and fake news. To demonstrate their proficiency, they recorded a short interview with Jean for the midday news, which informed viewers that this distinguished son of the University of St Chinian would be making an important announcement at his *alma mater* the following morning. Claire Macon interrupted the interviewer when he tried to question a rather puzzled Jean for his views on the controversy raging throughout the university about the election of the new president of the student union. She explained that they had to leave at once for urgent meetings at the School of Viticulture Oenology and Agriculture.

They drove through delightful countryside to the beautiful six hundred-hectare Domaine de Lacan, home to the experimental farm and vineyard of the university's School of Viticulture, Oenology, and Agriculture. It is situated near the village of Berlou, fifteen kilometres from the main campus — sufficiently remote from the electoral political turmoil of the other Schools.

Here the activities of both staff and students are deployed in genuine and necessarily cooperative physical exercise rather than in agile adversarial mental gymnastics. These relaxed pastoral academics are not much interested in university politics and, in general, are as content with the present order of things in the university as they are with the unchanging cyclical rhythm of the seasons. They see the role of the school as one of educating and training young local vignerons and farmers and accommodating a sprinkling of "matures" who are welcomed as an exotic distraction. They would be much more concerned were they aware of plans for the school which were being envisaged by Lotti Beausang's more extreme campaigners!

Marc Tavel, professor of viticulture, and Marie Latour, professor of animal husbandry and poultry, welcomed the visitors. 'We are delighted,' said Marc, jokingly, 'that you have found time to visit the poor country cousins of the university. We don't often have the pleasure of such distinguished company. I know that you, Jean, as a student, were too preoccupied and busy with urban extracurricular activities to have time to travel to our rural outpost. But perhaps your secretary, Miss O'Brien, with such a distinctly Irish name, is more familiar with country life and agricultural pursuits?'

'I'm afraid not,' replied Molly. 'I'm strictly a New York city girl, born and bred, so all of this is a great adventure for me.'

This was no more than the truth. For Molly had been born and reared in downtown Manhattan and had never before seen anything much larger than a poodle or a pigeon. She looked somewhat apprehensively at the herd of Friesian cows that had approached them inquisitively, straining their necks over the fence of the field beside which they stood.

'Shouldn't they be in cages?' she asked. The two academics thought that this was a splendid joke. But poor Molly was not joking.

'Before you head off to view the vineyards,' said Marie Latour, 'I would like to give you a quick tour of my own domain of animal husbandry.'

Again, Molly was somewhat puzzled. She knew what "animal" meant. She had experienced some enjoyable encounters with of a number of entertaining human male animals in her day. But she wondered what the "husbandry" bit might involve. 'Could it be an animal version of marriage counselling?' she speculated. Certainly, in her experience, the inhabitants of Fifth Avenue or Times Square didn't have to conjure with the concept of animal husbandry!

They drove for about ten minutes in a converted roofless van until they reached the section of the estate devoted to the care of poultry and farm animals. The scene, which gradually unfolded, astonished Molly. In nearby fields there were not only more cattle but also sheep and goats wandering casually around, grazing, and, occasionally, approaching to inspect the visitors in an alarming and entirely uncontrolled manner.

The poultry section was not much better. Admittedly the hens and ducks seemed harmless enough. They appeared to be more interested in pursuing their own interests than engaging with the visitors. In one corner of the area, Helga Kerstin, the former wife of Hans Kerstin, the formidable chairman of the notorious external Quality Appraisal Committee that had been imposed upon the university a few years previously, was busily engaged in conducting experiments for her PhD.

Her aim was, through selective cross-breeding, to produce a strain of Rouen ducks that could fly. It seemed outrageous to her that there were ducks that could not or had forgotten how to do so. The visitors watched her standing on an elevated platform over a pond into which she dropped, one by one, a dozen imaginatively bred Rouen ducks. Unfortunately, despite her ingenious cross-breeding, her academic objective eluded her as each of the recalcitrant birds landed with a splash in the pond.

This tolerable and mildly entertaining spectacle was unexpectedly disturbed by the appearance of a gaggle of geese. These were decidedly more truculent customers. They clearly resented the intrusion of strangers into their own quarters and advanced menacingly, necks stretched and hissing loudly. Molly was visibly intimidated. She had not expected such a literal encounter with what it meant to be goosed. She was greatly relieved when Professor Marie Latour declared, 'Finally, you must visit my pride and joy.'

The professor led them cheerfully to an extensive enclosed pen behind the henhouse. Its treasured occupants were about forty pigs of various hues and dimensions, grunting and sloshing happily around in the mud. 'Welcome to my piggery,' Marie exulted. 'These wonderful animals are greatly underestimated and they are my special interest. I know them individually and they are my particular friends. Moreover, they are much more intelligent and amiable than people realize. Indeed, my research involves seeking to breed a slender pig which can be adopted as a domestic pet and I will name it, even if I cannot christen it, Porcus Chinianus. One of my particular academic aspirations is one day to see smart ladies strolling down the Rue de Rivoli in Paris, leading their Porcus Chinianus by a silver lead.'

As though to confirm her high estimation of their amiability, a number of the pigs ambled over close to where the visitors stood and inspected them inquisitively and expectantly. As Jean regarded them with interest and amusement, poor Molly, already quite unnerved by her goose encounter, backed breathlessly away from this further intrusive initiative. 'Oh dear,' exclaimed Marie, taking her arm, 'don't be frightened. They are decent sociable fellows and only want to be friends with you. Just remember,' she continued, 'dogs look up to you; cats look down on you; but the honest, friendly pig looks you straight in the eye.'

Molly was not reassured by the evidence of several earnest snuffling attempts on the part of Marie's pride and joy to establish such straightforward eye contact. She was much relieved when Marc Tavel intervened to say that they would have to tear themselves away from this porcine paradise and proceed to visit the vineyards before lunch.

They left the tumultuous setting of animal husbandry, manoeuvred their way through a complicated labyrinth of farm tracks, and arrived eventually at a magnificent panorama of rolling hectares of vines which, in turn, led on to a veritable forest of olive trees. This inanimate vista was much more to Molly's liking and Jean was fascinated by Marc's lucid exposition of the characteristics of the various kinds of vine being cultivated on the estate. As he thought of all the wine consumed in his various pubs, hotels, and clubs, a genial entrepreneurial idea began to form in his mind! He listened with interest and intelligent questioning to the distinguishing characteristics and hazards of various vines — Sauvignon Blanc, Chardonnay, Syrah, Merlot, Cabernet Sauvignon, Grenache and, a local favourite, Carignan.

The vines, which had been pruned early in spring, showed a healthy fresh growth and the first clusters of new grapes. Teams of students, almost all of whom were young, undergraduate men and women, revealing a noticeable absence of "matures", moved systematically between the rows. They were spraying sulphur and copper sulphate to combat the risk of oidium, downy mildew, and the dreaded phylloxera, which, having been transmitted by vines imported from America, had devastated most European vines at the end of the nineteenth century.

'Why,' asked Molly, 'are all those pretty rose bushes planted at the end of the vine rows?' Marc explained that, nowadays, they were mainly for decoration but in earlier times they had been very useful in providing early signs of the same fungal diseases to which both they and the vines were susceptible.

Having completed their open-air inspection of the vines, the group moved to a large stone building nearby where the fruit of the vine was processed into various types of wine and stored, according to type and vintage, in large vats and stacked rows of bottles in the capacious underground cellar. This is the location, where open-air viticulture morphs into indoor oenology. The manifold oenological activities include regular sampling and appraisal of the wine at various stages of its transformation from grape to inspirational liquid. Unsurprisingly, many more mature students generously devote their time and impressive bibulous experience to this stage of the production — inspecting, sniffing, swirling appreciatively within their mouth and, only very occasionally, spitting.

The visitors were ushered into an elegant dining room for lunch. They were joined there by Luc Dupuis, the professor of farm management, who also managed the commercialization of the school's produce. After enjoying an appetizing sparkling aperitif of Blanquette de Limoux, which Marc explained was the very first naturally effervescent white wine produced in the sixteenth century by the Benedictine monks of Saint-Hilaire monastery at nearby Limoux, an enjoyable lunch prepared from the school's own produce was served. The menu offered pâté de foie gras, courtesy of the domaine's resident geese (which Molly surmised might explain their earlier indignation), rack of a lamb, that would hardly be missed from the large flock seen cavorting earlier, a mature pélardon goat's cheese, and tarte aux abricots — all agreeably lubricated by excellent house Sauvignon Blanc and Merlot.

During the meal, Jean aired the thought that had occurred to him when viewing the vineyard, namely, that he would like to have a signature wine for his many hospitality outlets. It provoked the lively interest of both Luc Dupuis and Marc Tavel. By the end of the meal, a provisional agreement had been reached for an initial order of five thousand bottles of blanc and five thousand bottles of rouge to be transported across the Atlantic to New York. The issue of a suitable title clearly identifying their provenance and owner was left for further discussion.

A little later, after their coffee and Armagnac, Claire delivered the well satisfied visitors back to their apartment to rest. She assured them that they would be collected in good time for the student theatrical performance in their honour later that evening. After a brief siesta, they strolled down to Capestang, the local village on the Canal du Midi, where tourists and small boats from northern France and the Netherlands were already much in evidence. They explored the rather splendid Collegiate Church of Saint-Étienne, frequented occasionally in the eighteenth century by Edward Dillon, the last archbishop of Narbonne. Dillon, of Irish parentage, liked to spend his summer vacation in his palace there during the years before he beat a hasty retreat to England, with his mistress, to avoid the threatening inconvenience of the glorious French Revolution.

CHAPTER FOURTEEN
Theatricals

As arranged, a university limousine was waiting outside
Jean and Molly's apartment building at seven p.m. to
convey them to the small theatre behind the university
library where Jean himself had performed in a couple of
unremarkable student productions. They were greeted
by President Boulanger and his wife, Lucy, and escorted
to seats in the front row by two members of the
university drama society, one a very mature lady and the
other a handsome young fellow, each clad as forest
children but with academic gowns over their shoulders.

The theatre filled up quickly with both staff and
students, curious to discover what on earth a show
entitled *Romeo and Juliet — St Chinian Style* might
have to offer. They would not be disappointed.

The curtains opened onto a stage designed as a
vineyard in which a number of couples locked in
various forms of intimate embrace, and clad in shorts,
white shirts, and St Chinian University blazers,
discussed issues of concern. A common characteristic
of the different couples was that, in various
combinations, they represented a possible pairing of a
"mature" and an "undergrad" student. In each case they

were also displaying exaggerated manifestations of solicitous attention. The "matures", both and male and female, were explaining mathematical theorems or solving crossword puzzles for their undergraduate partners. These, in turn, helped their mature counterparts over stiles or lifted them up to pluck an apple from an adjacent tree.

'As wise Pythagoras showed us, the square on the hypotenuse is equal to the square on the other two sides,' explained a retired quantity surveyor.

'But why would you ruin a nice hypotenuse by putting a square on it?' demanded his young companion, tossing her blonde hair incredulously.

'At three down can you give me a five-letter word naming our midday meal?' asked a former teacher.

'That's easy,' her eighteen-year-old footballer responded, 'it's "pizza".'

Close by, a handsome young man lifted up a sturdy former physiotherapist to reach some low-lying fruit. 'Oh, I hope you don't strain yourself,' she said, smiling, 'but if you do, I can give you a nice massage.'

The issue which concerned all of them was the dilemma in which the leading couple found themselves. They were Romeo, a sixty-five-year-old "mature", a plumber in a previous life, and Juliet, a twenty-year-old undergraduate student of social science. They were obviously deeply in love but their liaison was fiercely opposed by their respective families. Romeo's elder sisters thought that their silly brother had lost the run of himself and was being entrapped by a scheming hussy. Juliet's parents had higher aspirations for their beautiful daughter than a retired plumber trying ridiculously to reinvent himself as a sports writer. They had formulated a plan to remove their daughter from St Chinian by force and confine her within their extensive dairy farm near Avignon.

The couples participating in the drama, having got news of the dastardly plan of Juliet's family, were determined to foil it. They persuaded one of the university chaplains, a Franciscan monk, who, because of an alleged friendship with the American president, had been given the nickname Donaldo, to join them in the vineyard and to subvert the plans of both families by marrying the lovers.

The wedding ceremony, performed on stage, was a splendid affair. The best man was a young trainee vigneron. The bridesmaid was a mature Dutch matron, inscribed at the university in courses on Celtic monasticism, the manufacture of French cheese, and early Italian erotica.

Friar Donaldo conducted the ceremony with spirit and style. To the great entertainment of the guests, he urged the happy couple not to let their enthusiastic dedication to producing many children to distract them from their university studies.

The bridesmaid spoke eloquently of the wedding as a symbol of the close links which bound all mature students and all young students together. This evoked hoots of laughter and jeers from both classes of students in the audience, which momentarily puzzled Jean who was enchanted by the solidarity and co-operation proclaimed by the bridesmaid.

The bridegroom, Romeo, thanked the guests, young and old, on behalf of Juliet and himself for celebrating the happy event with them. 'Unfortunately,' he said, smiling, 'I didn't have the opportunity to invite our families or to ask her father for her hand in marriage. In fact, we must leave at once to catch a plane to Lanzarote before the news gets out, but please continue the celebration.'

The pair departed safely in high spirits. Unlike Shakespeare's original script, there would be no poisoning or suicides. Champagne arrives. A three-piece rock band strikes up, playing music from the sixties and seventies. The dancing begins with the gyrating golden codgers manifesting much greater proficiency and rhythm than their young partners. A mood of reckless abandon and joyful camaraderie prevails as the curtain comes down.

The audience, with delighted cheering, hooting, and laughter, applauded the show enthusiastically and accorded it several curtain calls. A few visitors, including Jean, took it as a wonderful expression of the co-operative culture prevailing throughout the University of St Chinian. For their part, the staff and students appreciated it as a hilarious travesty and caricature of the poisonous atmosphere which actually obtained throughout the campus. President Boulanger was well satisfied that the actors had excellently fulfilled the proposal he had discussed with the young auditor of the drama society a few weeks before Jean's arrival.

Jean and Molly were led backstage to meet the cast. He congratulated them and recounted some of his own experience on the same boards. Then Guy escorted them to the car waiting to convey them back to their apartment. Jean thanked him for a memorable experience. 'It dramatically confirms,' he enthused, 'everything I have heard about the wonderful atmosphere in the university between the mature students and the young undergraduates. It was wonderful to see how they complement and assist one another. What a pleasure it was to see an old accountant helping a young mathematically-challenged social science student grapple with her incomprehension of some statistical data. And equally charming to observe the young *vigneron* gracefully lifting a mature nurse, enchanted by her recently discovered part-time academic interests, over a fence.'

Molly was not quite as convinced or enthusiastic but was careful not to say so. Moreover, as they settled into the car, she noticed a gleam in Jean's eye, which intimated that, on their return to the seclusion of their apartment, he might wish to follow the mature accountant's exemplary solicitude and help her to grapple with her own statistics! She would be glad when they returned to the peace, calm, and tranquil predictability of downtown Manhattan, far removed from the hazards of agricultural life and student dramatics. She began to appreciate that "longing makes the heart grow fonder" and longed for the inanimate mechanical clamour and regulated chaos of Broadway and the Bronx.

CHAPTER FIFTEEN
Money from America

The sun shone brightly on the Saturday morning of the formal announcement of the Jean Martin Foundation. The president had ensured that it would be well-attended and enthusiastically applauded as a munificent donation to the University of St Chinian; which indeed it was. The ceremony was arranged to take place in the university's Aula Maxima which was used for distinguished guest lectures, the conferring of degrees, and other special events. It filled up quickly. University staff and local dignitaries occupied the main hall. Students crowded into the balcony area, attracted not only by the event but also in anticipation of the generous reception scheduled for afterwards.

As the guests arrived, they were confronted outside the building by small half-hearted groups of protestors, all attired in the requisite "yellow vest". A few waved banners denouncing America's global imperialism. Others were equally vehement in their outrage about America's lack of involvement in the global environmental programme agreed recently at the Paris Conference. A solitary protestor's banner asked, enigmatically, "What Would Napoleon Say?"

Smiling, Jean waved to them as he entered. 'We organized better protests against the Common Market, the Berlin Wall, and South African oranges when I was here in the seventies,' he informed them cheerfully.

Realizing that nobody was paying them much attention, most of them soon folded their banners, discarded their "yellow vest", and discreetly joined the celebration, confident that there was no conflict between principled protest and enjoying a glass of capitalist champagne.

The temporary suspension of electoral hostilities, tactically agreed between the rival student camps, remained in place at least until the endowment money was securely transferred.

The mayor of St Chinian, a benign socialist and part-time pork butcher, was escorted to her place in the front row. She is as renowned for the exceptional quality of her sausages as for her all-embracing socialism. She exhibits an ecumenical capacity to entertain contradictory propositions sympathetically, and defines her socialism as meaning that if she is unable to do a fellow citizen a good turn, she wouldn't do her a bad one. A senior official from the Ministry for Research and Universities was invited to sit beside her. Also seated in the front row were Claire Macon, Henri Campion, the deans of the university's four Schools, and Molly.

The representatives of various political parties placed themselves appropriately on the left- or right-hand side of the auditorium. The landladies of Languedoc were well-represented, as were the Concerned Mothers of St Chinian. There were a few local *vignerons* and a number of representatives of the Hérault Chamber of Commerce. There was gratifying interest from the local and national press corps. And the university's radio and television Service was geared up to convey the good news to the surrounding region.

President Boulanger led Jean onto the raised stage, escorted him to his seat, and walked to the nearby microphone to introduce him.

'*Monsieur le Maire*, distinguished guests, fellow academics and students, ladies and gentlemen,' he began, 'it is my great pleasure to greet you to on this special occasion when we welcome home a most distinguished alumnus, Jean Martin. Jean spent a junior year abroad with us in 1975. He has not had the opportunity to visit us since. He has been wholly engaged in developing his father's modest entertainment business in Louisiana into a nationwide chain of theatres, cinemas, nightclubs and hotels. But when I met him in America last summer, he spoke warmly of his year with us and proposed to mark it in an appropriate manner. It is to facilitate this desire that I have invited him here today. So, without further delay, I ask our dear alumnus, Jean Martin, to address us.'

To enthusiastic applause, Jean rose and faced the expectant audience. 'President Boulanger, ladies and gentlemen,' he began, 'it is such a pleasure to return, after more than forty years, to the University of St Chinian, where I spent such a happy year. My mother was a native of this region and it was during a tour of America, pursuing her artistic career, that she met and married my father who was in the entertainment business in Louisiana. I am the result of that happy liaison.

'Twenty years later, when I was attending college in Louisiana, she persuaded my father to send me on a junior year abroad programme to the recently established University of St Chinian, to discover for myself some sense of my French provenance. It proved to be the most enjoyable year of my life.'

'Officially, I was meant to be studying business, public relations, and marketing. And, in a way, I suppose you could say that this is what I was doing, but not in a very academic way. I had little aptitude for trying to make sense of academic lectures. Also, I found more than half an hour in the library to be a very claustrophobic experience and so bad for my health that a restorative litre of beer would be urgently required.' (Polite laughter from the front rows, and hoots from the student balcony.)

'However, I compensated for my academic ennui by practical participation in various highly entertaining social activities. I received a sterling education in personal relations, both in the broad sense of cultivating team spirit on the rugby field and in the more intimate sense of negotiating the logic and mysteries of very

152

personal relationships with the beautiful girls of St Chinian, and with one in particular.

'My marketing skills were finely honed by my participation in several theatrical productions of the university's drama society. There is hardly a better marketing education than convincing an audience of the authenticity of a piece of sheer make-belief, which one enacts on stage in the glare of revealing footlights.

'My business acumen was greatly developed by my conscientious attendance at various venues devoted to social revelry. I soon identified the more popular places in which to party into the early hours. I also discovered those that were better value, and those best adapted to changing fashions and fads. This practical fieldwork, dedicated to the study of business in action, has been a significant resource in the subsequent development of my own business activities, even if it did not translate at St Chinian into respectable academic grades

'When President Boulanger visited me in New Orleans last summer, it reminded me of my happy time here. I was also aware of his internationally acclaimed genial initiative of making the resources of the university accessible to a new cadre of mature, part-time students at the university. I resolved to show my appreciation by making a gift to the university at which I had passed such a memorable year, and I accepted his kind invitation to come here today to announce it. I had indicated to him in advance that the bequest would take the form of a gift of thirty million dollars to build a new student centre and restaurant, a new theatre for the drama society, and a new student residence complex, consisting of one hundred three-bedroom apartments. I expressed the wish that each of these apartments be shared by a combination of mature and younger students in whatever configuration they find appropriate or agreeable. A further attraction implicit in this arrangement is that the rent of the apartments will provide a helpful ongoing discretionary income stream for the university. However, since my arrival here, and my experience over the past two days, I have decided to modify this gift.'

As he paused to take a sip of water one could see signals of alarm on various faces. *My God*, thought Guy, *has he discovered that a far from cordial relationship obtains between the golden codgers and the young Turks? Is the money going to be delayed or diminished?*

Replacing the glass and wiping his lips, Jean continued his remarks. 'Yesterday morning, I spent a delightful, and informative few hours, as a guest of your excellent School of Viticulture, Oenology and Agriculture, at nearby Berlou. And last evening I experienced a wonderful theatrical production of *Romeo and Juliet — St Chinian* by the student drama society of which I am so proud to have been a member. It provided a most moving dramatic confirmation of the wonderful co-operative spirit obtaining between the older and younger students of St Chinian.

'Consequently,' he said, smiling, 'I have decided to enlarge the scale of the endowment to a sum of thirty-five million dollars. This will enable me to purchase, each year, for an initial five years, ten thousand bottles of St Chinian wine from the university vineyards and to establish annual year abroad scholarships at St Chinian for four Americans, two mature and two junior students. And so, without further delay, it now gives me great pleasure to present your president with a cheque in the sum of thirty-five million dollars. I hope it is in good time to be lodged to the university's bank account this afternoon.'

To tumultuous applause, he walked over to Guy and handed him a greatly magnified cheque on which the number thirty-five million was clearly visible. As the pair embraced, radios whirred, TV cameras swept the exultant audience, and a hundred smartphones flashed.

Guy moved to the microphone. 'My dear Jean,' he exclaimed, 'what a wonderful and greatly appreciated endowment. It is the most munificent and generous gift that this or any French university has ever received from an individual alumnus. I know that you have not sought to have your name associated publicly with the new buildings you have endowed. However, for a start, I propose to recommend to the governing body of the university that the new student theatre be named the Jean Martin Theatre and I am sure we can devise a similarly appropriate name for the wine from our

155

vineyards which will adorn your various enterprises on the other side of the Atlantic. Perhaps we can work around an initial suggestion of "Domaine Jean Martin". I'm sure our professor of marketing will have interesting refinements to propose.

'I know,' Guy concluded, 'that you must leave in about an hour for your flight to New York. So, for the next fifteen minutes we can receive a few remarks from the audience and then I hope you can join us, if only briefly, at the reception in your honour which is sure to continue in a joyful spirit of appreciation and celebration long after your departure for your flight.'

The mayor was the first to speak from the audience. She was decidedly of the opinion that the wonderful gift to the University of St Chinian was a splendid confirmation of the intrinsic harmony of entrepreneurial capitalism and practical socialism. She intended to propose to her fellow councillors that the freedom of St Chinian be awarded to Jean and she hoped to be still mayor after the forthcoming local elections in order to confer the honour personally.

Not to be outdone, the president of the local *vignerons'* association, a prominent Republican Party candidate in the same elections, declared that he hoped, on Jean's next visit, to induct him as a *Chevalier* of the *Confrérie des vignerons de St Chinian.*

The president of the Landladies of Languedoc hoped that the new student residences were intended to cater for additional students who would be attracted to the university and would not adversely affect the meagre income of the local landladies.

The chairwoman of the Concerned Mothers of St Chinian hoped that the unusual arrangements envisaged for tenants of the new student apartments would not constitute a moral hazard for the modest female students of the university. She hoped that the new three-bedroom apartments, even if shared between mature and young students, would only be occupied by persons of the same sex. Her comment provoked an outburst of unseemly mirth.

Guy thanked the contributors and, bringing the ceremony to a close, invited all present to enjoy the fine reception being offered in honour of Jean's munificent gift. The audience needed no encouragement. They moved with alacrity to the large reception area adjoining the lecture hall and soon were busy washing down oysters, canapés, *pâté de foie gras*, and sausages, with brimming glasses of Sauvignon Blanc, Merlot, and Blanquette de Limoux.

Jean rejoined Molly and circulated through the crowd, acknowledging congratulations and thanks. Didier Ritz, professor of marketing, buttonholed him for a couple of minutes. He promised to work on a sensational title for Jean's wine and proposed himself as a marketing consultant for the promotion of Jean's enterprises throughout Europe.

Shortly before they had to leave for their plane, a handsome woman approached and said, 'Dear Jean, how lovely to see you again after all these years.'

Looking closely, he recognized, with great emotion, his former particular girlfriend, Claudine, the leading lady with whom he had acted publicly in a production of the drama society, and more privately in the seclusion of his bedsit. They embraced warmly. She had married a young doctor a couple of years after he returned to America. Her husband had died recently. Jean promised that they would meet again on his next visit. Molly was relieved when they had to leave for their flight and would be in no hurry to suggest an early return visit!

Later that evening, Guy met with Claire Macon and Henri Campion in his office. They agreed that the visit had been a great success and Henri confirmed that the cheque had been safely lodged. 'A very good day's work,' said Guy, smiling. 'Our next challenge may not be quite so enjoyable, namely, coping with the electoral fallout of the evolving adversarial relationship between the golden codgers and the golden youths.'

CHAPTER SIXTEEN
Business as Usual

The plane transporting Jean and Molly back to New York had barely risen off the tarmacadam at Beziers when the two student election machines sprang back into action with renewed commitment.

Rewriting the narrative, retired detective, Louis Dupre, chairman of Lotti Beausang's election committee, issued a statement claiming that the Jean Martin endowment would never have happened without the significant presence and achievements of mature, part-time students at the university, a presence which had so impressed the donor.

Andre Leon, the public relations student, who had been elected as spokesman for Yves Leroy's team, issued a press release claiming that the motivation of the gift was Jean's fond memories of his time at the university, a simpler, more authentic time, uncomplicated by the unpredictable behaviour of ageing "wannabe" swinging students.

As the election date drew closer, the differences between the two camps intensified. Each sought to claim the high moral ground of serving the best interest of the University of St Chinian and the future course of higher education therein. The various social events and competitions scheduled for the coming week between the different categories of students took on an added significance.

Both Lotti and Yves, although each was fully committed to their respective campaigns, began to think that the antagonism, which was escalating, was excessive. This misgiving may have something to do with the fact that she herself was among the younger members of the "matures", and he among the older of the "youngsters".

At the great reception celebrating Jean's bequest, she saw him talking with a group nearby and smiled at him. It reminded him of their brief, previous, private meeting, which he had initiated and which he had greatly enjoyed. He returned her smile but the noisy convivial atmosphere of the reception provided no opportunity for conversation. He decided to email her and to invite her to meet him for breakfast the next morning in the same discreet out of the way café in which they had previously met. She replied that she would be happy to meet him there at nine a.m., as suggested. After the usual Saturday night entertainments and diversions, it was unlikely that many students would be about at such an ungodly hour on a Sunday morning.

He was already discreetly seated at a table at the back of the café when she arrived. He rose, greeted her warmly, their cheeks touching. 'That would make a great photo in the "*St Chinian Trumpet*",' she laughed. 'Young footballer, Yves, kissing "golden codger", Lotti. Imagine the indignation of our respective campaigners, who would expect us to be scowling or at least coldly ignoring each other.'

'You're not that easy to ignore,' he replied. 'What would you like to have?'

'A skinny latte and a croissant would be lovely,' she said.

'That suits me, too,' he agreed.

Over breakfast they discussed the highly charged and sharply adversarial nature of the exchanges that the campaign had provoked. They both regretted it but realized there was little either could do to temper it. Any conciliatory remarks at this stage by either would be interpreted and used by the other's campaigners as evidence of the weakness and indefensibility of their opponent's case. For the ringleaders in both camps, it was a fight to the death which must not be relieved by sentiment, however generous and well-intentioned.

'I'll be happy when it's over, one way or the other,' Yves declared.

'Yes,' Lotti agreed, 'and whatever the outcome, eventually some viable *modus vivendi* between the factions will have to be reached.'

'Well,' he said, 'whatever that outcome may be, one good feature of the exercise for me is that it has provided me with the good fortune of meeting you and

I hope that after it's all over we can keep in touch as friends.'

'Yes, indeed,' she said, smiling, 'and I hope maybe not just keep in touch, but also get to know each other better and, perhaps, become more than just friends.'

'What a good idea,' he agreed. 'And now, before our secret tryst is discovered by one of our supporters seeking to quench a raging thirst after last night's revelry, I suppose we better return to our respective headquarters and continue our preparations for battle.'

'Yes, indeed,' she laughed, 'and may the best mature woman win.'

A university chaplain, Dom Placebo, preaching at mass in the local church that morning, expressed his hope that the students would conduct a good-humoured, friendly, Christian campaign. Somewhat to the mystification of those students attending, he evoked, as evidence of the mature students' right to avail themselves of the benefits of university education, the example of the elderly gentleman attempting to enter the healing pool at Bethesda for a cure. And he followed this with the example of the child Jesus debating with the elders in the temple as conclusive evidence of the compatibility of different categories of students in the life of the university. The general consensus outside the church afterwards was that the poor man had become somewhat deranged by the intensity of the election campaign.

Later that day, each side publicized their own results of a pre-election poll that they had conducted. The different results provoked further acrimonious recriminations and charges of deception, distortion, and downright skulduggery.

Each party, as agreed, had canvassed one thousand students — five hundred part-time matures and five hundred full-time undergraduates. The declared results were very different, far greater than any conceivable margin of error might explain.

According to the mature students' poll, 48% of those asked supported Lotti Beausang, 42% supported Yves Leroy, and 10% supported the invisible Alex Denton. According to the undergraduate students' poll, 34% supported Lotti Beausang, 68% supported Yves Leroy, and 8% supported Alex Denton.

Each side vehemently defended their own results, appealing, in each case, to their own statistical experts. Eventually, the source of the disparity was uncovered. The undergraduate poll had ascribed only half a vote to each of the mature students asked to participate. This provoked outrage in the part-timers camp, but was stoutly defended by the full-timers as corresponding to the electoral weight officially accorded to a mature student's vote in the forthcoming election. This weighting had been determined by the regulations adopted some years earlier by the university when mature students were somewhat of a rarity.

The mature students' camp was aroused to new levels of indignation by such extended application of a discriminatory regulation. It intensified their determination to elect Lotti Beausang and eliminate once and for all the outrageous marginalization of mature students. They were now in a decisive numerical majority at the university and should not be treated with such contempt as only half a student. Reproductions of old American and South African placards, demanding "One Person One Vote", were widely distributed.

The "crooked pre-election poll" added further fuel to the already combustible atmosphere in which the final week of campaigning would unfold. Each category of student sought to fan the flames of confrontation.

The only putative, but unconvincing, evidence of inter-group harmony and solidarity was the news, recently publicized in the *St Chinian Trumpet*, that a feisty fifty-eight-year-old mature student named Naomi, with irregular attendance at a number of courses including one on the history of Greek lesbianism, had abandoned her seventy-year-old husband. She told the interviewer proudly that she was now living with her new partner whom she hoped to marry — Angelique, a third year, twenty-two-year-old undergraduate student of poultry farming!

Naomi's husband was demanding Angelique's expulsion and Angelique's parents were demanding the same for Naomi. A university committee, chaired by the dean of women students, took the view that any such action was undesirable and unnecessary as the university had no role to play in how consenting adults organized or disorganized their private lives. This decision was widely approved with only The Maternity of Concerned Mothers of St Chinian registering their disapproval.

Dr Thomas Van Velsen, lecturer on the history of sociology, and president of the St Chinian Community of Latter-Day Albigensians, warmly invited the couple to join the community, assuring them that therein they would encounter many kindred spirits in quest of sexual authenticity. The invitation was cordially, but firmly, declined on the grounds that, in their circumstance, and for the present, at least, the happy couple had as much sexual authenticity as they could cope with!

The stage was set for an interesting final week of public events and encounters. These were scheduled to culminate in the greatly anticipated public debate between the two candidates just two days before election day. Meanwhile, however, Professor Didier Ritz, professor of marketing, had arranged a far from public, indeed strictly confidential, meeting with a few colleagues in his home to discuss a matter close to his heart.

CHAPTER SEVENTEEN
Black Marketing

Didier Ritz welcomed his five guests to his ostentatious imitation chateau overlooking St Chinian. Having seated them in comfortable armchairs in his ornately furnished salon, he popped a magnum of champagne and charged six glasses. His third wife, Farah, a beautiful Persian woman, the daughter of a minor prince at the court of the late and last shah, deposited dishes of Bouzigues oysters and smoked salmon *canapés* on strategically placed small tables. Having greeted her husband's guests graciously, she withdrew discreetly. Didier was reputed to have claimed that he preferred having wives rather than children.

At first sight, the five guests appeared to have little in common other than that they were all members of the governing body, which is the ultimate decision-making body of the University of St Chinian. As well as dealing with its own agenda, it confirms recommendations of the other bodies of the university, including the academic council, and the buildings and finance committees. It determines fees and salary scales, and makes all appointments, including that of president.

The eldest of the visitors is a local councillor, Paul Comps, a dog groomer by profession. He has succeeded in persuading the good citizens of St Chinian, ardent dog lovers, to elect him for the past twenty years to the seat on the governing body of the university reserved for a local councillor.

Next, somewhat surprisingly, is Simone Blondel, professor of social administration and fiery self-proclaimed Marxist. She is the staff trade union representative on the governing body. Although a voluble critic of capitalism, she admires Didier's absolute lack of principle and reckons that he is a man with whom she could do business.

The third guest is Rodrigo Gonzales, professor of Spanish, who has come to St Chinian from Barcelona. He is preoccupied with determining whether it would be to his advantage to remain stoutly pro-central government or declare himself as passionately in favour of an independent Catalonia. He also considers that his own academic excellence has been inadequately appreciated by the university authorities. However, he has a strong following amongst mature students, eager to acquire a few strategic romantic phrases for holidays in sunny Torremolinos, Benidorm or Magaluf. Politically ambitious, he had persuaded members of the School of Arts, Media and Communication to elect him as their representative on the governing body.

The fourth guest is Monique Dubray, the head of computer science in the recently merged departments of computer science and library studies into the new Centre for Library and Information Studies. She is still highly indignant about this shotgun wedding. She considers her domain of computer science to be the voice of the future and is disgusted to be shackled to the library. 'In my estimation,' she frequently declares, 'the library is simply an historical graveyard for obsolete pen-pushers.'

However, as everybody in the university, particularly those technologically challenged, have need at some time or other of her expertise, she is able, through intimidation or by demanding repayment for a favour, to secure repeated re-election by both academic colleagues and non-academic administrators to the governing body.

Finally, there is Maxim Proust, the youngest of the group. He was appointed six years ago as a junior lecturer in Didier's department of marketing. Having completed his PhD under Didier's benign direction, he has recently been promoted, again with Didier's goodwill, to the post of senior lecturer. Having calculated on which side his bread is buttered, he has accepted the role of serving as Didier's Trojan Horse in various delicate initiatives and has linked his own ambitions to those of Didier. Indeed, the other four guests were of a similar, if not yet publicly acknowledged, disposition.

Topping up their glasses, Didier, standing with his back to the ornate marble mantelpiece, addressed them benevolently. 'My dear friends,' he began, 'so good of you to tear yourselves away from the bosom of your families. I appreciate your sacrifice, knowing that it is your only opportunity of the week to enjoy their incomparable company, away from the otherwise all-absorbing demands of your academic responsibilities.'

The five colleagues tried both to smile self-deprecatingly and convey their agreement that he had hit the nail on the head. Privately they thought that he was stretching the "bosom-tearing" and "incomparable" language a bit far!

'However,' he continued, 'my invitation to you this evening is more than a purely social one. I wish to discuss with you a matter of great importance. At the last meeting of the academic council, as Simone and Rodrigo who were present know, I sought to introduce a discussion about the future of our university. Such a discussion at senior academic level is urgently required in view of the conflict of views about this future, concretely being debated throughout the student community. It is the core topic in their current campaigns to elect their new president of the student union.

'I indicated clearly my belief that the University of St Chinian needs to revise its profile and organization. The time is ripe for it to declare unequivocally, its intention to be a university of the *troisième âge,* devoted primarily to cultivating the academic and cultural needs of mature people who have devoted their working lives

169

to the good of their country. I detected a measure of support for my view from some colleagues including yourself, dear Simone.

'However, our esteemed president, Guy Boulanger, who, with my inspirational support, several years ago initiated the recruitment of mature students to our beloved university does not, I fear, support my vision. He appears to be still committed to the view that the primary role of the university is to educate the young. He seems to believe that the presence of mature students is to be welcomed only in a very subsidiary role. He terminated the discussion before the debate achieved the fervour that it deserved. But not before I had made my view clearly known and had pledged my support to the campaign of Madame Lotti Beausang. She, as you know, is seeking election as president of the student union to promote the objective of transforming the University of St Chinian into a primarily third age institution.'

'I think that this campaign could be the first step in a revolutionary transformation, not only of the nature of our beloved university but also of its organization and administration. Moreover, it is important, I believe, that we should be seen to be involved in it from the outset. With this objective in mind, I have already contacted Madame Beausang personally to assure her of my wholehearted support.'

As Didier paused to take a sip of champagne from his glass on the mantelpiece, it was clear that his

170

remarks had aroused the alert attention of his audience who followed his example and raised their glasses to their lips.

Clearing his throat, he continued. 'In eighteen months, the statutory election process to appoint the president of the university for a four-year term of office must be put in train. I believe that Guy Boulanger, who has been elected several times to this office, may not be disposed to seek re-election as president of a university for which there is a groundswell of support to transform it into a third age institution. And even if he does seek re-election, I believe he would not be successful.'

In the room, a palpable hush prevailed. Even the glasses of champagne remained temporarily suspended. The group leaned forward in eager conspiratorial anticipation. Didier, the consummate marketeer, knew he had his audience where he wanted them. 'Consider the following hypothetical scenario,' he mused. 'The election of a university president must be initiated eighteen months after the dramatically successful election of a student president totally committed to a radical transformation of the university into a haven primarily for mature students. The incumbent president is unwilling to seek re-election in such circumstance. An enlightened team of university academic and professional staff, that has supported the mature students' case from the outset, decides to put a candidate forward for election as president. Their specific aim is the implementation of the proposed transformation of the university and the consequent reformation of its academic and administrative organization.

'Consider this hypothetical scenario more concretely. Suppose that the group present here this evening decides to be the basic caucus to propose the election of the professor of marketing, who just happens to be myself, as president of the university. In the likely circumstance of my election, there would inevitably be a dramatic renewal of personnel in the new organization of the university.

'For example,' he continued, 'if Boulanger does not seek or does not succeed to be re-elected as president, it is unlikely that the academic vice president and the current deans of Schools will continue in office under a new regime. Consequently, you, dear Simone, may feel obliged to replace Claire Macon as academic vice president. It would provide you with such a splendid opportunity to give wider currency to your passionately held views. Your academic colleagues would pay you devoted and respectful attention and you and the president would, I know, work harmoniously together.'

Sidelong glances at Simone indicated that she was already imagining herself as a Stalinesque vice president for academic affairs, issuing diktats and reforming curricula to ensure revolutionary political orthodoxy.

'And you, dear Rodrigo, as an influential source of the reform would doubtless be warmly welcomed as the new dean of the School of Arts, Media, and

Communication. You would be in a position to ensure that Spanish was accorded the importance, which I know you believe it should have in this university. Doubtless, if you are not too preoccupied with the thorny issue of Catalonia, you could have very fruitful co-operation with Simone in her desire to promote Marxist revolutionary activity in Spanish speaking regions of South America.

'A further inevitable consequence of the proposed hypothetical change would be a vacancy in my chair of marketing. It would be entirely reasonable to presume that you, Maxim, a senior lecturer in the department, and one of my most accomplished doctoral students, would be a clear favourite to succeed me as professorial head of department.'

That left just Monique Dubray, director of computer service, and local councillor, Paul Comps. They both looked rather uncertain about what the new regime might have for them. However, Didier now turned his benign attention to them.

'Dear Monique,' he said smiling, 'you have provided such a wonderful computer service for the university. It must be very distressing to have your agile and dynamic performance linked with the ponderous activity of the library. The computing service is the medium of communication par excellence of the future and its pre-eminent importance must be recognized as such by this university. In the future organization, I envisage you as director of an autonomous centre for communication of which the library would be merely a sub-department. Needless to say, your activities would have to be greatly extended, and appropriately recognized, in view of the very likely institution of a massive programme of online courses which a new university of the third age will inaugurate.

These honeyed words left Monique in a state of euphoric delight. But Councillor Comps was looking increasingly crestfallen. What role could he play in the unfolding drama? But Didier came promptly to his rescue. 'My dear Paul,' he said, 'in this wonderful transformation of our university I see a most important role for you who have been such a dedicated member of our governing body. It seems to me that, in view of your long association with the university, you should sit on our governing body not just as an elected local councillor but as the *ex officio* mayor of St Chinian. The university will seek to ensure that the ever-increasing number of mature students who qualify as electors in St Chinian cast their vote for you as mayor to grace our governing body in that capacity.' Paul straightened his shoulders and began to look solemnly mayoral!

'Now that I've finished my little monologue,' Didier said, smiling, 'I would be interested to hear your views on the image of the university which I have indicated, which is, of course, only a hypothetical scenario. But before I sit down to enjoy the discussion let me recharge your glasses.' He popped another magnum of Dom Pérignon. 'Curious, isn't it,' he remarked, 'to think how that rascal, Pérignon, from the Champagne region stole the method for producing naturally effervescent wine. The method was originated in the sixteenth century in Limoux, here in the Languedoc region, by the Benedictine monks of the monastery of St Hilaire. Pérignon, who was allegedly on a fraternal visit to the monastery, learnt their technique and hoofed it back up to his own monastery in Champagne with the wonderful new method in his pocket. I'm sorry I wasn't around then to advise the local Languedoc monks and help them market their bubbling creation. If I had been,' he modestly reflected, 'throughout the world today people would be toasting each other with sparkling Dom Hilaire Limoux instead of Dom Pérignon Champagne.' Having replenished their glasses, he sat down and encouraged their comments.

Simone Blondel was first out of the trap. 'Thank you, Didier, for your splendid remarks,' she declared. 'I think history will record our strictly confidential meeting here this evening as an axial moment in the revolutionizing of the University of St Chinian.' (She failed to make clear how history could record such a strictly confidential meeting unless perhaps she herself had already decided to be the mouthpiece of history in her own memoirs.) 'I think we know one another, and trust each other well enough,' she continued, 'to drop the pretence that we are talking about a possible or hypothetical scenario. Our discussion should concentrate on how to make the scenario, that Didier has described, a concrete reality. Instead of hypothetical speculation, we need unambiguous practical action, what comrade Marx called "praxis", namely, the concrete political action whereby the dictatorship of the proletariat will accomplish a revolutionary ideal.'

She paused for a moment to savour her own eloquence. Only Monique Dubray had the nerve to intervene. 'Simone, dear,' she said, 'please keep the Marxist claptrap for your Party meetings. Tell us in plain language what you suggest we do. I agree with you that we must seek to make the scenario which Didier has described a concrete reality. I'm with him 100%. But how should we proceed?'

'Well,' replied Simone, more temperately, 'if we are to achieve the ultimate goal which Didier has described so well, we must begin by succeeding with the immediate challenge which will greatly promote its realization. In other words, we must concentrate upon ensuring that Lotti Beausang is elected as president of the student union in order to bring the issue of a radical transformation of the university openly onto the political agenda. Her success will provide us with the opportunity and justification for pursuing the radical change that will hopefully include the change of administrative regime which Didier has described.'

'That's more like it,' said Monique encouragingly. 'And I, although I will have to be careful, will avail myself of my computer service facilities and expertise to send an enthusiastic anonymous email to all students urging them to vote for Lotti.'

Not wishing to appear less committed, Rodrigo declared that in his weekly column in the Barcelona newspaper, *Vangardia*, which would appear next Friday and which all the Spanish students read, he would feature Lotti and the remarkable initiative of the mature students to transform the University of St Chinian.

Councillor Comps offered to leave a bundle of Lotti's election pamphlets on the table at the entrance hall of the *mairie* and to encourage any students who brought their dogs to him for grooming to vote for her.

Maxim proposed that, in view of Didier's inspiring vision, they should, without delay, formulate and sign a brief but strong declaration of support for Lotti which they would publicize widely. This proposal was agreed.

The discussion continued for about another hour. As the champagne flowed, increasingly audacious suggestions in support of Lotti's election were advanced, including a suggestion by Councillor Comps that a helicopter trailing a supportive slogan might fly around the town on election day. This suggestion was welcomed with delight but no one quite knew how to implement it. Monica Dubray offered to consult with her scientific friends to ascertain whether, instead of a helicopter, a couple of ground-controlled drones might do the job.

Finally, with Didier's guidance, the short declaration of support proposed by Maxim was formulated for publication and signed by each of them. He urged them to rally support among their colleagues and thanked them for their advice and commitment. They agreed to meet together again in a few weeks to review the result of the election. They departed in high spirits, in the two taxis which Didier had summoned to return them to the neglected bosoms of their families — where, doubtless, their pained laments about having to devote even their weekends to tiring academic meetings would be greeted with some scepticism.

CHAPTER EIGHTEEN
Meetings

Meanwhile, the two main campaign committees of Lotti and Yves also held their final pre-election meetings. Nobody had any idea what might be going on in the Alex Denton camp, although increasing numbers of posters appeared throughout the campus displaying graphic images of shafts of sunlight, Tsunami waves, and avenging angels over the stark reminder that "Alex says No".

Yves' committee, chaired by Andre Leon, the third-year student of public relations and media studies, reviewed with satisfaction the various sporting and cultural events scheduled for the coming week. 'I think we can be pretty confident,' he remarked, 'that we will have a rather resounding victory in nearly all events. I don't see our mature companions giving us much competition in the touch rugby or the rowing. Our teams should be equally successful in the tennis, the high jump, the half marathon and the basketball. The success of our teams in these physically challenging events will give practical witness to the intrinsically youthful nature of a real university and should convince any wavering voters.'

Marie Regis, the tennis star, was particularly pleased about the subliminal message which the sponsored lecture on the merits of breast feeding would convey about the appropriate age profile of a real university student. 'The lecturer has promised,' she said, 'to show a video of young women students, having completed their examination papers, lifting their infants to their breast from the cradles beside them in the examination hall. Not many of our mature visitors will be able to match that performance.'

Jeanne Mandel expected that her active participation in Yves' campaign would yield a rich harvest of recruits to the National Front party, which was her own primary interest. She judged that zealous, French nationalists, were more likely to be found among increasingly conservative university youngsters than among the seasoned, mature, old codgers, some of whom liked to comfortably indulge heroic left-wing fantasies.

Henri Lemaitre, the postgraduate economics student, said that most of his friends considered the campaign to transform the university into a playground for old codgers would be funny if it were not so ridiculous. Young Jacques Delon, who had originally suggested Yves' nomination, admitted that he was inexperienced in electoral campaigning. However, he promised to faithfully execute any tasks he might be deputed to perform during the coming week, such as distributing pamphlets and encouraging his less politically committed companions to vote.

The remainder of the meeting was devoted to framing questions and assigning interjections to be made during the crucial television debate before the election. Yves, who attended the meeting, and had listened encouragingly, rather than seeking to direct proceedings, thanked them for their support. He told them that he was pretty confident that the students of viticulture, oenology and agriculture would abandon their sprayers and shovels and would vote for him in large numbers. The meeting ended on this confident note and the group retired in good spirits to the student bar for a little well-deserved liquid refreshment.

Around the same time, Lotti Beausang's campaign committee was meeting in Detective Louis Dupre's apartment. As the self-appointed chairman, he had invited them to review the campaign as it entered its final week. Lotti was there, as was Pierre Moulin, the former Toulouse weatherman, who had accompanied her on the cruise last year. Also, present were Luc and Marie Dupront, the retired beauty consultants from Narbonne, who, together with Dupre and Moulin, had originally invited Lotti to contest the election. There were also a couple of recent additions to the committee, a retired tax inspector and a midwife, who, even at this stage of their lives, were eager to engage in the cut and thrust of student politics.

Welcoming them warmly, Louis informed them that he had a couple of new supporters waiting in his kitchen to be introduced. 'I think,' he said, 'you will find them an interesting addition to our group.' As they looked expectantly around, he opened the kitchen door. 'Nicolas and Louise,' he called, 'come in and meet the team.'

To the surprise of the assembled elders, two attractive young students entered, smiling broadly. 'This is Louise Amard,' he said. 'A brilliant third-year student of archaeology. For the past few months, Louise has been the partner and constant companion of our friend, Rudi Bruggerman, the retired very successful German businessman who, as you know, is a dedicated part-time, mature student of two of our more popular university courses, "Life in an Oriental Harem" and "The History of the Papacy".

'And this is dear Nicolas Plon,' he continued, 'a special friend of mine. We met some time ago in a delightful bar in nearby Capestang, discreetly named "*Le Coq et Taureau*". Nicolas, a student of history and politics, is a remarkable striker, or "number 10", on the university's first soccer team and is also the current president of the university's gay and lesbian society.

'I have been talking with them over the past few weeks and they both, each for their own particular reasons, are keen to declare their commitment to dear Lotti's campaign and to work to assure its success. They have each experienced, in their own way, the revelations and raptures which a mature perspective and a relaxed approach can bestow upon their university studies. They are as determined as we are to make this indulgent approach the established norm at their beloved University of St Chinian. Having experienced our relaxed approach to academic requirements they are convinced that all work and no play makes Jack a dull boy, and that a mature approach to life at the University of St Chinian must be promoted and institutionalized.

'The revelation that Louise's new partner, Rudi, has made a most generous donation to our campaign fund, and Nicholas' remarkable football achievement, will certainly temper our undergraduates' youthful adulation of Yves Leroy, and provide additional lustre to their surprise commitment to our campaign.'

These remarks were greeted with delight and the two new recruits were warmly welcomed to the committee. It was agreed that their public declaration of support would be a great advantage. 'Perhaps they can play for us on our mixed touch rugby team,' suggested Luc Dupront, 'that would certainly even things up a bit.'

'And,' Pierre, the former weatherman, remarked, 'Nicolas' endorsement should swing the gay and lesbian vote for us. This would probably provide us with a winning 10% swing.'

'Yes,' agreed Louis, 'and I think they should both play a prominent role from the audience during the crucial TV programme next Friday evening.' He served drinks to the group and they got down to serious discussion of final preparations.

It was agreed not to announce Louise and Nicholas' involvement in Lotti's campaign until they made their appearance, togged out as reserves, on the "matures" rugby team on Wednesday. That would create a sufficiently dramatic statement and not leave enough time for an effective reaction by the "youngsters" campaign.

The committee was a bit anxious about the range of competitions to which the young, full-time students had challenged their seniors, with the aim of demonstrating their crumbling anatomy. However, Louis, with Lotti's support, convinced them that, although the "matures" would probably have some difficulty trying to put up a good show in the more energetic sports, one could be confident that they would score well in the more relaxed and sedentary competitions.

'I'm a bit worried about the lecture on the merits of breastfeeding, which Yves Leroy's band of female admirers has organized,' said Cathy, the midwife who had recently joined the committee. 'It will seek to portray us more mature ladies, who are no longer candidates for that maternal exercise, as a bit past our sell-by date and somewhat of an anomaly in university life.'

'Don't be worried about that,' said weatherman, Pierre Moulin, who was Lotti's cruise companion last year and ardent supporter, 'you can leave that little matter to me.'

'What do you mean?' Cathy asked, clearly puzzled. 'How can you, so obviously and convincingly male, deal with an issue like that?' But he just smiled enigmatically and assured her that everything would be all right on the day.

The committee then concentrated its attention on its strategy for the all-important television debate and discussion. Lotti provided a summary of what she intended to say in her introductory presentation. The committee members were delighted with it and suggested merely a few minimal modifications and additions.

She went on to remind them of the meeting she had with Didier Ritz in his office and of his pledge of support for her campaign. 'He told me,' she said, 'of his intention to renew his support of a radical transformation of the profile of the university, in favour of its mature students, at the next meeting of the academic council. Do you think,' she continued, 'I should invite him to be in the audience during the television programme and to renew his support for our position there?'

This gave rise to some lively discussion. A couple of members thought an intervention of staff in a student election debate might turn some voters off but eventually it was agreed that an open declaration of support from the influential dean of the School of

Economics, Business Studies and Tourism would have a dramatic and very positive effect. Lotti decided to invite him to attend, although she was well aware that Professor Didier Ritz's solicitude on her behalf also served longer term ambitions of his own. However, she admired his initiative and judged him to be a man with whom she could work effectively.

The remainder of the meeting was devoted to allocating to designated individuals' specific spontaneous interventions from the audience, and to anticipating those which the opposition might propose. Finally, shortly after nine o'clock, the group, having decided that they had covered as much ground as possible, departed in good spirits, looking forward to the unfolding of events in the coming decisive week.

CHAPTER NINETEEN
Fun and Games

Monday morning, the commencement of the university midterm break, dawned bright and sunlit. Good weather was forecast for the week ahead. It would feature the various sporting competitions and cultural events involving the two groups seeking to win the hearts and minds of the students of St Chinian, the mature, part-time "golden codgers" and the traditional, full-time undergrads.

The first challenge was the rowing regatta, which had been arranged for that morning on the River Orb, in the nearby village of Roquebrun, where the university rowing club boats, or "shells", were kept. Three events were scheduled, a "quad" a "single" and an "eight".

The quad race got under way first. Three racing shells, each with a crew of four, participated. There was a male undergraduate crew, a women's undergraduate crew and a male mature student's crew. All twelve had been active members of the club for some time, enjoying the competitive sport on the river and the camaraderie afterwards in the club's small pavilion.

A pistol shot signalled the start and the three boats sculled forward smoothly, the crews rowing rhythmically and supporters striding the riverbank shouting encouragement. Although all three boats performed energetically, it was obvious at a couple of hundred meters from the finish that the most which the "matures" could achieve was a respectable third behind the women undergraduates who finished some distance behind the stronger male crew.

The next event was the singles race in which one person sculls a twenty-seven-foot racing shell the entire length of the two-kilometre race. Three undergraduate students had entered for this competition. It was generally expected that Martin, the captain of the club, a third-year, strongly-built agriculture student, who was a superb athlete, would be the clear winner. There was some surprise and mild amusement when it was announced Thomas Delon, a sixty-five-year-old retired engineer, had offered to represent the "matures" in the race. Thomas was rather reclusive and not well known. However, a few people had sometimes noticed him practicing on the river early in the morning or working out during the evening in the university gym. In a previous life, he had worked for a large international engineering company. It had included in its corporate provision for its staff, free membership of a local rowing club. Thomas had gladly availed himself of this facility.

The race proceeded at a respectable but measured pace for the first kilometre and a half with no obvious winner. Then, in the final few hundred meters, to everyone's astonishment, Thomas' racing shell surged ahead and Martin, despite most strenuous efforts to get in contention, could only finish a poor second. The "matures" were euphoric with delight and Thomas' glowing body was showered from top to bottom with the reckless kisses of "golden codgers" who had happily abandoned all sense of propriety.

The unexpected win, which left each side with a victory, provoked intense interest in the final decisive contest, the "eight race", in which each team would launch eight rowers and a cox in a nineteen-metre racing shell to compete in the two-kilometre race. Because the "matures" were decidedly short of seasoned boat people, it was agreed that the teams would each involve four men and four women and that the cox could be either. Supporters of each side assembled near the start to encourage their sporting heroes.

A bell chimed and the two teams emerged from the boathouse to rousing cheers. The younger contestants created quite an impression. The eight young men and women and their female cox, all togged out smartly in white shorts, singlets, and boat club blazers, presented a picture of youthful exuberance and athletic prowess. They waved in acknowledgement of the delighted reception which their supporters gave them.

The team of "matures" presented a rather different picture. Two of the men wore snug fitting shorts and sports jackets. The other two, more used to a bowling alley, were in white flannel trousers and woollen sweaters. The four ladies, by mutual agreement, and with due regard to their diverse dimensions, were attired in pale blue tracksuits. To proclaim their team identity, all eight wore green baseball caps.

They had experienced some difficulty in identifying a coxswain of sufficiently modest stature and capable of directing their unpredictable rowing rhythm. Eventually they had persuaded a retired jockey, who weighed only fifty-five kilos and was attending courses at the university on Italian poetry and cuisine, to undergo a crash course in coxing. He was charmingly attired for the event in jodhpurs and the scarlet and gold racing silks in which, many years before, he had won a minor classic at Saint-Cloud, near Paris.

The eight young students and their cox slipped gracefully into their boat. The crew of "matures", brandishing their eight oars, boarded somewhat less gracefully. They contrived diplomatically to achieve an economic distribution of their collective weight of nearly sixteen hundred pounds along the length of the narrow two-hundred-pound racing shell. The two boats steadied parallel to each other. The starter raised his pistol in the air. A shot rang out. A great cheer rose from the crowd. The crucial race got under way.

Everything went well for the first few hundred meters. The students stroked slightly ahead, but the "matures" remained in close contact. Hunched in the stern of the boat, facing its bow, the jockey's native equine skill combined successfully with his few lessons on guiding a shell. His authoritative call steadied the

190

nerves of the rowers, coordinating, surprisingly effectively, their power and rhythm. It looked as though, by availing himself of his professional riding expertise in steadying frisky thoroughbreds, his gallant team of golden codgers would pull together, energetically and smoothly, and make a good race of it.

However, at the five-hundred-meter stage, disaster struck. The number four crew, a particularly enthusiastic lady and a supermarket manager in a previous existence, hit the water with her oar at an oblique angle, catching what in rowing terminology is called a crab. The boat heaved over sideways taking water on board. At this stage all the oars on her side became entangled and the four on the other side rowed so strenuously that the boat began to turn and lurch over even more alarmingly. It filled with water, turned upside down, and deposited all of its crew in the river; except for the agile coxswain who, anticipating the inevitable outcome, jumped ship and swam ashore. Fortunately, the supporting crowd who accompanied the team along the riverbank had access to a number of lifebuoys. These were cast into the river to rescue four of the crew who were unable to swim.

As the other boat sculled to a seamless victory, a forest of smartphones flashed, recording for posterity the antics of the mature water sprites swimming, splashing, clutching lifebuoys and trying to scramble ashore as their boat bobbed merrily upside down in the river. They huddled together on the river bank, water

191

dripping into puddles at their feet. They sought, not very convincingly, to convey an image of composure, detachment and *sangfroid* — *"sangfroid"* being the only literally appropriate description.

However, they were significantly aided in their endeavour to appear unconcerned by the warm and indulgent reception they were given by both groups of supporters. Later that evening in the local pub, dressed more conventionally, they were already rewriting the narrative, conveying the impression that their aquatic performance was a carefully calculated and heroic response to an unpredictable act of God.

The next day, Tuesday, the young Turks continued their winning streak with victories in tennis, swimming, and the half-marathon. They were also awarded victory in the uncontested men's wrestling competition despite the unsuccessful attempt of three energetic mature ladies to engage.

The "matures" fared slightly better in the touch rugby with the contesting teams winning a game each. Their victory was greatly facilitated by the surprise participation of Louise and Nicholas, the two young students, who, at Louis Dupre's invitation, had pinned their colours to the matures' campaign. Their involvement with the campaign came as a big surprise, particularly in view of Nicholas' celebrity as a hero of St Chinian's soccer team. However, they defended their new allegiance robustly and encouraged their friends to share their conversion.

'The new university organization being proposed by the mature students,' declared Louise, thinking of the delights she shared with Rudi, her new, wealthy, mature, German lover, 'will enable all students to enjoy a much more agreeable balance between studies and social life.'

'And,' added Nicholas, 'it will provide a wider support base, not only for our sporting life, but also for greater exposure and extended extracurricular activity of the members of our LGBT society, of which I am the proud elected chairperson.'

'The extended extracurricular activity will be fine,' laughed one of Lotti's supporters, 'but you better be careful about that greater exposure of your members!'

Later in the day, the "matures" scored, as expected, another victory, this time in the *pétanque* contest, the ball game similar to bowling, which originated locally in the Occitan region of France. They manifested great skill and expertise in projecting their steel ball, or *boule,* to hit the small wooden jack, or *cochonnet,* which was the object of the game. But they also displayed exceptional mercilessness and calculated cunning in displacing their opponent's *boule* whenever it appeared likely that it might reach the intended jack. In retaliation, the opposition sought to trivialize the contest by offering the "matures" a magnet attached to a length of string to lift their hollow steel *boule* from the ground. The offer was made in simulated concern for their presumed senile rheumatic inability to bend down.

Notwithstanding the strenuous and protracted endeavours of both teams, no award was made in the rock-climbing contest in the nearby Caroux hills. Two flags, one red and one green, had been placed on the summit. The red was to be claimed by the team which reached the summit first and this team would be declared the overall winner if, showing the red flag as proof of its victorious ascent, it also finished first on the descent. However, the contest would be declared a draw if the other team, on securing the green flag as proof of reaching the summit, overtook the other team on the descent and arrived first at the finish. These elaborately constructed rules of engagement were utterly undermined. For, on reaching the summit, there were no red or green flags to be seen. They had disappeared, presumably stolen. Instead, fluttering in the breeze, there were two identical black flags, each bearing a slogan printed in large white letters: "Alex Says No — Vote for Alex".

The following day, Wednesday, was devoted to less physically demanding activities. The competitions involved were table tennis, billiards, bridge, poker, chess and baking. The results were for the most part predictable and the awards fairly evenly divided.

The table tennis contest was won easily by a trim "mature" who had been a sports mistress in a junior school. Two third-year undergraduate students of philosophy, putting many hours of ill-spent youth in snooker halls to good use, secured the billiards award.

Surprisingly, the youngsters also won the bridge contest. However, the "matures" retaliated by winning the poker game, displaying a convincing but breathtaking ability to bluff.

The chess competition evoked considerable interest, particularly in view of the signalled intention of Alex Denton to participate. However, the anticipation that his or her identity would at last be revealed was dashed. The draw determined that two players, one representing the "matures" and the other the undergraduates, would be the first to play. They would each then play against Alex Denton. Presenting themselves in the hall where the contest was scheduled, they sat opposite each other at a small table on which the chessboard and pieces were located. Because of the size of the audience, it had been agreed that the moves in the game would be displayed on a large screen in the front of the hall.

The game proceeded in a lively and impressive manner, each contestant introducing imaginative initiatives which were equally skilfully repelled. It ended after forty-five minutes in a stalemate with neither player able to secure a decisive advantage.

The eager audience now began to look around for Alex Denton to take his or her place to play the other two contestants in turn. At last, they hoped, the mysterious identity would be revealed. However, Thomas Mansion, his/her nominator and chief promoter, took the microphone and addressed them.

'Dear Alex,' he explained, 'is so happy to express his or her solidarity with you by a token participation in this week's contests. However, in accordance with the conviction that the forthcoming election should be characterized by reliance upon arguments rather than personalities, he or she cannot be with you today and will not address you in person until the morning of the election. He or she has deputed me to act as agent to implement on the chessboard the strategic moves which will be conveyed to me electronically.'

The games proceeded and Alex competed with each of the other contestants in turn. The moves which were relayed to Thomas Mansion's earphones were recorded by him on the chessboard and projected onto the screen at the front of the hall. Alex played brilliantly and within an hour and a half had dispatched both opponents decisively.

Thomas turned to the assembled crowd. 'Alex,' he said, 'has instructed me to convey his best wishes to you all and to tell you how much he or she is looking forward to addressing you personally on May 1st, just before voting commences. I will convey your congratulations on two fine victories to Alex who continues to say "NO" and would value your vote.'

Ignoring the demands from all sides to come clean and disclose Alex's identity, Thomas buttoned his coat straightened his spectacles and, trying to appear important, marched resolutely and tight- lipped from the hall. Greater curiosity than ever, combined with mounting frustration, prevailed about the identity of the enigmatic Alex.

The baking contest was won, as expected, by the "matures". They were represented by a retired couple of professional bakers. This artistic couple produced a beautifully concocted and elaborately iced three-tier wedding cake which they generously sliced and distributed to an appreciative audience. The undergraduate contestants, appreciating that serious competition was futile, wheeled in on a trolley a huge tubular white edifice, festooned with coloured ribbons representing the university's rugby team. Suddenly, as people surveyed it perplexedly, out of the white cardboard top burst a lightly clad beautiful girl, a first-year student of viticulture. She was accorded a rapturous reception but the retired bakers were the acknowledged winners.

Later that evening, in the main hall of the Student Centre, the group of Yves Leroy's enthusiastic, young, female campaigners staged their special lecture, which they expected would attract major support for his candidature among young voters. They had persuaded a pharmaceutical company in Toulouse to sponsor a lecture by the celebrated paediatrician, Dr Gillian Dubonnet, on the superiority of natural breastfeeding over powder milk baby products. Incidentally, mindful of the generous fee which the company had agreed, she would also imprint on their eager young minds the benefit to nursing mothers of the company's profitable vitamin tonic "Lactoboost".

The lecture had been advertised under various engaging titles such as "Keep Abreast of Our Time" and "Give Baby a Break — Keep Your Powder Dry". It attracted a wide audience, mainly of women, young and not so young, but also a good representation of men of all ages who seemed magnetically attracted by any mention of breasts! Pierre Moulin, the retired weatherman and active member of Lotti Beausang's election committee, made sure to secure a prominent place in the hall for himself and his fellow committee members.

The lecturer was in splendid form and played strongly to the hidden agenda of correlating fertile young breastfeeding motherhood with fertile young academic and social achievement. She referred triumphantly to research conducted in Belarus, involving seventeen hundred babies, which claimed to have established that those who had been breastfed were less likely to develop pimples when they reached adolescence and were more likely to succeed at university.

She illustrated her lecture with a large number of eye-catching photographs, projected in magnified images onto a large screen behind her. These included images of young matrons discreetly nursing their babies between lectures or while busily consulting electronic documents or ancient manuscripts in the library. There were also enchanting images of the same young matrons cheering the university rugby team or participating in games of hockey or tennis while their healthy and replete offspring gurgled and chuckled contentedly on the side-line.

By way of contrast, there were also a couple of condescending images of worried, more mature ladies, late for their classes or tutorials, anxiously trying to compile bottles of powdered milk for their petulant and emaciated IVF progeny. The most compelling image was of a group of young mothers in cap and gown, and with smiling babies clamped to their bosoms, triumphantly receiving the award of their university degrees.

Finally, in case anyone was in doubt, the lecturer concluded her discourse with an unambiguous statement. 'Whereas I fully agree,' she declared, 'that a university must provide a comprehensive contraceptive service for its students, I am also convinced that it is also the ideal location for those who wish to combine youthful intellectual pursuits with carefree natural mothering. The simultaneous transfer of knowledge to the brain and of milk from the breast is an exchange of incomparable beauty and efficacy. It accomplishes a sublime academic equilibrium which no mature, part-time student powered only by powdered milk transfusion, can match.'

The applause of the younger members of the large audience was enthusiastic. It culminated in a standing ovation which the lecturer graciously acknowledged.

Questions and remarks after the lecture contributed further to the newly acquired conviction that there was an intrinsic and highly beneficial connection between university academic achievement and having been powder-free breastfed. It was implied that those who had not been so privileged would have to struggle academically and socially. One enthusiastic young wit jovially suggested that perhaps the next sponsored lecture might be devoted to the academic benefit of incontinence nappies for mature students. Her remark was greeted with a combination of indignation and hilarity.

However, just before the discussion was brought to a conclusion, Pierre Moulin rose to his feet, reached for the microphone, and addressed the greatly inspired audience. 'I have listened,' he said, 'with close attention, but increasing bewilderment, to this evening's proceedings. I have heard an ever-expanding outpouring of adulation and praise for the mystical academic properties and unquestionable life enhancing benefits of breastfeeding, not only for the mother but also as contributing decisively to the health, beauty and intelligence of the fortunate suckling infants. By contrast, the mundane administration of a chemically composed powder milk product allegedly deprives the mother of an intellectual transfusion and her child of a brilliant, handsome and prosperous future. Is this brief description an accurate synopsis of this evening's discussion?' he asked. A chorus of enthusiastic affirmative responses greeted his query.

'Very well,' he said, 'I would now like to ask you another couple of questions. Please take a good look at me. Would you agree that I am a nicely proportioned, well set-up, and even rather handsome fellow?' Good humouredly, the audience agreed, urging him to continue. 'And might you grant that I seem to be a fellow intelligent enough to develop an argument, engage your interest, and who might even be agreeable company on an exploratory date with one of the many beautiful women gracing this occasion?'

Again, the audience laughingly agreed and urged him to continue. They were keen to find where his curious line of questioning was leading. 'Well,' he said, 'listening to the learned exposition and the enthusiastic discussion which it provoked, I find myself in a somewhat puzzled condition. For I must frankly confess to you that I didn't get my handsome eager lips near a woman's breast until I was twenty years of age.' Smiling broadly, he sat down.

The hall erupted in a discordant uproar. Although, from some of the more mature members of the audience, there was a minor ripple of applause and laughter, the general reaction was one of outrage and indignation. There were loud cries of "shame", "disgraceful", "chauvinist pig" and "throw him out".

The magical illusion that had been created of an intimate bond between benevolent youthful maternal fecundity and authentic university participation was shattered. The great boost to Yves Leroy's election campaign, envisaged and carefully planned by his ardent young female supporters, was lost in a noisy disarray of indignation, contention, abuse, and amusement. The audience dispersed, many heading to local hostelries to discuss the unanticipated conclusion to an inspirational evening. Pierre Moulin, smiled and winked at the other members of Lotti Beausang's committee members who were present, pleased that he had honoured his assurance that he would throw a spanner into the works which would counter the intended impact of the event.

The outcome of the election was still very much in the lap of the gods, if no longer in the fantasized fecund bosoms of academically brilliant young women. The next few days would be decisive.

CHAPTER TWENTY
Academic Distractions

With the election looming ever closer, the next day, Thursday, witnessed some cheerful and entertaining canvassing by the different groups of supporters, eager to attract to their cause the rapidly decreasing number of undecided students. Mature supporters of Lotti gathered, with their guitars, ukuleles, and trumpets, near the main entry to the university. They provided enthusiastic musical backing for an energetic old swinger who crooned out favourite songs from Elvis, The Beatles, U2, The Beach Boys, and The Rolling Stones.

Nearby, in the main square of the university, a lively group of Yves' supporters invited passing students to participate in an impromptu version of *Dancing with the Stars,* featuring heroes of his victorious rugby team and a few much-admired members of the women's hockey team. They tangoed and boogied to exhortations to "Make St Chinian Great Again with Yves!"

A couple of kites fluttered overhead trailing banners inviting votes for Alex who steadfastly continues to say "NO".

Meanwhile, in the late afternoon, the academic staff was invited, some would say coerced, by President Boulanger to attend a lecture by a visiting bureaucrat. The lecture was allegedly proposed, but in fact imposed, by the Ministry for Higher Education and Research in Paris. Its title, "A University Fit for Purpose Today", was hardly one to entice a group of seasoned academics, keen to enjoy the respite of the midterm break without having to endure such a propagandizing distraction.

The lecturer, Dr Vincent Soulages, was an assistant secretary at the ministry. He himself had failed to secure an academic appointment in the sociology department of his own university in Normandy. He was a man of modest dimensions and intellect. After six years of painstaking research, he had presented his doctoral thesis, which was offered as a devastating analysis and copiously referenced refutation of Aristotle's claim in his *Nicomachean Ethics*, that "small men, even if pretty and well proportioned, could never be deemed beautiful". Vincent Soulages was a living confirmation of the claim he sought to refute!

Several years at the ministry, adroitly manipulating the corridors of power to achieve his current exalted position, had transformed his conception of the university and the role of its various occupants. He was now convinced that its alleged commitment to the pursuit of truth for its own sake by the conservation, transmission, and creation of knowledge was altogether out of touch with current sensibility. The university

204

needed to be re-educated in order to realize that its primary purpose was to serve the economic and political objectives of the society which funded it.

The central theme of his lecture this afternoon was the role of an academic in a genuine university today. 'My simple claim,' he declared modestly, 'is that a truly contemporary "with-it" academic should become invisible. His or her role is to be an impersonal functionary, enabling students, in various non-directive ways, to find things out for themselves, ideally in co-operative group projects with fellow students. The outdated idea of a good lecture as a product of a professor expressing her personal convictions, for her own admiration and the incidental illumination of students fortunate enough to be eavesdropping, must be abandoned.

'Ideally, all university discourse henceforth,' he announced, 'should be amenable to digitization and should contribute to a fully digitalized self-educated community, animated by the slogan, "Don't Speculate — Digitilate". The role of the academic is to convey impersonal digitized information and to enable students to use it. The goal of university education is to transform a speaking or reading culture into a digital culture. The library will be gradually absorbed within the computer centre. The entire corpus of human knowledge is to be translated into a Boolean game of "noughts and crosses" or "ones and zeros".

'The professor must learn,' he exhorted, 'to take a backseat and confine her activity to outlining useful digitized questions, enabling students, non-judgmentally, to formulate universally accessible and acceptable digitized answers in the laboratory, the computer service, and the library until it becomes redundant.

'These support services must be recognized as the real centres of gravity of a university where students, supplied by the professor with appropriate digital know-how and direction, would find things out for themselves. They would be enabled to fashion themselves to function efficiently and impersonally as free and equal members of a technological society.

'In such a university fit for purpose,' he exulted, 'there will be no need for any increase in the number of expensive academic staff. Possibly more researchers may be required but this requirement can be accommodated by a reduction in the cohort of those assigned to teaching. Academic teaching will become a technique not an art. Research will be inspired and oriented by the indications and requirements of the economic development projects of national governments.

'There will, of course,' he explained, 'be a real requirement in a genuinely "fit for purpose" contemporary university for many more well-qualified administrators to ensure that the university functions smoothly and effectively as a shining example of good corporate management. They will devise wonderful rules and regulations, governing every aspect and division of the university, and they will institute various ingenious mechanisms to ensure that these rules and regulations are implemented meticulously. They will be vigilant in their coercive regulation of conduct, speech codes, and political correctness. They should no longer be known as mere administrators but rather as academic regulators.

'The most exciting feature of such a "fit for purpose" contemporary university,' he continued, 'is the manner in which all its aims and objectives and their due implementation, appraisal, and verification becomes the responsibility of such an expert administration, which will report regularly to the Ministry for Higher Education and Research in Paris. Apart from the various questionnaires and reports which each of you will have to answer and compile, as academic teachers you will be encouraged to concentrate upon your task of teaching in an uncontroversial, non-assertive and student-centred manner.'

With a self-satisfied smile, Dr Soulages bowed to his astounded audience. He sat down to a very muted reception. President Boulanger invited questions but the audience seemed too nonplussed. Eventually, a bright young economics lecturer took up the challenge. 'It seems to me,' he said, 'that what you propose amounts to hanging a top-heavy administration around the necks of the academics and diverting them from their proper task of providing a liberal and challenging university education for their students. Lecturers' time will be absorbed proving that they are conforming to an administrative regime which has little to do with what they should be about, namely, a committed dedication to the pursuit and promotion of truth for its own sake.' He sat down to approving applause and loud exclamations of "Hear, hear".

'Not at all,' replied Dr Soulages complacently. 'You mustn't look on a rigorous university administration as a burden. Consider it rather as a protective shield which enables you to fulfil your responsibilities appropriately. You could look on it as like the shell on a tortoise's back, which enables it to pursue its tortoise activity safely if somewhat sedately. There are so many factors which have a bearing upon the desirable and politically correct operation of a university fit for purpose that academics, absorbed in their futile intellectual preoccupations, are notoriously prone to absent-mindedly ignore. They need an alert administration to protect them from falling into serious error in the exercise of their academic responsibility.'

'What in the name of God are you talking about?' asked the clearly outraged professor of mathematics. 'My academic responsibility is to develop my research interests, to teach mathematics as a rigorous discipline to the best of my ability, to challenge my students to excel, and inspire in them a love of the subject. I have no need for or interest in fashionable trends or political posturing.'

'Oh dear, oh dear,' sighed Dr Soulages, 'what an inadequate conception of your role. You are too preoccupied with the mere content of your subject and obviously insensitive to its sociological and political implications. This is precisely why a vigilant administration is an absolute necessity in a university today. Otherwise, who will attend to counteracting the decidedly sexist nature of the mathematics that you research and teach, and which has been conclusively demonstrated to be such in papers delivered at our international conferences for university administrators?

'Unless appropriately monitored by vigilant administrators, in the interest of inclusiveness and diversity, recourse to academic rigour in mathematics and allied sciences will perpetuate undeserved white, male, heterosexual privilege. In the interest of inclusiveness, previous standards and goals must be adjusted in a more all-embracing manner. Mathematical programmes, amongst others, must henceforth be based less upon talented individuals seeking to solve difficult quantitative challenges and more upon broadly attractive qualitative group projects, such as are already widely accepted by many, as the norm of good education in the social sciences.'

"Bloody nonsense,' replied the professor. 'Most of my best students are women and they are more committed than the men to establishing their individual mathematical reputations than fooling around with touchy-feely group projects.'

President Boulanger moved quickly to bring the proceedings to a conclusion before Dr Soulages was subjected further to the evident outrage of the audience. In fact, he himself wasn't looking forward to the dinner to which, as a matter of courtesy and propriety, he had invited the lecturer later this evening. Indeed, he was asking himself, if what he had just heard is the shape of things to come, whether he would be interested in seeking re-election as president of the university? Of late, he had been feeling a little tired and somewhat lacking the enthusiasm with which he had embraced the post more than ten years ago.

Some months ago, his doctor had increased his blood pressure prescription and advised him to take things a bit easier. Tomorrow he had an appointment with him to learn the result of the range of tests he had undergone at the hospital in Beziers a few days ago. He had been sent there after experiencing some mild chest pain. He was looking forward to a nice holiday during the summer break. He planned to return with his wife to a hotel in Connemara in the west of Ireland where they had stayed a number of years ago and enjoyed two weeks of salmon fishing on the beautiful river nearby.

Meanwhile, the audience dispersed, most of them to the academic staff common room, in urgent need of restorative drinks and to give vent to their indignation.

There was general accord that the lecture was a ridiculous caricature of what a university should be.

'Absolute piffle,' declared the professor of geography as he added just a small splash of water to his double Scotch whisky. 'Treating the university like a school for social engineering, offering degrees in political correctness. No appreciation of true academic values, standards, and commitment.'

Although there was broad agreement with his sentiments, they would have received a more enthusiastic reception if he himself was a more credible witness to the values and standards he so fervently espoused. In fact, it was a long-standing source of some amusement among his colleagues that the professor of geography seemed to believe that his academic responsibility involved leaving most of the teaching to his junior staff while he spent much of his time on extended visits to places which he claimed to be of great geographical interest, but which also always happened to boast a state-of-the-art golf course. A joke which went around was that the difference between God and St Chinian's professor of geography is that, whereas God is everywhere, the professor of geography is everywhere except St Chinian!

The only person who voiced a word of support for the lecture was a young woman, a newly appointed lecturer in the recently established controversial centre for equality studies. People took her feeble defence in a comradely spirit of those who understood that she felt under an obligation as a new colleague to proclaim her professional egalitarian loyalties. Somebody even jovially suggested that Dr Soulages might be offered a job in the centre for equality studies to remove his malign influence from the ministry in Paris.

It was Rodrigo Gonzales, the professor of Spanish, also a member of the group that had attended the caucus convened by Didier Ritz, who brought the discussion round explicitly to the forthcoming election of a president of the student union. 'The election of a mature student as president of the student union,' he said, 'could have a crucial bearing on the future of our beloved university. The orientation of the university in favour of mature students would provide it with sufficient financial independence to counter the sort of academic intimidation which we heard earlier. Professor Didier Ritz, who has another engagement this evening, raised this issue at the last meeting of the academic council. He courageously declared his support for the candidacy of Lotti Beausang. She is the mature student who is running for the office of president in order to transform the university into one in which mature students and their intellectual requirement play a dominant role. It seems important to me that this programme is successful. It will provide us with the independence and the resources to challenge and defeat the ambition, which we heard prefigured this evening, to convert the university into a political instrument of the Ministry for Higher Education and Research.'

This intervention provoked a lively reaction, some in favour of the radical change advocated by Lotti and Didier Ritz, some heatedly against — and the silent majority cautiously wondering where it would all lead. However, one thing was clear; the university was heading into uncharted water. The genie was out of the bottle and would not be re-encapsulated.

CHAPTER TWENTY-ONE
Final Preparations

The sun shone brightly over the University of St Chinian on Friday morning, just forty-eight hours before the crucial election. Later that evening, the much-heralded debate would take place in the aula max of the university, which is usually reserved for public lectures and degree conferring ceremonies. When fully occupied it can accommodate about twelve hundred people. However, as it was evident that a much larger audience wish to attend the debate, further arrangements had to be made.

In the main square of the university, Square Marcelin Albert, work is underway to erect an enormous television screen on one side of the square which can accommodate several thousand students comfortably. The square was named in honour of Marcelin Albert, the leader of the early twentieth century vignerons revolt against the importation of cheap wine from Algeria. The wily President Clemenceau had tried to dishonour him by falsely insinuating that he had accepted a bribe.

'What is all this in aid of?' asked a labourer who was helping to assemble the supporting scaffolding for the screen.

'It's to show a televised political debate,' replied the foreman, a Moroccan immigrant whose daughter was the first member of his family to attend a university. She was aiming for a degree in tourism studies in the School of Economics, Business Studies and Tourism.

'Who's debating?' asked the labourer. 'It might be interesting to see Macron and Le Pen knocking sparks off one another. More fun than watching Sarkozy and Hollande shadow-boxing.'

'It's not that sort of debate,' said the foreman, 'it's a debate between students about what sort of university they want. It's mainly between an old bird and a young fellow, whom my daughter thinks is great.'

'It's well for them,' said the seasoned old labourer, 'they should be reading their books, drawing their pictures, and doing their sums instead of trying to play politics. There's enough of that already in France. A few months on a building site would soon straighten them out and teach them how lucky they are.'

However, throughout the university, a more exalted view of the impending debate prevailed. Interest and excitement were mounting in anticipation. The supporters of both Lotti and Yves had each erected gaily decorated information booths from which free coffee and biscuits were offered. These were dispensed with advice and promotional literature to allegedly

215

undecided voters, who were often more interested in the relative merits of the proffered refreshment. Alex Denton's contribution was limited to a couple of rather forlorn looking supporters distributing leaflets reminding students that "Alex Says No".

The Concerned Mothers of St Chinian also had a stall advising students how to vote. They warned them of the moral dangers inherent in granting mature students more influence in determining the extracurricular activity of student life. However, their warnings fell on deaf ears or tended to have the opposite effect. The students rather relished the prospect of embracing the moral hazards which the concerned mothers predicted. The more lurid the temptations which the anxious matrons portrayed, the more interesting they seemed to the students. After all, if adults in public life could find happiness with a more mature partner why should they be deprived of the same possibility? In their opinion, the concerned mothers could peddle their admonitions elsewhere. The undecided students, whom they sought to influence, became distinctly more decided as they listened to the imaginary scenarios of revelry and seduction outlined to them.

Lotti's team met in Inspector Louis Dupre's apartment for a light lunch and to review the main points of her address. They spent some time discussing which interventions should be made in the period after the debate that would be open to remarks from the audience.

Particular individuals were designated to make specific observations. It was agreed that Louise Amard and Nicholas Plon, the two young undergraduate students, whom Louis had recruited to the committee, should make enthusiastic interventions in her favour. This would embarrass her opposition's election committee, which although chaired by a young student of public relations, had overlooked the public relations effect of Lotti having a couple of popular youngsters supporting her programme. They had not thought to compensate by producing a couple of "matures" to champion the election of Yves, and the Concerned Mothers of St Chinian were not much help!

Throughout the intensive rehearsal, Lotti herself remained composed and even a little amused. Eventually, at around three o'clock, she excused herself and returned to her own apartment for a relaxed siesta while her team continued with their scheming as though she was still there listening to their brainwaves. She had, however, arranged with Luc and Marie Dupront, the semi-retired beauty therapists, to come to her apartment at half past five to give her the gold standard beauty treatment which they claimed would enchant her audience. She found herself hoping, a little guiltily, that it would have a similar effect on her co-debater, Yves Leroy! She found that he was much in her thoughts and not simply as an electoral opponent!

Yves' team had assembled at noon on a secluded bank of the nearby river. As they relaxed and threw a ball around, they took it in turns to fire questions at Yves which they supposed might be directed to him during the debate. When the most likely ones had been rehearsed the exercise began to degenerate. When some of his more ardent supporters good-humouredly began directing decidedly improper proposals to him in the guise of innocent enquiries, the meeting had to be called to order by its young chairman, Andre Leon, the public relations student who still had a lot to learn about his subject. Proceedings returned to a more decorous and business-like format until it broke for a picnic lunch at two o'clock. Shortly after four o'clock, the gathering dispersed, buoyed with youthful confidence that the doddery old opposition would be demolished.

Yves went to the sports centre where he had a workout, a sauna, and a swim, before returning to his own room to gather his thoughts together again in advance of the meeting which was scheduled for eight o'clock. To his surprise, he found himself wondering, a little affectionately, how his co-debater, Lotti Beausang, was feeling! It promised to be a very interesting evening.

CHAPTER TWENTY-TWO
Anticipation

From about seven o'clock, the aula max, or great hall, began to fill up. A few of the front rows had been reserved for academic staff and invited guests. Prominent seats were allocated to local dignitaries and senior executives of commercial enterprises. Their support or financial endowment of various student cultural and sporting activities was always in demand and much appreciated.

The event itself, which would be transmitted by the university television studio over an area of about twenty-five kilometres, had captured the local imagination. Although not familiar with the finer implications of the topic of the debate — "Whither the University of St Chinian?" — the local community had a sense that something important was happening at the university, an institution of ever-increasing importance in the region.

Paul Comps, the local councillor on the university's governing body who had attended Didier Ritz's *soiree,* was seated prominently. He was here this evening not only in his own capacity but also as representing the mayor. The mayor, as a part-time pork butcher, had a prior engagement and a personal preference to attend the annual general meeting of the *Confrérie des Boucheries de Languedoc*.

The Concerned Mothers of St Chinian were also well-represented. Their chairwoman, a formidable matron in a patriotic red, white and blue ensemble, was escorted to a seat in the front row by one of Yves' supporters. She had recently written a blistering attack on the corrupting influence of mature students to the local newspaper, *Midi Libre*, signing herself simply as "An Indignant Mother of Ten".

However, she had to play her hand carefully when expressing her dire warnings about the malevolent influence of mature students. For whereas most of her colleagues would be righteously indignant at the prospect of their fine young sons succumbing to the charms of a predatory golden-haired mature beauty, they were more open-minded about their daughters establishing a permanent liaison with a comfortable retired bank manager. Their chairwoman considered this subtle distinction to be a blatant expression of sexism but experienced some difficulty in formulating her objection!

There were representatives also of the local *vignerons* and of various organizations and enterprises whose business interests were affected by the course of university events. Dom Placebo, the local priest who had preached the inscrutable sermon the previous Sunday about the election, was also in benign attendance. Also present, were a journalist and a photographer from the *Midi Libre* newspaper — each looking for an angle from which to report or record.

There was a respectable representation of academic staff from the various schools. Some of them had very decided views but most simply wished to learn more about an issue which seemed to be convulsing the student body. At the back of the hall and on the balcony, hundreds of students, both young and mature, crowded into the limited space available. Most just wanted to observe the spectacle but some were keen to have direct engagement in the proceedings. Initially, the young, full-time students tended to sit together on the left of the hall and the mature, part-timers on the right. But, as the hall filled up, latecomers of both groups sat wherever they could find a space. On the stage there were three desks and a microphone stand. At the back of the stage, a large screen had been erected on which the reactions of both the large crowd assembled in Square Marcelin Albert and the subliminal messages of the mysterious Alex Denton could be portrayed.

In anticipation of the ceremony, the noise level in the hall was surprisingly subdued — an almost devotional hush prevailed, broken only by an occasional burst of laughter. Things were rather different in the large open Square Marcelin Albert. As it filled up with throngs of students of all ages, a carnival spirit prevailed. On a makeshift stage, while waiting for the debate to begin, alternating musical groups, supporting the different candidates, entertained the crowd with musical hits ranging, in turn, from the 1950s to the present day. A black-gowned and hooded individual played a dead march on a trumpet to remind them of the candidature of Alex Denton. One wag remarked, 'He or she should have been a bit livelier to get my vote!'

A few entrepreneurial business studies students had set up stalls and tables from which they conducted a brisk business selling beers and hamburgers. Others were discreetly selling cigarettes from which a surprisingly sweet-scented smell permeated the air! One enterprising "mature", a retired bookmaker, was offering odds on the result of the election. Colourfully attired, he offered an equally colourful range of exhortations, recalled from his professional racecourse activity in Britain. 'Roll up, roll up,' he exhorted, 'if you don't speculate you can't accumulate!' He was attracting a gratifying number of punters. It looked as if it was going to be a profitable evening for him, as he was offering odds of only four to five on each of the main candidates and ten to one against an Alex Denton victory.

The crowd was in an increasingly happy mood as they awaited the formal opening of proceedings, even though these would be available to them only electronically on the huge screen at the back of the square. The scene was set for a lively and entertaining evening which would extend long beyond the scheduled programme.

CHAPTER TWENTY-THREE
Opening the Debate

As the clock on the nearby library tower chimed eight o'clock, the two main personalities providing the evening's entertainment, Lotti and Yves, who had been waiting in a small reception room off the great hall, made their entry. They were led in, to enthusiastic applause, by Professor Claire Macon, to whom Guy Boulanger had committed the task of chairing the debate. For the occasion she had donned her scarlet doctoral gown. Lotti and Yves were less formally attired, she in a pale blue dress, he in green sports jacket and grey slacks. Strange images and remarks began to float along the screen at the back of the stage, confirming the spiritual presence of Alex Denton.

As Lotti and Yves seated themselves at their desks, Claire Macon walked to the microphone at the front of the stage, tapped it to ensure that it was operational, and addressed the audience.

'Distinguished guests, dear colleagues and students,' she began, 'it is my great pleasure as chairperson to welcome you here this evening to this important debate and discussion. It is a significant feature of the democratic process by which the students of the University of St Chinian select the president of their student union. The successful candidate will play a key role during the next two years in organizing official student activities in the university and in representing the students on all of its official bodies. In all previous elections to this important post, there have never been more than two official candidates. This year, exceptionally, there are three. Two of the candidates are present this evening to debate their respective views. The third candidate, Alex Denton, whether as a matter of discretion, or for some other undisclosed motives, has declined to participate personally. He or she, as agreed with the secretary of the university, will project a number of images and observations on the screen behind us during this evening's proceedings.'

As she spoke a large image of Charlie Chaplain, waving his trademark walking stick, floated across the screen. Ignoring the titters of laughter which this provoked, Professor Macon proceeded with her introduction.

'The agreed topic of our discussion this evening is the challenging question, "Whither the University of St Chinian?" The two candidates for the post of president who are with us this evening, are both remarkable students of the university. However, in addressing the topic for discussion, I understand that they will be presenting very different responses to the question which they are invited to address. These two candidates are Yves Leroy and Lotti Beausang.

'Monsieur Yves Leroy is a young, full-time third-year student in the School of Viticulture, Oenology, and Agriculture. As captain of the rugby team, which won the prestigious inter-university De Gaulle trophy, he has brought great honour to his university. Although devoted to his studies, he is also a keen supporter of all the sporting activities of the university. In addressing the topic for debate, he wishes to argue that the primary role of the University of St Chinian is the higher education of the youth of the Languedoc region.' Youthful approbation rippled through the hall.

'Madame Lotti Beausang,' Claire continued, 'is the other candidate with us this evening. She is a mature, part-time student from the north of France who has come to live here in St Chinian to pursue the university studies she was unable to avail herself of when she was younger. For over thirty years, she enjoyed a distinguished career in a publishing company before taking early retirement to pursue her intellectual interests with us. This is her third year at the University of St Chinian and she is an enthusiastic and popular member of many of the university's societies and clubs. In addressing the topic for debate, she wishes to argue that the primary purpose of the University of St Chinian should be to be a ground-breaking international pioneer in the higher education of mature students.' Refined murmurings of mature support were clearly audible!

'Each candidate,' Claire explained, 'will be accorded half an hour to present their case. Then there will be a short break after which the remaining period of the evening will be devoted to exchanges between the candidates and to offering you, the audience, an opportunity to comment on the views you have heard and to add your own observations to the discussion. I would ask you to do so in a measured and responsible manner. I now call upon our first speaker, M. Yves Leroy, to open the discussion of "Whither the University of St Chinian?"' Polite applause from the various supporters accompanied the chairperson's remarks as she returned to her seat.

The reaction of the much larger audience in Square Marcelin Albert was far less temperate and respectful. Well-fuelled by hamburgers, beer, and reinforced tobacco, they were not merely willing but eager to express their engagement with the proceedings. As each candidate was introduced by Professor Macon, there had been sustained cheering from their respective supporters. When the different views which the two candidates would argue were announced, the supporting cheers were accompanied by sustained jeers and expressions of mockery from the opposition.

Her concluding remark, in which she pleaded for a measured and responsible discussion, was greeted by the assembled extramural occupants of Square Marcelin Albert, with derisory hooting and laughter. They may not have secured a place within the hallowed precincts of the aula max, but they had every intention of making their views emphatically known. A great opportunity for the spontaneous and democratic expression of wit, repartee, and contradictory prejudices was eagerly and happily anticipated.

CHAPTER TWENTY-FOUR
Yves Leroy

Acknowledging Professor Macon's gracious introduction with a polite bow, Yves raised his elegantly proportioned frame, and, smiling broadly to the audience, strode casually to the microphone podium. His movement seemed so calm and relaxed one would not have suspected that, because he was more accustomed to scoring rugby tries than public speaking, he had nervously practiced this opening challenge several times the day before. It had reminded him of the more agreeable hours he had spent practicing how to kick a penalty score from various positions on the field.

To warm applause from the aula, and raucous shouts of encouragement from Square Marcelin Albert, he commenced his address. 'Madam Chairperson, ladies and gentlemen, fellow students of St Chinian, thank you for your much-appreciated invitation to address you this evening. It is an honour to have an opportunity to engage with you in a discussion about the future of our beloved university.

'My message is a simple one. The University of St Chinian should continue to be that which it was originally intended to be and which, since its inauguration over fifty years ago, it has continued to be, notwithstanding various economic constraints and more recent social distractions.'

The significance of his reference to "recent social distractions" was not lost on either the aula audience or the large crowd in the square. From the "tut-tutting" of the one to the "booing" of the other, it was obvious that the "matures" were not happy to be considered social distractions.

'Our university,' he proclaimed, 'was established to provide quality higher education for the young people of Languedoc and, by so doing, to enhance the economic, social, and cultural quality of the region. To be diverted from this objective would not only be absurd but would also betray the brave and imaginative decision of the generous people of this wonderful region to establish and promote a university in St Chinian.'

Yves was getting comfortably into his stride. The "brave, imaginative, and generous people" in the front few rows beamed with satisfaction. One could almost read the lips of the chairperson of the Concerned Mothers proclaiming, 'Good boy, Yves, sock it to them!' The mayor would regret that she was not there in person to acknowledge the compliment.

Among this complacent audience, few would be so small-minded as to point out that the people of the region had nothing to do with the decision to establish the university. The decision had been taken in 1948 by the political authorities in Paris. They had considered it an expedient measure to contain the fecklessness and agitation of the young and notoriously rebellious descendants of Cathar heretics who inhabited the region. It was judged that it would probably be more effective to provide them with a few years of carefully planned low-cost higher education instead of building the *gendarmeries* and prisons which would otherwise probably be required to contain them.

'The wonderfully successful and now prestigious University of St Chinian,' Yves continued, 'is rooted in the same great tradition of French scholarship that characterizes that of Europe's second university, the Sorbonne, in Paris, which was founded in the thirteenth century. It belongs also to the great tradition of renewal of university life under Napoleon at the beginning of the nineteenth century. It is an integral part of the French centralized, continuous, and hierarchical model of education for its young citizens. It involves a conception of higher education as closely connected with, and evolving naturally out of, its system of secondary education. The young teenager, studying for his or her baccalaureate at a *lycée* during the final three years of secondary education, is serving there the necessary novitiate for seamless admission into the full glory and responsibility of youthful undergraduate university studies. From these essentially youth-oriented university studies, he or she may enter the world of work as a well-qualified and appropriately prepared young citizen. Or he or she may continue for a time, naturally and organically, to engage in postgraduate studies which will qualify him or her further for entry into professional, public, or academic life.

'Since Napoleonic times, the whole process of French university education is focused essentially and irreplaceably upon its aspirations for the appropriate formation and well-being of the youth of the Republic who are the future of France. Any attempt to distort or obfuscate this essentially youth-oriented conception of university life must be resolutely resisted as a travesty of the true idea of a French university.' With this remark there was spontaneous applause from the younger members of the audience in the aula max and jubilant uproar in the Square Marcelin Albert.

Meanwhile, on the screen behind the stage in the aula, images floated by of tsunami waves, melting icebergs, and mystifying mathematical formulae relating to the prediction of entropic chaos by the second law of thermodynamics. These were interspersed with the exhortation to "Vote for Alex — Who Says No and Promotes Negative Entropy". The viewers remained mystified by what this might mean.

Realizing that he had at least one part of the audience enthusiastically on his side, Yves continued to play to his strength. 'The young students and graduates of the University of St Chinian,' he declared have made and continue to make a wonderful contribution to the economic, social, and cultural life of Languedoc. We are at the beginning, not the end, of our productive lives.

We are the future *vignerons*, teachers, business people, journalists, hoteliers, social and political leaders of Languedoc and further afield. In any section of the university which you may visit, you will find us exerting our youthful energy and enthusiasm in industrious attention to the studies which prepare us to serve our region and our country.

'I invite you, for example, to visit our campus at Berlou where our School of Viticulture, Oenology and Agriculture is located and where I am privileged to be a student. There you will see us toiling in the fields, day and night, under the wise direction of our learned professors. Whatever the weather, we are there, pruning the vines, tending the bees, herding the cattle, weighing the pigs, guiding the geese, grading the eggs. We are dedicated to acquiring the skills to provide the region with the future *vignerons* and farmers who will continue to be the backbone of its economy. You don't see many old dears sloshing about in melting winter snow to feed buckets of turnips to a herd of hungry pigs, or climbing a ladder to spray the olive trees.

'And this brings me,' he said, 'to the key issue in this election of a new president of the student union of St Chinian. It is the issue of addressing and containing the role of mature students in our beloved university.'

As he broached this delicate topic, a frisson of apprehensive anticipation passed through the audience. How would he handle the issue which had been convulsing the student body, and exercising the minds of many academics for the past six weeks?

'Let me make it clear at the outset,' he declared, 'that I have no objection in principle to mature students at our university. I welcome them, I like them, and I even admire them. Indeed, it would not be pushing it too far to say that a few of my good friends are mature students. They lend a little colour to the local landscape with their quaint views and unpredictable reactions. Although often quite pleasant company, they can also be a salutary warning to the young student, indicating how he or she might turn out if not careful.' (This provoked a good-natured combination of laughter and dissent.)

'Yes, I can happily agree that it may be good for the *esprit de corps* of a university to have a few mature students in the mix, a bit like an occasional raisin or nut in a birthday cake. They may remind us of our parents and may even at times impart some sensible advice. They are always welcome touchline supporters at the performance of our young, full-time students in various inter-university sporting contests.

'So, you will understand that I am not opposed in principle to mature students as to an undesirable university phenomenon. They are there to be accepted, or at least endured, as a given feature of the landscape, like early morning lectures or end of term examinations.

'However, I do object when, although well past their reproductive life, they appear to breed like rabbits

233

on the campus. I do object when I find that there are twice as many mature old dears, parading as students of the University of St Chinian, as there are young, full-time students. I have to remind myself that a French university exists primarily to educate and prepare the young for life, not to reward and indulge those who are past it. That is why I am seeking your vote for election to the important post of president of the student union.

'A stranger,' he cautioned, 'coming from Australia or China and chancing upon our campus would be puzzled when told that the pride and joy of St Chinian is its wonderful university. In the cafes and bars, he would see mainly old greybeards and suicide blondes, dyed by their own hand, guzzling their Pernods. Likewise, at the queue for the university restaurant, he would join mainly old dears in designer jeans and brand-new glittering Nikes. He would have to visit the library or the sports centre to find a few young, full-time students huddling together.'

Delighted by the impact of the image he was conveying, Yves further elaborated. 'Suppose,' he said, 'you wished to visit an aquarium to look at all the beautiful gleaming agile fish moving gracefully and speedily around in the water. Now imagine, upon arriving at the indicated location, all you saw, apart from a few small fish in a pool, were thousands of monkeys swinging lazily from branch to branch. Wouldn't you wonder had you come to the right place?'

This was a step too far for some of the mature ladies in the aula. One of them shouted, 'You cheeky young pup — have you no manners?' Four of them stood up and marched resolutely towards the exit.

'Oh, my goodness,' exclaimed Yves, seemingly contrite, 'dear ladies, please don't take offence. It was only a figure of speech to make the point that at a university you usually expect to see young students rather than venerable and, of course, deeply respected elderly citizens. If you wish, I will gladly change the figure of speech. Instead of swinging monkeys, I am perfectly willing to substitute aviaries of multicoloured birds of paradise, or flocks of pink-feathered flamingos perched on one leg and the other tucked under. I might even have referred to strutting peacocks were it not for the fact that only the male of the species has a tail worth talking about. The argument remains the same. At a university, you expect to see more young students than pensioners.'

The alternative images he suggested provoked mild amusement, which helped to restore calm to the audience in the aula. In the Square Michelin Albert, however, a much rowdier atmosphere prevailed as robust exchanges of mirthful delight and indignant outrage were traded between the opposing factions.

Availing himself of the temporary restoration of peace, Yves continued his remarks. 'I come now, by way of conclusion, to recall the measures I will pursue if elected as president of the student union.

235

'As I have made clear at various meetings, I will devote myself to securing better arrangements and conditions for all students. This will include greater appraisal by students of the academic courses which they endure. It will also involve demanding longer opening hours of the library, the restaurants, and the student bars. It will include significant improvement of the university's sporting and cultural facilities, strict rent control, and the provision of additional student residences. These are issues which concern all students and which should always have the dedicated commitment and attention of any student president.

'However, as I have indicated, at this particular time, the threat to the very identity of the University of St Chinian, which the recent mass inundation by mature student poses, must be addressed. Accordingly, I will use all my influence on the various bodies of the university, to which my office accords me membership, to secure the following three decisions.

> 'Firstly, the number of mature, part-time students must not exceed that of young, full-time students. This will mean a gradual increase over the next few years of the number of full-time students and a corresponding calculated reduction in the number of part-time students.

> 'Secondly, because of full-time students' onerous schedule and their exemplary dedication to their studies, they must be

236

accorded prior access to the various college facilities, such as bars, restaurants, cinema, and sporting facilities. It is an affront to see them having to queue behind a group of chattering, old part-timers, debating where to buy their winter ensembles.

'Lastly, a levy of fifty euro to be added to the fees which mature students are currently charged for each course they attend. This fund to be administered by the student union to improve campus facilities for all students. In return, the union will support the attempts of mature students to secure tax exemption for their fees.

'These simple measures will, in my view, restore harmony and equilibrium to student life in our beloved University of St Chinian. I seek the support of your vote to help me to make them a reality. If we do not take these simple steps to restore the ethos of the university, the French government may take more drastic steps. Recall how the revolutionary government suppressed all French universities from 1793 because it disliked their conservative culture. They were only restored a decade later, under strict government control, by Napoleon. I would not wish to witness the suppression of the University of St Chinian because it is perceived as more like an old folks' home. I hope I can rely upon your vote and I thank you for your kind attention.'

Yves bowed to his audience, waved to the screen behind the stage which, besides displaying Alex Denton's images and exhortations, transmitted the reactions of the great crowd in Square Marcelin Albert.

The reaction of the audience in the aula was predictably very mixed. The younger members were enthusiastically delighted. The bloc of mature students was uniformly outraged and sought, unavailingly at this stage of the proceedings, to express their indignation. The invited guests, for the most part, weren't quite sure whether to look concerned or amused — the more experienced among them managing to convey both reactions simultaneously.

The atmosphere in Square Marcelin Albert was a combustible combination of euphoria and outrage. However, it was temporarily contained by the more pressing need of many of the audience to relieve themselves, obtain more beer or reinforced tobacco, and to consult their smartphones before the next speaker approached the microphone.

CHAPTER TWENTY-FIVE
Lotti Beausang

As the reactions to Yves' remarks subsided, Chairperson Claire Macon called the aula to order and invited the second speaker, Lotti Beausang, to the microphone. She asked her to present her argument that the University of St Chinian should exist as a ground-breaking academic milieu devoted primarily to the academic, social, and cultural requirements of mature students.

Having clearly benefited from a comprehensive makeover earlier that afternoon by her beautician friends, Luc and Marie Dupront, Lotti strolled gracefully to the podium. She smiled broadly at the aula audience and, looking back at the screen behind her, waved cheerfully to the larger and more exuberant audience in Square Michelin Albert. In her smart, low cut and close-fitting blue dress, she conveyed an attractive aura of a maturity which was more one of pleasing physical proportions than of *Anno Domini.*

'Dear Chairperson, distinguished guests, and all students, both young and mature, I am delighted to share a few thoughts with you this evening.

'For me, as a recently retired executive in my fifties, it is a rather unusual experience to find myself seeking your support for election as president of the student union of the University of St Chinian. I'm sure that some of you also may find it a pretty odd request. Therefore, I am glad to have this opportunity to convince you that at this crucial time in the life of our beloved university that I am the right person for this important post.

'As our gracious chairperson indicated, I am seeking this role in order to promote the claim that the University of St Chinian should exist as a unique and innovative milieu devoted primarily to the academic, social, and cultural requirements of mature students.

'Does this mean that I am challenging the view that a university may rightfully claim that the higher education of young people is its primary mission? Certainly not! I do not count myself amongst those who say that young people in general should be treated only as apprentices who are expected to learn, by on-the-job training, the various trades and occupations required by society. I reject the view that young people should only be adapted to societal needs, rather than society adapted to theirs. I do not subscribe, therefore, to the view that the more liberal objectives characteristic of university life should be available only in one's spare time or later in life. Nothing could be further from my mind. I wish to promote a larger not a narrower conception of university higher education.

'By a larger conception of university higher education, I mean a more inclusive, open and innovative one. I am happy to accept that most universities should be focused primarily on the education of young students. But surely this does not mean that all universities must operate according to this norm? It seems obvious to me that the very notion of liberal university education should include the possibility, indeed the desirability, that at least one such institution be dedicated primarily, though not exclusively, to meeting the requirements of mature students. And I want to commend to your favourable consideration that the University of St Chinian is uniquely positioned to fulfil such a role.

'A few years ago, our enlightened President Boulanger, prompted undoubtedly by financial considerations, but also, I would like to believe, inspired by generous and liberal intentions, decided to welcome to this wonderful university its first cohort of mature students. What a momentous decision. Nobody could have anticipated its long-term implications for the university.

'The invitation, so generously extended to mature students, was eagerly accepted. It was welcomed as though by a group of thirsty travellers, traversing a sun-baked barren desert, who suddenly chance upon a gently flowing river of sparkling clear water.' (The eloquent image generated both a few lace handkerchiefs to stem emotional tears and a number of discreet groans. From the crowd in Square Marcelin Albert acclamations of joyful agreement were countered by clearly audible declarations of "*Merde*").

'The offer of university education for mature, and, for the most part, recently retired, hardworking citizens was responded to not only by the worthy people of Languedoc, but by thousands of French citizens from every corner of the Republic and its territories. People who had laboured industriously all their adult lives suddenly saw an opportunity to kindle or refresh their neglected cultural aspirations. And not only French citizens availed themselves of this beautiful possibility. There was an eager response throughout Europe and the Americas. Also, people from Australia, Asia, China, and Japan, in the gloomy winter of their burdensome working life, suddenly saw, at St Chinian, the welcoming light of what, in an earlier century, the great educationalist, John Henry Newman, called a "Second Spring". Something unsuspected, but of cosmic significance, was stirring in the academic groves of the University of St Chinian.

'For the first time,' she continued enthusiastically, 'men who had been bricklayers their entire adult lives could study classical architecture. Retired nurses could toy with the Italian Renaissance. The celibate bachelor clerk, whose working nose had been buried in an office ledger, could bury the same rejuvenated nose in the delights of the Roman Empire and German romantic literature. The weary electrician, whose working life down cellars and up poles had been a maze of wires and plugs, could test, through electrifying tuition in live model classes, his secret ambition to paint young women dancing joyfully on a sunlit beach.

'These are just a few of the verified instances of the liberation of mature adventurers made possible by the initiative at the University of St Chinian, which has captured the world's imagination. I see it as my role to help this wonderful initiative, not only to persist, but to develop to its full potential as a shining example of a university dedicated primarily to the talents and academic requirements of mature students. Such recognition of their lives of dedicated service to society in the world of work is richly deserved and long overdue.

'I want,' she continued, 'to help the University of St Chinian to fulfil the destiny which a happy combination of chance and necessity has ordained for it, namely, to be the first *grande école* for mature students. It can open a new path of exuberant university life for our troubled times.

'Nor, indeed, are we without significant precedents which anticipated in their modest way the revolution to which St Chinian is invoked. At the very origin of higher education, Plato's Academy, in the fourth century B.C., included a majority of older students, including women. A little later, the gymnasium, founded by Aristotle, also favoured older students. I quote the great man himself, where he states in his

Nichomachean Ethics, "Hence a young man is not a proper hearer of lectures on political science; for he is inexperienced in the actions that occur in life... And further since he tends to follow his passions, his study will be vain and unprofitable... For to such persons, as to the incontinent, knowledge brings no profit" (*NE* 1, 1095 a 2-11). And elsewhere, elucidating this claim, he concludes that the mind is at its best from about forty-nine. "Young men," he wrote, "have strong passions and tend to gratify them indiscriminately. Of the bodily desires, it is the sexual by which they are most swayed and in which they show absence of self-control... As for Men in their Prime, clearly, we shall find that they have a character between that of the young and that of the old, free from the extremes of either... To put it generally, all the valuable qualities that youth and age divide between them are united in the prime of life, while all their excesses or defects are replaced by moderation and fitness. The body is in its prime from thirty to five-and-thirty; the mind about forty-nine" (*Rhet.* 1389–90).

'Likewise, as demonstrated in his breathtaking lectures, our esteemed professor of Latin has shown us how, in Roman times, Cicero, in his *De Senectute* made it clear, that mature students are more reliable than headstrong youths. Moreover, the medieval schools which were the precursors of our modern universities were peopled mainly by mature theologians. And the great philosopher, Emmanuel Kant, didn't publish *The*

Critique of Pure Reason, the first of his several masterpieces, until he was nearly sixty.

'However,' she cautioned, 'if the University of St Chinian is to achieve its destiny as one dedicated to mature students, certain important changes will have to be implemented. If elected as president of the student union, I will devote myself to promoting these changes.'

Just as she was about to outline her proposed changes, she was slightly disconcerted by an outburst of laughter from the audience. On the screen behind her, Homer, Marge, and Bart Simpson were depicted dancing down the street waving banners exhorting to "Vote for Alex — Who Says No and Promotes Negative Entropy". Seeking to ignore the distraction, she proceeded with her presentation.

'In the first place, it is clear that, if the University of St Chinian is to be devoted primarily to the requirement of mature students, the vast majority of the student body should be mature students. I suggest that this means that at least 75% must be mature students. This could easily be achieved, either by raising the number of mature students to twelve thousand, or by raising their current number from eight to nine thousand and reducing the number of young students from four to three thousand.

'Secondly, the current regulation which accords only a half vote to mature students must be abolished immediately. I would not favour a corresponding reduction in the value of a young students vote. Young students should be recognized as valuable although ancillary members of the student body. Indeed, I would support a proposal that mature students might adopt a young student, preferably of the opposite sex, for guidance, cultural exchange, and social interaction.' (This latter proposal provoked frowns on the faces of the Concerned Mothers of St Chinian. It was greeted with hilarity and lewd comments by the crowd in Square Marcelin Albert.)

'Thirdly, if the potential of the wonderful new conception of the University of St Chinian is to be fully realized, certain important institutional and organizational changes will have to be implemented. These changes must all be animated by the determination that, henceforth, the primary purpose of the university must be to serve the interests of part-time, mature students. This means that, henceforth, the university, in all its organization and arrangements, must primarily serve the interests of mature students, and only accommodate those of full-time students as an important but subsidiary consideration.

'This change will be reflected in a wholescale reform of the academic programme. All courses will be provided as fifteen lecture units to facilitate the average mature student's attention span and their interest in sampling a number of very different courses each year. How these units can be combined to meet the interests of young students wishing to pursue a full-time degree can be worked out by discussion and sensible planning.

'Negotiations must also be entered into with the state to secure the funding of all the university's activities. In particular, unless it agrees to continue funding all the full-time degree programmes, for which there may not be many mature candidates, the university may exercise the option of discontinuing some of these courses. This might involve the now internationally renowned University of St Chinian declaring itself to be a private institution totally independent of the state. I think the authorities in Paris would not welcome this development particularly as they would have to make provision elsewhere for the thousands of young, full-time Languedoc students.

'Fourthly, the University of St Chinian might initiate an attractive menu of distance learning programmes to facilitate mature students who wish to avail themselves of its wonderful courses but who, for various reasons, may be delayed from attending them personally. This, however, should be envisaged as only an interim option, intended to encourage those students to plan eventual participation in the wonderful experience of living in St Chinian itself.

'Finally, as well as the above-mentioned academic and administrative reorganization, there will have to be a reconfiguration of the university's cultural and social facilities, one which reflects the age profile of the great majority of its students. This will include giving a higher priority to activities such as golf, bowling, bridge and ballroom dancing. Attention must also be devoted to organizing academic cruises and study holidays in interesting sunny locations, particularly during the winter.

'As president of the student union I will devote myself tirelessly to making this imaginative renewal of the University of St Chinian a reality. Thank you for your attention and, in anticipation of Sunday's election, thank you for your vote.'

As she returned to her seat, she was accompanied by enthusiastic applause from the mature students both in the aula and in the Square Marcelin Albert. However, from the mainly young audience in the square, there were some rude exclamations, and offers of a wheel chair or a walking stick to assist her back to her seat.

The chairperson thanked Lotti for her vibrant contribution. She then announced that there would now be a twenty-minute break but urged people to return to their seats promptly at nine twenty for the open discussion between the speakers and the audience. She confirmed that there would be a television link enabling members of the large gathering in the Square Marcelin Albert to participate.

Coffee and tea were available in the large vestibule into which the audience filed patiently from the aula. The crowd in the square sought more invigorating sustenance from the various impromptu installations established by the novice entrepreneurs from the School of Economics, Business Studies and Tourism. A lively young rock group, availing themselves of the free television exposure, belted out noisy interim entertainment on the makeshift stage. The suspect scent of the rising haze of blue smoke mingled incongruously with that of "Joy" and "Chanel No 5", favoured by some of the more sophisticated mature students.

CHAPTER TWENTY-SIX
Audience Response

As the library tower bell chimed nine fifteen, the audience began to reassemble in the aula and the square. A little before nine thirty, Chairperson Macon recommenced proceedings and invited comments from the audiences in both locations. She had a small television and interactive device on her desk which enabled her to communicate with a colleague in the square who had the challenging task of trying to organize the communication from the large and boisterous crowd there.

The first to seize the microphone was Thomas van Velsen, the Dutch lecturer in history of sociology and chairman of the St Chinian Latter Day Albigensians. He declared that in his role as chairman he must request that if there was any reduction in the number of younger students, as envisaged by Madame Beausang, it should be confined to male students. For young women students were the most enthusiastic members of the St Chinian Community of Latter Day Albigensians. Indeed, their lively and engaging participation in the life of the community was one of the main reasons which attracted a number of otherwise somewhat less enthusiastic male seekers of enlightenment to the community. Any reduction in the number of young women students would have a very adverse effect on the life of the community which was such a wonderful component of the university.

Sandra Ricoeur, the editor of *The St Chinian Trumpet,* reminded the audience that there was a third candidate, Alex Denton, whose brief election slogan's recent inclusion of a reference to "negative entropy" might contain a profound message. She wondered had either of the other candidates any comment to make for her readers. Neither had!

However, a serious looking young man, a student of mathematical physics and one of Alex's nominators, offered some illumination. 'Negative entropy,' he said, 'is sometimes called negentropy, and it refers to the capacity, especially of rational beings, to generate order, for example, scientific, technological, literary, aesthetic, or religious order, which counteracts the cosmic tendency to entropic disorder, and chaos. Perhaps Alex is advocating a more creative role for the president of the student union than the divisive and destructive programmes of the other two candidates?'

This enlightened observation evoked little enthusiasm from the partisan audience in the aula and even less for those in the square who were quite well disposed to a little randomness and chaos.

The next person in the aula to obtain the roving microphone was Jeanne Mandel, a keen supporter of

Yves and fiery chairperson of the St Chinian students' *Front National* society. 'I think,' she said, 'that the attempt by mature students to undermine the University of St Chinian's commitment to traditional French university values is disgraceful. Since Napoleonic times, French universities have cherished the intrinsic link and natural transition between the secondary school baccalaureate programme and university studies. This bond embodies an inalienable and essential link of university life with youthful hopes and aspirations. To attempt to transform our university into an international playground for old codgers is just another move in the relentless drive to destroy France's glorious history and distinctive culture. We see it everywhere, in creeping Americanization, in the expansionist claims of the European Union, the domineering influence of the English language, the craven worship of globalization, uncontrolled immigration. Let us be resolute and at least keep our university faithful to its essentially French tradition as a place dedicated primarily to the higher education of French youth. *Vive Le Front National —Vive Marine Le Pen, Vive la France.*'

Lotti responded briefly. 'The allegedly glorious French tradition of higher education,' she remarked, 'is hardly very robust if it cannot include, by way of exception, even one university devoted to the further education of mature citizens who have devoted their working life to the welfare of the Republic.' Polite applause was recorded from the golden codgers in the aula maxima. A livelier reaction was expressed by both the opposing factions in Square Michelin Albert.

However, the argument in favour of a young student body was pursued from a different, less political, angle by Marc Tavel, the professor of viticulture. He pointed out that the wine industry, so important to the region, depended upon the continuously renewed education of a cohort of young people. 'They undergo,' he explained, 'an arduous programme of practical, professional training in the most up to date techniques and procedures of contemporary viticulture. This programme involves not only attendance in the lecture hall and laboratory but also strenuous physical outdoor work in all seasons and all kinds of weather. These are the young students who have the responsibility of carrying on to the next generation the proud tradition of producing quality Languedoc wine.

'To seek,' he continued, 'to deflect the orientation of this crucial educational programme in favour of the interests of mature students would be a grave economic, social and regional mistake.

'In my experience,' he said, 'mature students are more interested in, and physically more capable of, sitting around in comfortable chairs comparing the "nose", "fruit" and "back of the throat flavour" of different wines. This is an honourable preoccupation but of very secondary significance in the education of a competent vigneron.'

Seated beside him, Marie Latour, professor of animal husbandry and poultry, just added briefly that, in her experience, mature students were happy feeding chickens but notable by their absence when it came to lambing or mucking out.

These contributions motivated Didier Ritz, professor of marketing, to claim the microphone. 'With the greatest respect to my cherished colleagues, Marc and Marie, and to adopt their own quaint bucolic idiom, we cannot let the tail wag the dog of the university. They are welcome to continue their viticulture and animal husbandry, mainly for the benefit of sturdy young men and buxom young women on the university farm in distant Berlou. The rest of the university is hardly aware of their existence or of their agricultural labours.

'They will, of course,' he insisted, 'be expected to facilitate the requirements of those mature students who wish to sample some of the more refined aspects of their rustic contortions, such as soothing broody hens or discerning the respective merits of Sauvignon Blanc and Merlot. But they must not be permitted to abort or impede the triumphant deliverance in due season of the great intellectual conception which it is the privilege of the University of St Chinian to be the proud expectant mother.

'I refer, of course,' he continued, 'to the birth of France's first multi-faculty university devoted primarily and specifically to meeting the pressing intellectual, cultural, and social requirements of mature students. As dean of the School of Economics, Business Studies, and Tourism, I have pledged my services as midwife to assist in every way possible with this auspicious birth.

'I urge you all to open your minds and hearts to the great transformation of life which is within the grasp of our university and which has been so prophetically described this evening by Madame Beausang. Let your minds feast upon the prospect of all the schools and departments of the university being radically reorganized and expanded to provide an astonishing and varied range of intellectual temptations to thousands of mature enquirers from every corner of the world. Hundreds of new programmes, ranging from "Amorous Drama" to "Zen Illumination" will flourish at St Chinian. It will be my privilege to help to market this astonishing development. I can foresee adjunct campuses of St Chinian being established throughout the world, welcoming our own professors as visitors to ensure the faithful delivery of the authentic St Chinian brand. The term "St Chinian" will become synonymous with quality mature university education. *Sursum Corda* and *Carpe Diem*!'

Didier sat down to euphoric applause from the "matures". However, it was tempered by looks of incredulity from the younger audience who found it hard to conjure with his depiction of himself as a dedicated midwife.

His remarks inspired Paul Comps, the local councillor on the governing body and member of

Didier's privately organized group, to rise to his feet. He declared that he personally agreed with everything that Lotti and Didier had said. However, he was also representing the mayor of St Chinian, who had asked him to convey her greetings and good wishes to the meeting. 'She wants you to know,' declared Comps, 'that she is extremely interested in the topic of this evening's discussion and wishes to assure you that she appreciates and sympathizes with all points of view and will strive to the best of her ability to help to have them all implemented,' This expression of quixotic ecumenical fervour provoked some badly needed laughter from both audiences.

Dom Placebo, the university chaplain, reminded the audiences that whatever decision might be reached it would be important to take spiritual values into account. When asked by one of Yves' supporters whether this should this include prayers for a happy death, he surmised that the formulation of these values might vary somewhat depending on whether the eventual decision favoured a university for the mature or the young.

At this stage, some of the crowd in Square Marcelin Albert sought to participate in the discussion, with supporters of each candidate making their preference clear. One young man jumped to his feet and introduced himself as a nominator and enthusiastic supporter of Alex Denton. He reminded the audience that, although Alex was commendably self-effacing, he had promised to address the crowd personally in Square Marcelin Albert on the morning of the election. Alex was a person of his or her word and he, as one of his or her nominators, could assure them that Alex would indeed address them in person that morning. He urged them to attend that communication in great numbers and then proceed to vote for honest "Alex Who Says No".

Next, a young woman, captain of the women's boxing team and an ardent supporter of Yves, got the microphone and made a point which evoked considerable discussion. She claimed that a university devoted primarily to "matures" would destroy the culture and the fine reputation that it had achieved for excellence in sporting activities; an achievement most significantly illustrated by last year's triumph in winning the Languedoc inter-university rugby competition under Yves Leroy's captaincy.

Yves thanked her and agreed heartily. He declared that ballroom dancing would be a poor substitute for a strong line-out or a tight scrum. Excellence in competitive sports, so important for the reputation of a university, was a vocation for young minds and agile bodies.

An irate "mature" retorted that dignified ballroom dancing was certainly preferable to the amorous slouching and smooching which passed for dancing at the student centre. She also maintained, to loud applause, that bowling, or its locally more popular French version, *pétanque*, was every bit as invigorating, demanding, skilful, and competitive as throwing an egg-shaped piece of leather around a field.

Before the argument got too heated, the chair moved on to acknowledge, from the front row of the aula, the urgent gesticulations of Madame Eveline Bombardier, chairwoman of the Maternity of Concerned Mothers of St Chinian. Rising to her feet, arms resolutely folded across her formidable bosom, she announced that she wished to address an astonishing suggestion of Madame Beausang.

'I refer,' she declared, 'to her alarming suggestion that a mature student, posing as a benign mentor, might adopt a younger student, preferably of the opposite sex, to initiate and guide them in their academic, social, and cultural pursuits. This strikes me as a very dangerous proposal. If accepted, it could open the gate to all sorts of questionable relationships. This would be especially the case if the suggestion is allied with another proposal, suggested by Jean Martin, and adopted in one of Madame Beausang's election pamphlets, that the new three-student apartments in the university should always comprise a combination of young and mature students.

'As the proud mother of two young men at the university, I would fear for their moral integrity if this suggestion is implemented. If I had a daughter there instead of sons, I might well see the point of her being adopted for mentoring service by a kindly and benevolent mature man. Daughters are much better than sons at handling such relationships and are quite capable, if they wish, of developing them smoothly into a happy marriage. But boys are so innocent and impulsive. I would hate to see one of my fine sons seduced into a torrid relationship by some scheming, widely experienced old dame. Even if, through her erotic charm, she managed to manipulate such an outrageous situation into a marriage, how could I ever fulfil my greatly anticipated involvement as an effective mother-in-law of somebody maybe older than me?'

She smiled grimly and sat down, quite convinced that she had delivered a devastating argument. She was particularly pleased about the compelling force of her concluding remark about her role, in due course, as an effective mother-in-law. Her remarks generated a lively response, especially from the crowd in the square.

The first to interject was a young man who introduced himself simply as Leon. 'I think Madame Beausang's suggestion is admirable,' he said. 'And I here and now offer myself unreservedly to be adopted by her as my mentor.'

Lotti recognized him as the young man who had departed in high spirits from her apartment one morning a few weeks ago after a very agreeable social encounter the previous evening. She smiled and said she would give his offer her serious consideration. But she warned him that if she adopted him, she would be a very strict mentor and ensure he took all his responsibilities, both academic and social very seriously. This comment evoked great mirth and unleashed an outburst of increasingly outrageous proposals and invitations.

Various young men, naming particular exotic or beautiful mature women, offered themselves for the great honour and indeed pleasure of adoption. They were matched by a number of mature men offering to mentor named delectable female undergraduates. The exercise, proceeding joyfully through all possible coupled variations of sex and age, terminated eventually with a sturdy young woman footballer requesting to be monitored by a mature woman with similar interests.

Thomas Van Velsen, fearing that the proposed mentoring regime might deflect prospective postulants from his Community of Latter Day Albigensians suggested that the community might serve as a sort of dating agency to implement the proposal. His suggestion was energetically declined.

Chairperson Claire Macon, perceiving that the discussion had begun to degenerate into increasingly hilarious proposals, decided it was time to bring the proceedings to a close. She thanked the candidates for their invigorating presentation, acknowledged the enigmatic contribution of Alex Denton, and expressed her appreciation of the lively participation of the audience, both in the aula and in Square Marcelin Albert. She hoped that they would reflect upon the evening's discussion and that it would help them in coming to a wise decision when they cast their vote on

Sunday. She wished them a safe journey home and formally concluded the meeting.

The audience in the aula filed out in a fairly orderly fashion, some to their cars, others to local coffee shops or bars. The university television station, having recorded a picture of the two candidates shaking hands, concluded its recording of the event. It followed with a pre-recorded reflection by a professor from the economics department about the pros and cons of Brexit. The viewing audience decreased promptly by eighty percent.

Activity was rather livelier in the Square Michelin Albert. Here it seemed as if the party was just beginning. The rock group had reoccupied the stage and was producing somewhat softer, more romantic noise. In the open space in front of the stage, some free spirits began to dance. They included some good-natured and expectant combinations of the young and the mature. However, their performance could hardly be termed ballroom dancing. "Amorous slouching and smooching", so forcefully descried by an earlier contributor, was more the order of the night.

Elsewhere, scattered groups, cans or bottles in hand, debated earnestly. Small crowds gathered cheerfully around the improvised bars and hamburger stands. Starry-eyed couples, hand in hand, drifted towards the seats along the back and sides of the square — and the band played on. It looked as if it would be a long night.

CHAPTER TWENTY-SEVEN
The Calm Before...

The following day was not spent, as recommended by Chairperson Macon, in tranquil reflection. It was devoted by the contending candidates to energetic last-minute canvassing.

When it became known that Lotti's team had somehow obtained the personal email addresses of all students, the other candidates, appealing to secretary bursar, Henri Campion, demanded that they be provided with them also. He agreed that this should be done. It was rumoured but unproven that Monique Dubray, the head of computer service, who had attended the conspiratorial gathering in Didier Ritz's home, had facilitated Lotti's campaign manager's access to the list of personal emails addresses. Whatever its provenance, now that the list was available to all, it generated lively attention and frenetic activity. In the brief time remaining, each group sought to get a personal email dispatched as soon as possible to the twelve thousand voters.

There was controversy among Yves' supporters about the message to be sent. Some argued for a short snappy slogan, such a "Score as Goal for St Chinian —

Vote Yves Leroy". Finally, however, a rather protracted message, repeating most of his television debate speech, was sent.

Lotti's supporters, heeding marketing advice from Didier Ritz, who was widely declaring his support for her, settled for something much shorter. Seeking to convey an age-indifferent approbation of maturity, the message stated simply, "She values your mature view — vote for Lotti Beausang".

A few of Alex Denton's nominators weren't sure what message to send. However, they claimed that on his or her advice it was agreed to adopt an iconic 1958 remark of General De Gaulle in Algeria. The message read simply: *"Je vous ai compris* — vote Alex Denton, who says No and promotes Negentropy".

The rest of the morning was devoted to getting these various "personal messages" conveyed to their recipients. However, in the afternoon, there was livelier canvassing by supporters. Various places where students tended to congregate, such as the student centre, the sports gymnasium, and local bars, were visited to make a final appeal to whoever might be still undecided. Literature was distributed and the support of identified individuals solicited. A group of Lotti's supporters even ventured to the campus in Berlou where the viticulture and agriculture students pursued their academic activities. They were greeted benignly and with some amusement but secured few promises.

Later in the afternoon, the university rugby club played an exhibition game in support of Yves. There was a large attendance of supporters, who were entertained at half-time with a song and dance routine, in American football cheerleading style, by a group of his beautiful, enthusiastic, female admirers.

At the same time, not to be outperformed, Lotti's supporters staged a widely advertised *pétanque* competition, in the course of which the elderly competitors exhibited remarkable feats of cunning, guile, and deception. They could not compete with the rugby half-time artistic performance but compensated by providing free wine and sandwiches for the audience.

Alex Denton's few supporters were not in a position to stage an athletic performance of any kind. However, an isolated drone, trailing a "Vote for Alex" banner, floated aimlessly around in the sky above.

When evening fell, everybody felt they had done as much as they could for their preferred candidate. It was a Saturday evening and the welcome end of a busy week. The beckoning restaurants, bars and cafes quickly filled with students of every age and political preference. Well-deserved relaxation, amusement, and much laughter prevailed.

There was a general consensus that the election campaign, although fiercely contested, had been a fair and reasonably good-natured one. There had been occasional snide remarks about senile dementia and gormless youth. Also, a few of Lotti's posters soliciting a mature vote had been defaced. The "t" in "mature" had been replaced with an "n". However, these were exceptions and, at the end of the campaign, participants on all sides believed it had been an exhilarating and worthwhile exercise, even if somewhat bizarre.

Tomorrow would be another day — but a very significant one for the University of St Chinian. Votes could be cast from nine thirty in the morning. Alex Denton would personally provide his or her much anticipated address at nine fifteen in Square Marcelin Albert.

CHAPTER TWENTY-EIGHT
The Vote

The fine weather, which had obtained over the previous two weeks, changed rather dramatically on Sunday morning, the first day of May. A low lying leaden grey sky was more suggestive of winter gloom than spring optimism. But, apart from a few drops, it had not yet begun to rain heavily. However, a few sombre rumbles of thunder and an occasional flash of lightning created an atmosphere of uncertainty. A chill wind replaced yesterday's fragrant light breeze. It seemed as though Nature herself might be signalling cosmic apprehension about what was about to be enacted by the students in St Chinian today.

However, the voters themselves displayed more a sense of curiosity and optimism than of apprehension; curiosity about the identity of Alex Denton and optimism about their preferred candidate. Their mood was one of anticipation rather than apprehension. An edition of *The St Chinian Trumpet* was on sale. Each of the candidates had bought a page to make a last-minute appeal to voters. Lotti had accepted the back page and Yves the sports page. They each portrayed charming photographs of themselves and brief summaries of their mission statements. Alex had somehow secured the front page which was completely blank except for, in very small print at the bottom, the message: "Alex Says No; Vote for Alex".

Shortly before nine o'clock, curious students assembled in considerable numbers in the Square Marcelin Albert. It was here that, at last, Alex Denton was expected to speak to them in person instead of by indirectly conveyed messages. The retired bookmaker, whose courses at the university included statistics, addiction, and the history of magic, was busy running a book on whether Alex would prove to be a man or a woman. From wagers, in notes from "matures" and coins from undergraduates, he had accumulated more than seven hundred euro. He offered even money if one wished to bet that Alex was a woman but one had to wager six to win four to bet that he or she was a man.

At ten past nine, the large white van skidded into the square and a group of Alex's nominators emerged. They opened the back doors of the van and lifted out what appeared to be a recumbent figure, draped in an all-encompassing black robe. They carried the figure up the steps and gently laid it down on the large table at the centre of the stage which had been temporarily erected, a couple of days ago, for the television debate. The crowd fell silent. The atmosphere resembled that of a crowd expecting a miraculous revelation. Thomas Mansion, the leader of the group, stepped forward reverently and removed the robe. What was revealed was not the much-anticipated incarnate subjectivity of Alex Denton, but a coffin-like box crowned with a row of small steel loudspeakers. Thomas walked cautiously to the back of the box and flipped a switch. Coloured lights lit up on the front of the box and created a mysterious technicolour halo. A passage from Handel's "Messiah" sounded briefly from the loudspeakers. After a pause, which seemed like an age, softer background music emerged and a husky voice began to speak.

'My dear fellow students, both young and mature, I offer you my warmest greetings. I am Alex Denton and I am hereby honouring the commitment which I gave you that I would address you personally on this important day when your vote will have a decisive influence on the future of our university.

'As I do not wish you to be overwhelmed by my physical attributes, which I modestly agree are exceptional, I have decided not to address you in the flesh. This is a manifestation which I reserve for your pleasure and delight when you have elected me as the new president of the student union. As I have today honoured my commitment to address you personally, I will likewise, upon my election to this important office, reveal myself to you, here in this Square Marcelin Albert, in a complete and unconcealed physical disclosure. All you have to do to enjoy this revelation is to vote effectively for me today.

'But despite such a tempting offer,' s/he continued, 'some of you might still perhaps be wondering why you should vote for me. Let me briefly enlighten you.

'Like you, I have listened attentively to the claims of the two other candidates for the office of president of the student union. I have heard Monsieur Yves Leroy argue that a university is intrinsically a place for the higher education of young people proceeding naturally thereto from their secondary level studies, and that mature students are only an incidental, if welcome, accessory in the university. What is my reply? My reply is: "Alex says NO — vote for Alex".

'I have also listened carefully to Madame Lotti Beausang's insistence that mature students, who have worked hard all their lives, also deserve, in the course of their retirement, to enjoy the experience of participating fully in the joys of university life. She argues strongly that at least one French university should be devoted primarily to caring for the academic, cultural and social requirements of mature students and that the University of St Chinian, in virtue of its brief but remarkable welcome to such students, is destined to be that university. What is my reply? My reply is: "Alex says NO — vote for Alex".

'"Is this all you have to say?" you may ask. And I reply you must learn to appreciate the power of negativity. I am the apostle of negativity. You will be astonished how negative I can be. Elect me and you will see the wonders that negativity can achieve. Alex says

No — vote for Alex, who promotes the creative power of negentropy.'

The voice fell silent as did the crowd until the group who had carried and placed the voice-recording instrument burst into loud applause. Some others burst out laughing. The view of others was economically expressed by a mature fishmonger from Bouzigues, who exclaimed indignantly, 'What a load of old cobblers!'

As the reoccupied van drove off at high speed, bearing its ethereal voice, another heated discussion broke out among the crowd. Was the voice they had heard the voice of a man or a woman?

There were those that declared that it was certainly the voice of a woman and cited as comparable voices those of singers Eartha Kitt, Nina Simone, and *'Non je ne regrette rien'* Edith Piaf. Others were equally insistent that it was obviously the voice of a man. They drew comparisons with Orson Wells, Humphrey Bogart, and singer Michael Davis. Somebody jovially suggested that it might be the voice of a transgender person.

The discussion took a serious turn when the pop-up bookmaker declared that, as there was no agreement about the gender of Alex Denton, everyone had lost their bet. He was almost mobbed by the punters and eventually agreed to return their wagers.

Shortly afterwards, everyone's attention was redirected by the solemn chiming of the library bell at nine thirty that signalled the opening of the various voting centres. There were three such centres. One was located in the Square Marcelin Albert. Another was in the aula maxima. And a third was in the campus at Berlou. When prospective voters had displayed their student cards at one of the centres, their names were ticked off the electronic voting register, and they were presented with a voting paper, a blue one for full-time students and a red one for part-timers. They were invited to cast their vote for the candidates in the order of their choice.

A group of mature, part-time German students, who had been attracted to St Chinian by the prospect of participating in a university devoted to the interests of older citizens, indignantly tore up their red voting papers which signified that the value of their vote was only half that of full-time students. 'A part-time student is not a half person,' they protested angrily. When their protest produced no immediate effect, they had to try to stick the bits of paper together again in order to vote.

The brisk early voting was sustained throughout the day and it looked as if it would be a record poll. Lotti's campaign manager, Louis Dupre, had organized an effective transport system. Eager volunteers drove other mature students from their homes or apartments to the nearest polling station. The younger, full-time students had to walk or rely on their bicycles. However, they had persuaded Secretary Campion to operate, exceptionally on a Sunday, the university bus which during the week transported students between the main campus and that

271

at Berlou. This was judged to provide a significant boost to Yves' campaign as most students at Berlou were young, full-time undergraduates energetically involved in viticultural and agricultural activities.

Supporters of all the candidates were actively canvassing outside the various polling centres and distributing supporting literature. Lotti's supporters, who were more financially viable, also offered small badges bearing her smiling image. Both she and Yves appeared several times during the day at each of the polling centres. Members of the Concerned Mothers of St Chinian were also outside each centre, distributing literature warning of the moral hazard to their sons if the viewpoint of the mature, part-timers prevailed. This, however, seemed to have the opposite effect as many of the targeted young men seemed to relish the prospect of exposure to the envisaged moral hazard. Alex Denton was not present in person. However, the drone bearing his slogan of negativity fluttered overhead.

In general, the election proceeded in an orderly and good-spirited manner. A few of the less righteous and politically experienced voters sought to act on the old Tammany Hall maxim: "Vote Early and Vote Often". They visited each of the polling stations and sought to register their vote three times. However, Secretary Campion's electronic precautions thwarted their nefarious attempts. There were a few others who, having borrowed the student card of those unavoidably absent, sought to vote on their behalf. However, the contrast between the visual appearance of those bearing the card and the image on the card itself was usually enough to abort the attempt.

At seven in the evening, to the relief of all concerned, the three polling centres closed. It had been a busy day and its result would become evident tomorrow when the count concluded.

By this time, most of the students had dispersed to their lodgings or to seek refreshment in St Chinian's various restaurants, cafés and bars. Several glasses of wine or beer helped to lubricate the discussion about the likely outcome of the vote. It was surmised that the Berlou vote would clearly favour Yves but that votes cast at the aula maxima, where most mature students voted, would favour Lotti. The vote at the Square Marcelin Albert was unpredictable. There were also widely diverging opinions about the influence of Alex Denton's voters. A couple of amateurish exit polls which had been conducted provided conflicting accounts of the likely overall outcome.

However, the day's work was not over for the election committees of the candidates. Representatives of each committee kept close guard at the three voting centres to ensure that the votes cast there were safely deposited and locked in the official steel containers and the keys lodged with Secretary Campion. In previous student elections, the mysterious disappearance overnight of packets of votes was not unknown.

Tomorrow morning, all the votes would be assembled in the aula maxima for the official count.

Eventually, with the votes safely secured, the election committees of both Yves and Lotti found themselves in the main bar of the student centre. Initially seated in separate groups, they soon appreciated that the campaign was over and by the end of the evening they had merged into one convivial party, exchanging stories about some of the more hilarious aspects of their campaigns. Lotti bought Yves a beer and remarked, smiling, 'I hope that after tomorrow when you will no longer be bothered by student politics that you will be able to return happily to playing rugby for which you have such a remarkable talent.'

'After my victory speech tomorrow,' he replied in equal good humour, 'I'll buy you a gin and tonic and you can get safely back to your knitting.' They were obviously enjoying each other's company.

However, there was no trace of members of Alex Denton's committee. They must have decided, following their leader's example, that their presence as a significant absence was the appropriate witness. They probably also appreciated that they might be forcibly required to reveal their candidate's identity. Their absence did not prevent lively discussion by the other two committees of the influence of Alex on the outcome of the election. Whereas few expected him or her to score well in the actual count, they feared that whatever support he did secure might play a significant role in the final outcome of the election.

As the party broke up in high spirits, Yves murmured to Lotti, 'Whatever the outcome, I would like us to keep in touch.'

'And I,' she said, smiling, 'would like to see a bit more of you than just cheering you on in St Chinian colours and white shorts on a rugby field.'

CHAPTER TWENTY-NINE
The Count

On Monday morning, as though eager to welcome a new student president of the University of St Chinian, glorious sunshine and a light spring breeze replaced the previous day's gloomy weather. A palpable atmosphere of unfolding drama prevailed. The nominators of the three candidates had arrived early to take their place in the large reception area of the aula maxima. Today would mark the culmination of their many weeks of intense political involvement. They would have an important role to play in monitoring and assuring the integrity of the count.

The locked steel chests containing the votes, which had been registered at the other two voting centres, were brought to the aula maxima. They were heavily escorted on their journey by supporters of all candidates, determined to ensure that no mishap befell them. Particular attention was paid by Jean's supporters to the transport of the votes from the Berlou campus. It was generally agreed that this would yield a rich agricultural harvest which would be greatly in his favour. It was important to ensure that it arrived safely, immune from any ambush! A group of five strong viticulture students crowded into the official van, which had been allocated to transport the ten chests of votes from Berlou. It would be very foolhardy of anybody to attempt to hijack that van, as it travelled the fifteen kilometres through the beautiful countryside, robed in vineyards, to the aula maxima in St Chinian.

In the reception area of the aula, ten tables were arranged behind a barrier which cordoned the count off from the interested spectators. Two officials, who would count the votes, were seated at each table. Also, at each table one observer from each of the teams of nominators was allowed to sit as a designated observer of the count. At a desk behind the tables sat the returning officer, Secretary Henri Campion. He planned to spend the day reading his newspaper and calculating how much the fees which the mature students had been charged for their various courses had contributed to the university's overall budget. The two candidates who were physically present, and other interested students, had to stand behind the erected barrier and hope to interpret the progress of the count from whatever signals they could receive from those actively monitoring it. The presence of Alex Denton, in fidelity to his or her disincarnate preference, was conspicuous by its absence.

At ten thirty, the caskets bearing the votes, which had been transported from each of the voting centres, were assembled to be unloaded together into a larger container from which they would be distributed to the ten count tables. Henri Campion gave the signal for this first preparatory stage of the count to commence. It would establish the total number of votes which had been cast.

But just before this began, the entire proceedings were cast into turmoil. It was discovered that only nine of the ten recorded and carefully protected caskets delivered from Berlou were available in the aula for the count. The accompanying record sheet declared unambiguously that ten caskets had been loaded onto the van and the five safeguarding passengers who had travelled with them confirmed that this indeed was the case. How had one casket of valuable votes been spirited away? Repeated counts, even one involving the secretary general, abandoning his newspaper to participate, confirmed that there were only nine caskets bearing the label "Berlou". Could one of the caskets have been accidentally given a label from one of the other centres? The caskets from these two centres were also counted and recounted. The numbers always corresponded to the numbers on the record sheets. A masterpiece of felonious skulduggery effecting the removal of a valuable casket of votes from the Berlou campus had somehow been achieved under the very eyes of all involved. Over a hundred votes, which most probably had been heavily weighted in favour of Yves Leroy, had disappeared into thin air. Who could be the Svengali of St Chinian?

After a momentary stunned silence, a confusion of opinions and suggestions soon found expression. Lotti's supporters proposed that the count should proceed as scheduled, ignoring the missing casket. Yves' supporters said the count should be delayed until the mystery of the missing casket was resolved, if necessary, with the assistance of the local *gendarmerie*. An unaligned observer suggested that the fingerprints of everyone present should be recorded.

'And compared with what?' enquired retired detective inspector, Louis Dupre.

'With the missing casket, of course,' replied the concerned observer. He could not understand why his pertinent reply was greeted with such hilarity.

A few of Alex Denton's supporters claimed that the situation clearly merited the election being declared null and void and that a new election must be held, perhaps in a year's time. In the meanwhile, they suggested the presidency of the student union should be exercised collectively by a triumvirate or, since at least one woman would be involved, a tripersonage of the three candidates. This suggestion evoked howls of derision and queries about what role Alex Denton might play in such an unholy trinity?

'He or she could perform the role of the Holy Ghost,' one wag proposed.

However, shortly afterwards, some light was thrown on the issue. One of the sturdy viticulture students who had accompanied the van with the votes from Berlou declared that his raincoat was also missing. Subjected to careful interrogation, he eventually recalled that he had placed it as a cushion over one of the caskets upon which he had sat during the journey from Berlou.

A delegation was dispatched at once to search the van. Unfortunately, it had already set out on its return journey to Berlou. Mark Tavel, professor of viticulture, was telephoned and requested to search the van when it arrived back at Berlou. He phoned half an hour later to say that it had arrived and that he had indeed found the missing casket covered by the missing raincoat.

Huge relief was expressed throughout the aula maxima. Mark Tavel agreed to send the van back at once with the casket and raincoat to St Chinian and offered to travel in it himself to ensure their safe delivery. Only Alex Denton's supporters seemed a little disappointed.

It was nearly one o'clock by the time the van arrived. The well-travelled casket was officially reunited with its companions and the raincoat safely returned to its owner. As lunch time was at hand, it was decided to delay the start of the count for another hour. However, those involved officially in the count were instructed to remain at their tables where they would be served coffee and sandwiches. The general body of students assembled in front of the barrier wandered out of the aula to enjoy the fresh air and to seek somewhat more stimulating nourishment in the nearby cafes and bars.

Eventually, at two o'clock, the count got underway, beginning with the calculation of the total number of votes before they were divided into equal bundles and allocated to the ten tables for attribution to the various candidates.

After a count and recount, it was established that the total valid vote was 9,922 votes. This represented a remarkable 82% of the 12,100 eligible voters. When the votes had been separated by colour, it transpired, that 6610 red ballots had been cast, by the part-time, mature students and 3312 blue ballots by the young, full-timers. It became clear that broadly the same percentage poll was registered by each group. Taking account of the relative value of the red and blue votes it seemed sure to be a very close contest. Much would depend on how many in each bundle of votes had voted for a candidate of a different age cohort to their own. There was the other imponderable of how many from either bundle might have voted for Alex Denton and thereby indirectly influenced the outcome. It was going to be a very interesting afternoon and evening.

The votes were distributed amongst the ten tables and at each the two officials began to conduct the count. They did so under the vigilant eyes of the nominated observers of each candidate. Gradually the red and blue ballot papers began to accumulate in the three containers on each table, most red ones in Lotti's basket, most blue in Yves', and a modest mixture of each in Alex Denton's.

During the afternoon, various people dropped in seeking to obtain some indication of how the count was going by deciphering the signals from official observers at the tables. There was a break for tea or coffee at four o'clock. The supporters of the different candidates, who had been observing the count from behind the barrier, used the break to share their observations and try to calculate the outcome. There was general agreement that, although Alex Denton clearly lagged far behind in third place, it was too close to call between Lotti and Yves.

Half an hour later, the count recommenced. It had entered its crucial final stage and it looked as though there would be at least a first count result within a couple of hours when the votes registered for the candidates at each of the ten tables were combined. During this period, the numbers observing the count increased greatly. The chairperson of the Concerned Mothers of St Chinian arrived, looking truly concerned, and attached herself to the group of Yves' supporters composed mainly of athletic young men and dedicated young women activists. They were joined by Thomas Van Velsen, the chairman of the Community of Latter Day Albigensians. He had now changed allegiance and was hoping for Yves' success in order to avoid the serious reduction in numbers of young undergraduates threatened by Lotti. Such a reduction would gravely affect his missionary recruitment of comely young maidens and their admirers to his Albigensian Community.

The mayor of St Chinian looked in briefly. She had a word of encouragement with each of the two candidates present. She assured each of them privately that, whatever the outcome, they had her full support. In her own mind, such comprehensive support was entirely reasonable.

Didier Ritz arrived at five o'clock and very pointedly joined Lotti's group of supporters. He told her that when her victory was declared he would like to invite her to dinner later in the week to advise her about the implementation of her programme and the central role he was eager to play in it.

The university chaplain, Dom Placebo, put in an appearance in case either of the candidates present might need spiritual consolation. He likened the large gathering to the miracle of loaves and fishes but declined to indicate which group he considered loaves and which fishes.

The retired bookmaker had re-emerged and was doing a brisk business, notwithstanding the wretched odds he was offering. To back either Lotti or Yves, one had to wager six euros to win four, and even the ten to one which he was offering against an Alex Denton victory could hardly be termed generous.

Meanwhile, the count proceeded in an orderly fashion. There was an occasional moment of light relief when the admissibility of a particular voting paper had to be decided by the returning officer. Votes for Donald Duck, Madonna, and Homer Simpson were easily dismissed. Slightly more problematic, but also disallowed, was a ballot paper which declared a willingness to vote for Lotti on condition that she agreed to be the voter's mentor. Another ballot paper gave a number two vote to Yves and a number three to Lotti. This allegedly created a dilemma about whether the unassigned number one vote should be allocated to Alex Denton. His supporters vehemently demanded that it be so allocated on the grounds that the votes numbered two and three could only be relative to vote number one and that the invisible Alex was the only person who could fulfil that requirement. The proposal was dismissed by the wise returning officer. When asked for a reason he simply murmured, '*Entia non sunt multiplicanda praeter necessitate,*' which effectively silenced the protestors without enlightening them.

By six o'clock, as the count drew to a close, the aula maxima was crowded with students of every age. They were joined by a number of interested academics. Didier Ritz, who was still there among Lotti's group of supporters, was joined by the conspiratorial colleagues he had entertained in his home the week before. Journalists and photographers from local newspapers were also in attendance. The memory was still alive of Yves' remarkable performance on the rugby field. It had played such a key and much publicized role in St

Chinian's dramatic victory in the inter-university rugby league the previous year, which delivered the coveted De Gaulle Cup to the university. Lotti was also newsworthy, not only for her striking mature Joan of Arc appearance, but also because of the innovative challenge to academic complacency which she represented. There were even a few "press stringers" representing some international newspapers and journals. They had been alerted by Lotti's campaign manager, Louis Dupre, that plans for the official recognition of the world's first university devoted primarily to the requirements of mature students hung in the balance.

Sandra Ricoeur, editor of The *St Chinian Trumpet,* joined the visiting reporters and briefed them about the various candidates emphasizing the significance of the nomination of the mysterious Alex Denton. It was a good opportunity for her to establish contacts that might be useful later in her anticipated professional journalistic career. The photographers sought to catch the two candidates looking balefully at one another. They were disappointed when all they could record was them smiling cheerfully.

At six thirty, the last two tables completed their count and record of votes. Secretary Campion rang a bell and called the proceedings to order. He instructed the two officials at each of the ten tables to bring him the recorded red and blue ballot papers, which had been distributed there in three separate candidate baskets and the signed record sheets of the numbers of votes per colour cast for each candidate. Aware that some of the officials, who were students selected anonymously, might be mathematically challenged by the demand to divide by two the number of red votes cast by mature students, he had not asked them to perform that operation. He had wisely reserved to himself the supervision of the addition of the number of differently coloured votes cast for each candidate at the various tables and the final total calculation of their relative value.

As this slightly complicated exercise was conducted and double-checked the assembled audience, which had been rather boisterous, became a little quieter. Even the pop-up bookmaker closed his book. He had recorded a substantial number of bets on both Yves and Lotti. Even a few loyal supporters had placed modest wagers on Alex Denton, whose odds had drifted out to twenty to one.

Eventually, at half past seven, Henri Campion, having completed his supervision of the calculation of the count, rang his bell again and strode purposefully to the microphone to announce the result of the ballot.

'Ladies and gentlemen,' he intoned solemnly, 'as official returning officer, appointed by the University of St Chinian to oversee the election of the president of its student union, it is now my duty and my pleasure to announce the result of the first ballot in this election. There are three nominated candidates for election to this important post, Lotti Beausang, Alex Denton and Yves Leroy. All three are registered students of the university and are therefore validly nominated candidates. By decision of the governing body of the university, the vote of a part-time mature student will be counted as being of half the value of the vote of a full-time student.'

'12,100 registered students were entitled to vote. Of these, 9,922 students cast a valid vote, representing 82% of the student body of the University of St Chinian. 6,610 votes were cast by part-time students on red coloured ballot papers. 3,312 votes were cast by full-time students on blue coloured ballot papers. These variously coloured ballot papers were allocated appropriately to the three candidates. The number of votes registered for each candidate was then calculated, with appropriate adjustments being made for the lesser value of the red ballot papers allocated to mature students. This calculation provides us with the following verified result of the first ballot of the election.'

Henri Campion paused for a few moments to allow an expectant hush descend upon the hall. Then, adjusting his spectacles, he read from a single sheet:

'Lotti Beausang: 2,973 votes.

Alex Denton: 803 votes

Yves Leroy: 2,841 votes.

'As no candidate has reached the quota of 3,309 votes, I propose to eliminate Alex Denton and to distribute those number two votes of his that have been cast for either of the other two candidates. We will now take a short break of twenty minutes and reassemble promptly at eight fifteen to proceed with the distribution and count of Alex Denton's number two votes.'

The temporary silence which had prevailed in the hall exploded into an excited clamour. Smartphones and pocket calculators were produced and agile fingers danced over them. A consensus emerged that Lotti had secured 45% of the vote; Yves had secured 43% and Alex 12%. It was obviously going to be a very closely contested outcome between Lotti and Yves. The various observers for the two remaining candidates at each of the tables were consulted in an attempt to calculate roughly how many red and how many blue votes had been cast for Alex. The presumption was that the red number two votes would be likely to go to Lotti and the blue ones to Yves. But the final outcome was impossible to call. However, the bookmaker had popped up again and now was offering even money on Yves but only one for two on Lotti.

Large groups of supporters gathered around both Lotti and Yves, extending good wishes and encouraging estimations. Professor Didier Ritz ostentatiously wagered a hundred euros on Lotti's success even though, as a member of the university's governing body, he should be demanding that the "book" be confiscated and the bookmaker's name recorded for disciplinary purposes.

Alex's nominators and a few supporters constituted a very modest gathering by comparison with the other two groups. They presented a rather pathetic picture, huddled around Alex's principal nominator and election agent, Thomas Mansion. He was deeply engrossed on the telephone with somebody; presumably relaying the gloomy news to Alex. Eventually he closed the phone and encouraged the group not to slink away but to sit together in the aula for the remainder of the proceedings.

At eight o'clock, returning officer Henri Campion's bell rang out again, the vote counters assembled at their post, and the various groups of supporters returned to their seats or stood close to the barrier which separated the general audience from the count.

The returning officer reminded everybody that they were about to embark on the final stage of the proceedings, namely, the distribution to the other two candidates of any second vote cast for them on the ballot papers for Alex Denton. However, as soon as he completed this simple announcement, Thomas Mansion rose to his feet and began to address him in a loud clear voice.

'Mr. Returning Officer,' he declared, 'I have been authorized to register an objection to your proposed procedure and to offer an alternative proposal on behalf of candidate Alex Denton. It is an objection and a proposal which has been scrutinized and approved by candidate Denton's legal advisers.' Gasps of astonishment and incredulity rippled through the audience.

'And what, may I ask,' said Henri irritably, 'is the precise nature of this objection and proposal? We have had a long day and I have no intention of subjecting the dedicated officials of this election count to distractions that I may consider to be simply futile or frivolous attempts to frustrate it.'

'They are neither futile nor frivolous,' replied Thomas calmly. 'The objection is necessary and unavoidable. The proposal constitutes a positive resolution of the dilemma occasioned by the objection. Allow me, sir, to state the objection and the proposal clearly, briefly, and in turn.

'The objection, which I lodge on behalf of candidate Denton, claims that as there has never before been more than two candidates for election to the office of president of the student union, there is no directive in the regulations governing this election about how to proceed when a candidate fails to be elected on the first count. This difficulty is compounded by the fact that the vote of the great majority of students of this university has been deemed to be worth only half the value of the vote of full-time students. This fact alone would render any automatic appeal to conventional second ballot procedures extremely questionable.'

Some of Lotti's supporters began to applaud vigorously, believing that the mysterious Alex was somehow declaring his or her support for Lotti even at this late stage. Thomas Mansion acknowledged the applause benignly and proceeded to his next point.

'Having indicated the intrinsically problematic nature of how to proceed with the next stage of the election process, I now propose, as instructed by candidate Denton, a solution to the difficulty which is delightful in its elegance and inspiring in its democratic generosity. Stated quite simply and unambiguously, it is the proposal that we proceed forthwith to the second ballot but that we include the number two vote cast by any student on their ballot paper, even though we are constrained by the odious regulation that limits the value of the votes of mature students. Alex Denton assures me that this procedure of including the number two votes of all voters in the second count works admirably in some of the islands in the Pacific Ocean, and that it had maintained the peace for centuries in several countries of the Ottoman Empire. Therefore, dear highly respected Returning Officer, I hereby present this proposal on behalf of candidate Denton and ask you to proceed with its implementation in your conduct of the second count.'

Thomas smiled broadly to the closely attentive audience and sat down to scattered and somewhat puzzled applause. It took some time for the significance of the proposal to sink in. For a while many in the audience were convinced that candidate Denton, graciously accepting that even though his low vote eliminated any hope of his own success, was generously determined that the outcome of this election, so crucial to the future welfare of the university, would be seen, in virtue of his all-inclusive proposal, to involve the most exhaustive and complete democratic procedure.

It was only when Lotti's campaign manager, Louis Dupre, jumped to his feet and intervened angrily that the real significance of the proposal eventually became evident. 'Honourable Director of election,' he exclaimed, 'I beg you to pay no attention to this unprecedented and outrageous proposal. It is a most egregious piece of chicanery. This so-called candidate, Alex Denton, has, from the very outset, sought to ridicule and trivialize this important election. He or she has played hide and seek with fellow students and has refused to participate in serious debate with the other candidates. Now that he or she is found to be the recipient of only 12% of the vote — 12% too many, in my opinion — a new and entirely unwarranted distraction is proposed. But it is not just a harmless distraction. It is a carefully thought-out ruse to distort to his or her advantage the entire outcome of the election.'

Warming to his topic, Louis continued energetically. 'Candidate Alex Denton's supposedly democratically inclusive second vote would include not only his own 803 votes but also Yves Leroy's 2841 votes and Lotti Beausang's 2973 votes. Since his negative slogan, "Alex Says No — Vote for Alex", is dismissive of the programmes of the two other candidates, it is unlikely that many of his supporters will have cast a second vote. Those that have will probably be equally divided between the other two candidates.

'However,' he continued, 'the situation is very different when we come to consider the votes cast for Lotti Beausang and the votes cast for Yves Leroy. The programmes of these two candidates are strictly opposed to each other, the one demanding a total change in the profile of St Chinian University, the other insisting on the maintenance of the status quo. It is therefore most unlikely that the voters for either of these candidates will give their second vote to the other. But it is very likely indeed, in order not in any way to advantage the other strong and radically opposed candidate, that they will both have awarded their number two vote to Alex Denton.

'Now consider,' he demanded, 'the outcome of the second count if Monsieur or Madame Denton's "democratic" proposal is accepted and implemented. Beausang and Leroy may each may obtain a couple of hundred, second preference votes from Alex, bringing the total of each to around three thousand votes. In the case of dear Alex, however, the probability is that he or she would gain about a further five and a half thousand votes. This would bring his total vote to over six thousand. He or she would thereby have comfortably exceeded the requisite quota and, consequently, would have to be declared the validly elected president of the university's student union.'

When the significance of this analysis sank in, loud whoops of delight emerged round the hall from small groups of Alex's supporters.

Jeanne Mandel, the National Front activist and influential nominator of Yves Leroy, jumped to her feet. 'I agree completely with everything that Inspector Dupre has said,' she proclaimed. 'The Denton proposal, far from promoting an exercise in extended democracy, is a total con trick. It is an integral piece of a long-term strategy beginning with the nomination of a candidate of whom we were told nothing. We didn't know whether the candidate was a man or a woman, a full-time, young student, or a part-time, mature student. We received no indication of any positive view advocated by the candidate. All we were given was the negative dismissal of the positive but opposed programmes of the other two candidates. All we heard was that "Alex Says No".

'The whole scenario was carefully planned to reach this grand finale which, by means of a spurious appeal to democratic inclusiveness, assured Alex Denton's election from the outset. Now we know what was meant by candidate Denton's reference to "the power of negativity". By force of sheer negativity and a cunningly devised appeal to democracy, two opposing but positive programmes would be overcome in favour of the anonymous Alex's nonsense. Further evidence, if it were required, of the great need to rediscover the true French political and moral values espoused by the

National Front under Marine Le Pen's enlightened leadership.' Jeanne sat down to loud applause.

Thomas Mansion rose to reply. 'Alex Denton is a validly nominated candidate for the office of president of the student union. He or she has made clear the reasons both for his or her temporary non-appearance in person, and the rejection of the programmes proposed by the other two candidates. I have presented a perfectly reasonable objection to having automatic mindless recourse to a so-called conventional procedure in conducting a count of second preference votes. And I have proposed, as instructed by candidate Denton, a perfectly reasonable and exceedingly democratic alternative. Candidate Denton has authorized me to declare that, if this legally approved proposal is not accepted, any such decision will be appealed to the highest court in the land and, if necessary, to the European Court of Human Rights.'

Sandra Ricoeur, editor of *The St Chinian Trumpet,* spoke next. 'I agree,' she declared, 'with everything M. Mansion has said. Alex Denton is a breath of fresh air in this election. He or she invests it with a new approach, one not based on cult of personality but imbued with an uplifting renewal of democratic aspiration. I heartily endorse Thomas Mansion's wise proposal.' Her endorsement did not come as a surprise to some members of the audience. They were well aware that Sandra's late-night encounters with her friend, Thomas, often lasting until daybreak, were not always focused on matters of journalistic interest.

Shouts and angry proclamations erupted from both Yves and Lotti's supporters. Both groups felt that the victory, which was within their grasp, had been snatched from them. Alex's supporters chortled with delight. It looked as though some nasty scuffles might break out. Keenly aware of the fraught situation, Henri Campion rang his returning officer's bell vigorously. Gradually the uproar in the hall subsided and people turned their attention to hearing what he had to say.

'It is obvious to me,' he declared, 'that the objection and proposal presented on behalf of candidate Alex Denton are quite untimely and very likely intentionally so. They should have been submitted before this election began when they could have been considered in a calm and dispassionate manner. However, now that they have been made in this inopportune manner, I have no intention of compounding the unfortunate situation by seeking to judge them here in this highly charged atmosphere. I intend to bring them to the attention of President Boulanger who will, undoubtedly, if necessary, in consultation with the university's lawyers, reach a carefully considered and judicious decision about how to bring this election count to a just and proper conclusion. Accordingly, I hereby suspend the meeting for two days and ordain that it is to reconvene to conclude its business in the light of President

Boulanger's instructions at three o'clock on Wednesday afternoon.'

The audience took some time to digest this decision, but as there was no viable alternative, they began to drift out of the aula. A few groups of dedicated supporters of the various candidates hung back, locked in lively discussion and debate. The pop-up bookmaker reappeared. He was now offering even money on each of the three candidates. The few supporters of Alex who had placed modest wagers on him or her at odds from eight to one to twenty to one smiled complacently and even smugly.

Yves Leroy went over to Lotti Beausang and invited her and Louis Dupre to join him and Jeanne Mandel in the student bar for a nightcap. They accepted willingly. 'I think we both need one,' she said, smiling. 'The invisible Alex Denton is proving more of a problem than either of us imagined. However, both Louis and Jeanne did a splendid job in revealing the subterfuge involved.'

As they strolled over to the bar, Henri Campion returned to his office and, as previously agreed, phoned Guy Boulanger and Claire Macon to inform them, not of the result of the election as anticipated, but of the dilemma which Alex Denton had occasioned. It was agreed that the three of them would meet in Guy's office at ten o'clock the following morning to evaluate the situation and decide on a course of action.

CHAPTER-THIRTY
Consultation

At nine o'clock, Guy Boulanger arrived at his office in the administration building of the university to prepare for the meeting at ten o'clock with his two close colleagues. His highly efficient office manager, Marie-Therese, who had been with him since his appointment as president, was already busy at her desk. He told her about the meeting that he had arranged the previous evening with Henri and Claire.

'Apparently, Marie-The,' he explained, 'in the regulations governing the election of the student union president there is no explicit regulation about the conduct of a second ballot. Perhaps this is not surprising as, heretofore, there have never been more than two candidates for this post. However, now the mysterious third candidate, Alex Denton, is demanding that the number two votes of all candidates be included in the second count, and he or she claims to have legal advice that this would be a valid and eminently democratic procedure, one enjoying some international precedents. If this procedure is agreed, it will most likely be to the considerable advantage, indeed victory, of candidate Alex Denton. Henri and Claire are coming at ten to discuss the situation with me and to advise me. Please try to get Attorney Chenu on the phone for me. He wasn't at home when I phoned him last evening but his wife assured me that he would be in his office by nine o'clock this morning.'

'I'll get him on the phone for you at once,' she said, 'and then, Guy, I'll look through the records to see if I can find anything that might be helpful.'

For the millionth time, Guy thanked God, to whom he accorded intermittent existence and with whom he had a precarious relationship, for having pointed Marie-Therese in his direction all those years ago. Her dedication, intelligence, and diplomacy had helped him through many a delicate situation.

Marie-The contacted the lawyer and put the call through on the phone. Guy explained the problem to him with typical clarity and precision. The ensuing discussion was inconclusive. Attorney Chenu could see both points of view, the one originally proposed by Secretary Campion and the alternative proposed on behalf of candidate Alex Denton. He asked Guy did he know the identity of this candidate. Guy replied that he did but it had been given to him in confidence and he intended to respect this confidence. Finally, the attorney said that he would look into the matter further and get back to Guy later in the day.

'My initial reaction,' he opined, 'is that it would be in order to proceed with Secretary Campion's initial proposal as it is in conformity with usual and widespread international custom.' However, with characteristic legalistic caution, he suggested that it might be necessary to have it confirmed by a specially convened meeting of the university's governing body. That was one piece of advice which Guy did not wish to hear and did not wish to implement. The intervening delay before such a meeting could be convened would only make an already difficult situation worse. Rumours, suspicions, and accusations, endemic to fraternal academic discourse, would be generated and flourish in the interim. He thanked the attorney and awaited the hopefully more pragmatic advice of his colleagues.

They arrived promptly at ten o'clock. Guy welcomed and seated them. Jerome, Marie-The's young assistant, delivered a tray of coffee and biscuits. 'Well, isn't this a nice turn of events,' said Guy. 'Not only have we the most controversial student election in the short history of the university, but now the election process itself is making the headlines, at least in *The St Chinian Tribune.* There is a special edition of it published this morning and Marie-The has left a copy for me on my desk. It is devoted mainly to yesterday's count and to the dramatic intervention on behalf of Alex Denton which brought the proceedings to a shuddering halt. It is effusive in its editorial praise of his or her "generous and profoundly democratic initiative in proposing that all second votes be included in the count". Such impartial appreciation of the "generous and profoundly democratic initiative" is, as we know, a bit rich coming from the editor of the *St Chinian Tribune.*'

'The proposal certainly left the aula in a state of uproar,' laughed Henri. 'I was glad to get away with my life.'

'Let's hope,' said Claire, 'that we can reach a sound decision about how to proceed in time for tomorrow afternoon's resumption of hostilities.'

'It seems to me,' replied Guy, 'that we have a number of options. Firstly, we could confirm the reasonable, conventional and common-sense decision proposed yesterday by the secretary, namely, that in the absence of an outright winner, the candidate with least votes be eliminated and the count proceed with the distribution of his number two votes. This has been our undisputed university practice in other elections and I believe that the governing body, at its next ordinary meeting, would retrospectively endorse the procedure in this case and be prepared to face any legal challenge. I believe that any such challenge would be most unlikely to succeed.

'Secondly, we could conduct two counts, one as initially proposed by the secretary and the other as proposed on behalf of candidate Denton. This procedure is likely to result in Alex Denton winning one of the counts and either Beausang or Leroy wining the other. We could then send the results of both counts to the governing body, with my recommendation, and let it decide. Even if it went against my recommendation and accepted Alex, we know it would not be the end of the world and might even help to diffuse a situation which would be comical were it not so confrontational and dangerous.

'Thirdly,' he continued, 'we could refuse to proceed with any second count, cancel the election and postpone a new one until the governing body has debated and confirmed an unambiguous regulation. I would be very opposed to such a delaying approach, which could only make a difficult situation worse.'

He poured fresh cups of coffee and was about to ask for their opinion when Marie-The entered discreetly and gave him a note, saying diplomatically, 'President, this is the matter which you asked me to research.'

He read the note and burst out laughing. 'You'll enjoy this,' he said. 'When the university was being envisaged in the middle of the last century, the government's bureaucratic planners, enjoying a theorizing extravaganza, drafted and codified literally hundreds of regulations. These included everything from temporary employment contracts for rat catchers to the frequency and format of required correspondence with the Ministry for Education and Research. Fortunately, when the university was actually established, our early predecessors devoted themselves in a practical manner to the formidable task of getting it up and running in accordance with local needs and in conformity with best university practice throughout the country. The planners' volumes of theoretical

302

regulations, irreverently deposited in the university archive, gathered dust over the years.

'Fortunately, however, it would seem that Marie-The makes them her bedtime reading because she has an encyclopaedic knowledge of them. This passionate interest has often been of invaluable help to me, and today again she has produced the goods with this note she has prepared. It reads as follows:

"Regulation 687: For election to any post in the university with more than two candidates, voters may rank the candidates in order of preference. If a candidate has not been elected on the first count, the candidate with least votes will be eliminated and the second vote ballots for this candidate will be distributed until one candidate is the top remaining choice of a majority of voters."

'Precisely what we have been doing all along but now we have it in gold-plated certainty from our bureaucratic masters in Paris. Henri, you can return to your returning officer's duties tomorrow afternoon, in a state of complacent infallibility, armed with the equivalent of a papal bull.'

Claire and Henri joined in Guy's sense of good-humoured relief. The issues involved in the student election were disconcerting enough without having them complicated further by legalistic distractions parading as democratic concern. This at least would settle that distraction, even if in the less hallowed form of a piece of bureaucratic indulgence!

303

'Now that I have you here,' said Guy, 'and as we have some time on our hands, perhaps we could discuss a few of the issues which will come up at the meeting of the governing body in two weeks.

'The first item on the agenda will be welcoming five new members to the governing body as a result of the election of a new president of the student union. I wonder who it will be. I suppose we can now safely discount our friend Alex Denton. It will be a close thing between Beausang and Leroy. She has a small advantage on the first ballot but if, as is likely, enough young students who voted for Alex give Leroy their number two, it could swing it for him, bearing in mind the double value of their vote. It would certainly make life a bit easier for the governing body. It won't know what hit it if it is faced with five experienced "golden codgers", brandishing a revolutionary agenda to transform the university. I am aware that our dear colleague and professor of marketing, Didier Ritz, a renowned altruistic supporter of populist causes, already has Madame Beausang clasped to his bosom and singing "Old Soldiers Never Die" to her. We might yet be wishing that Alex's clever strategy had worked.'

'I think we better prepare ourselves for a Lotti Beausang victory,' said Henri. 'It is my impression that even with the superior value of the full-time students' vote, it will be difficult to overtake her.'

'Well, we'll just have to wait and see,' said Guy, 'and try to make the best of whatever happens.'

Claire brought them through a few more academic matters on the agenda. These included a number of appointments, promotions, and renewals of contracts, and a request from Georges Fabre, professor of social anthropology, for a year's paid leave of absence to return to a Polynesian island and renew the hands-on research he had happily conducted there on the relaxed sexual mores of the inhabitants.

Guy reminded them that there would be the good news of Jean Martin's munificent endowment. The governing body would have to discuss and establish a committee to oversee its implementation. 'I intend, 'he continued, 'to propose that during the next academic year the university confer him with an honorary doctorate. He deserves it, not just for the generous endowment but in his own right for his remarkable entrepreneurial achievement and the employment he has created both in the US and proposedly here in Europe.' They both agreed that this would be a fitting recognition.

Finally, Guy informed them of another matter which he intended to convey to the governing body at its meeting. They heard it in an astonished silence. It overshadowed everything else which they had discussed.

When they left quietly some ten minutes later, Guy asked Marie-The to come into the office. He thanked her for her sterling detective work about the election regulation. He dictated a few letters and then discussed what preparation would be required for various items on the agenda of the upcoming governing body meeting. He then told her about the additional matter, of which he had informed Henri and Claire and which he would be bringing to the attention of to the meeting. She looked at him in disbelief and, most uncharacteristically, fell silent as tears trickled down her cheeks.

CHAPTER THIRTY-ONE
Second Round

Shortly after lunch the next day, students began to assemble in the aula max, intrigued to learn, at first hand, how the election drama would unfold. By two thirty it was full and others began to congregate in the Square Marcelin Albert nearby which was linked by microphone with the aula. Everybody wanted to witness the outcome and nobody wanted to miss the fun.

At three o'clock precisely, returning officer Campion strode onto the stage where the official group of counters, and the candidates' designated observers of the count, had already stationed themselves. He advanced to the microphone and the crowd in the aula fell silent. Those in the Square Michelin Albert were still joking and laughing until they heard Henri's voice sounding over the microphone.

'We now resume,' he said, 'the count of votes for the election of the president of the student union of St Chinian University. Because of an objection which was lodged on Monday, I delayed proceeding with my instruction on how to conduct the second ballot. Since then, I have consulted with President Boulanger. He not only confirmed my instruction but provided me with a copy of regulation number 687, formulated in 1954 by the Ministry for Higher Education and Research in preparation for the establishment of the university.' Henri, read the regulation aloud and declared, 'I now instruct the count to proceed with the elimination of candidate Alex Denton and the distribution of his second votes to the two remaining candidates.'

After a couple of seconds' silence, the aula exploded into loud and prolonged cheering. The scene was even rowdier in Square Michelin Albert, where some of the undergraduates began dancing with mature students old enough to be their mother and, in some cases, their grandmother. Thomas Mansion appeared to be desperately trying to contact Alex.

The count proceeded with the distribution of Alex's 803 votes. These were composed of 850 "half-value" red ballot papers cast by mature students (equivalent to 425 full votes) and 378 blue ballot papers, cast by full-time students. When those votes which had recorded just a number one preference had been discarded, there remained the equivalent of 760 full votes which had registered a second preference. These were distributed between the two remaining candidates. They were counted and recounted, with the complication of the lesser value of a mature student's vote carefully factored in. Eventually a final result of the second count was confirmed and agreed.

Henri strode purposefully to the microphone. 'The result of the second count,' he declared solemnly, 'is as follows: Yves Leroy received an additional 345 votes, bringing his total vote to 3186. Lotti Beausang received an additional 415 votes, bringing her total vote to 3338. I therefore declare Madame Lotti Beausang to be the duly elected new president of the student union of St Chinian University.'

A huge cheer erupted in the aula maxima and an even louder one in the Square Michelin Albert. Lotti's supporters were exuberant and Yves were very downcast. However, he was the first person to move across the aula to her and to embrace her warmly. This much photographed embrace evoked even louder cheers from all sides. Before the meeting closed, Sandra Ricoeur walked onto the stage and grasped the microphone.

'You haven't heard the last of Alex Denton,' she announced. 'Exercising what I might modestly call my remarkable investigative journalistic skill, I have tracked down the real identity of candidate Alex Denton. All will be revealed tomorrow morning in a special edition of *The St Chinian Trumpet.* Make sure to buy your paper early before they are all sold out.' Her announcement was greeted with more cheers and laughter. Everybody would want to read this latest turn in the Denton drama by an editor who had always, until this point, spoken and written of him or her in such glowing terms.

The crowds gradually moved away from the aula and the square. Lotti's mature supporters and some of her adventurous younger ones moved on to enjoy one or more of the many impromptu parties which celebrated her victory. Yves' supporters dispersed in small groups to various bars and cafes to drown their sorrows and analyse what went wrong, and what might have been done differently. The large white van with Alex Denton's ten nominators on board was seen speeding away but now no music was issuing from it.

The pop-up bookmaker was settling his accounts with those who had backed Lotti. She had been the most heavily backed, and mostly by mature students who had more money than young undergraduates. However, he still made a satisfactory profit, thanks largely to the late rush of money on Alex immediately after the challenge to the election count procedure was proposed on his behalf.

Henri walked with Claire Macon over to Guy Boulanger's office to discuss the result with him. He, of course, had already been informed by the omnicompetent Marie-The. She had sent her assistant, Jerome, to the aula with instructions to phone her as soon as the result was announced.

'Well, that is a most interesting outcome,' said Guy, 'and it will certainly bring the discussion of the future of our beloved university to a new level of intensity. Future meetings of the academic council and governing body will surely be livelier and less routine affairs. I can envisage how some of our colleagues are probably already planning their alignment with the new student president in the upcoming debates.'

'It was certainly a most impressive victory by Lotti Beausang and her team,' said Claire. 'Especially when one considers that the part-time, mature students' vote had only half the value of that of a full-time student.'

'Well, that's one regulation which will certainly be challenged.' replied Guy.

They continued their discussion for a while and, as it was well after six o'clock, he poured them each a measure of Irish Redbreast to charge their spirit and help them on their way.

CHAPTER THIRTY-TWO
Aftermath

The following morning, after a late night celebrating with her team and friends, Lotti woke in her comfortable apartment to the challenging awareness of how very different her life would be for at least the next two years. Her new post as president of the student union would commence officially in two weeks when she would be welcomed and endorsed at her first meeting of the governing body. She was determined to make her programme for the transformation of the University of St Chinian a reality, but was under no illusion about how difficult this might be. For many academics, as well as students, the *status quo* had a comfortable feel to it, which they would not like to see disturbed. The previous student president and his team had made very few waves on the various university bodies. For the most part, they seemed content to enjoy the fruits of office. Her aim was very different.

She showered, dressed simply in blue jeans, a white shirt, and a cardigan slung casually around her shoulders. As she nibbled her toast and sipped her tea, she read a host of congratulatory emails on her iPad. There was one which pleased her particularly. It was from Yves Leroy. He renewed his congratulations, wished her every success, and hoped, now that he was merely one of her constituents, they might keep in touch openly and more frequently. He claimed that after his interesting foray into student politics he was happy now to return to the gym and concentrate on getting back into shape for next year's rugby season. She smiled as thoughts already began to form in her mind about her future relationship with Monsieur Leroy. Not all of them were of a professional character!

A little later, as she walked to the university, she was warmly greeted and congratulated by many students. She went directly to the shop in the student centre. She wanted to get her copy of the special edition of *The St Chinian Trumpet,* not only to read its account of the election result, but also to learn the identity of candidate Alex Denton. Many others had the same inquisitive idea. The shop was crowded and the newspapers were flying off the shelf.

She got her copy and went to the student café to read it leisurely over a cup of coffee. She was very happy with its generous account of her election campaign, its unexpected endorsement of her victory, and its best wishes for the success of her term as president.

At the bottom of the front page, she was informed that the two centre pages, which were sealed, revealed the identity of Alex Denton. They were sealed, she was advised, to ensure that the paper was bought and not merely flicked through for free information. Intrigued, she tore around the perforated edges and opened the pages.

She found herself looking at the smiling face of the editor, Sandra Ricoeur, under a headline declaring "Now Alex Says Yes — This Is Me". It took Lotti a few seconds to realize that the mysterious Alex, "Who Says No", was none other than Sandra Ricoeur, third year student in the School of Arts, Media and Communication, and the popular editor of *The St Chinian Trumpet*. Interested and amused she continued reading.

I decided, wrote Sandra, *that this important election provided an excellent opportunity to sell more newspapers. But the opposing positions of the two well-regarded candidates seemed to me too clear-cut, honest and unambiguous. They lacked the potential for rumours of intrigue, mischief, scandal and skulduggery, which sell newspapers. I thought it would be interesting to introduce an element of mystery and ambiguity, even if it might be construed as "fake news".*

I told my boyfriend, Thomas Mansion, that I was thinking what fun it would be to enter as a mysterious candidate in the election. I was convinced that it would not just be fun but would increase popular interest in the contest, and also, most importantly from my point of view, sell more newspapers!

He was delighted with the idea and said that he would have no difficulty in securing the necessary ten nominators who could be relied upon to keep my identity as a mystery candidate a secret.

My father, Paul Denton, died in an accident six months before I was born. My birth was registered officially in the name of Alexandra Denton. When my mother married my stepfather, Jean Ricoeur, a year later, I became known, though not officially, as Sandra Ricoeur, a name I grew up with and happily bear today in my social and personal life. When I decided to present my candidature for president of the student union under the name of Alex Denton, I had to explain the grounds for this to Secretary Bursar Campion, who knew me only as Sandra Ricoeur. He said he would have to discuss the proposal in confidence with President Boulanger and Academic Vice President Macon. A couple of days later, he told me that my proposed candidature would be accepted. He even seemed amused by my claim that my candidature was inspired mainly by my journalistic enthusiasm to increase the sales of The St Chinian Trumpet. He acceded to my request to observe my anonymity throughout the election and assured me that the president and academic vice president would do likewise.

My little initiative worked even better than I expected. The mysterious and anonymous Alex Denton, aided by very favourable editorial comment by myself in The St Chinian Trumpet, became a celebrity throughout the electoral campaign. His or her intriguing candidature sold many newspapers, and even attracted a small but loyal group of enthusiastic supporters. The additional reference to "Negative Entropy" in my election slogan endowed my candidature with a deceptive gravity.

It was a most entertaining and, at times, hilarious experience. I was wickedly amused by the frustrated and baffled reaction I attracted from the other two very serious and very public candidates. I particularly enjoyed the images of Donald Duck and Homer Simpson, floating nonchalantly by on the screen behind the stage during the great debate between Lotti and Yves, and urging everyone to "Vote for Alex, Who Says No and Who promotes Negative Entropy"! The 12% of the vote I obtained was an even better result than the 10% I thought I might achieve.

It was my beloved boyfriend, Thomas Mansion, a doctoral student of political science and an expert on different voting procedures, who came up with the bright idea of challenging the presumed conventional second count, and proposing instead the allegedly more democratic procedure of including every candidate's second preference. This would have had the sensational result of electing the anonymous Alex Denton as president of the student union. This possibility had a very positive effect on sales during the two anxious days before President Boulanger eventually conveyed the authoritative decision which resulted in the valid election of Lotti Beausang.

I can now, with relief, devote all my free time to my true love which is journalism. I believe that Madame Beausang will be an excellent president of the student union and I wish her every success. However, I will of course be keeping a critical journalistic eye on her performance. Alex Denton can still say no!

Lotti smiled, finished her coffee and folded the paper which she would keep as a cherished souvenir. Meanwhile, she had to attend to the business of making arrangements to assume her new post and to begin the task of trying to implement her programme. She telephoned her campaign manager, Louis Dupre, and asked him to arrange a meeting with her election committee the following afternoon in the office of the president of the student union, which the outgoing president told her was available and which he was glad to vacate.

When the committee met the next day in her new office, they were still in jubilant form about Lotti's victory. They were delighted by the generous way in which Yves had conceded defeat, and the encouraging remarks in *The St Chinian Trumpet* by the recently identified Alex Denton. It looked even as though a number of the full-time students might be ready to accept the sea change advocated in her programme.

Having outlined certain administrative arrangements for the routine running of the student union, and the roles which various named people might

317

play in it; Lotti focused the attention of the meeting on the matter which interested her most. This was the appointment of the five student members to the governing body. For, if there was to be real change in the profile of the university, this was the body which ultimately would have to implement them. The student members would play a crucial role in persuading it to do so.

'Besides myself,' she said, 'I am entitled to nominate four other members to the governing body. I have given the matter careful consideration and would like to inform you of my decision.'

Louis Dupre raised an eyebrow, but it was clear that Madame Beausang was not going to lead simply from behind by negotiated agreement.

'I think,' she declared, 'that Marie Dupront will be an excellent member. With her husband, Luc, she has run a very successful beauty salon in Narbonne. I noticed during the campaign that she is a very good judge of people. I suppose it may have something to do with the many years she spent gazing intently into their faces as she tried to recompose them.'

Marie smiled and said, 'Thanks, dear Lotti. It is a great honour and a great responsibility and I will do my best to further your objectives.'

'Next,' Lotti continued, addressing Louise Amard, one of the two young, full-time students whom Louis Dupre had introduced to the team, 'I intend to invite your new partner, Rudi Bruggerman, to be a member.

He was of great help during the campaign, not only in virtue of his generous financial assistance but also as a retired very successful business man, with many years of experience in dealing with difficult situations, his wise advice was of considerable value. I think his experience will be a very useful asset to the governing body. It will also be of great assistance to me on that body in evaluating the alliances which I will be invited to make with other members who may have their own agenda, for example, with the well-disposed but very ambitious Professor Didier Ritz.'

At this stage, retired Inspector Dupre began to look distinctly alarmed on his own behalf. But, smiling, Lotti turned to him saying, 'And, of course, dear Louis, I hope that you will join our little group of student governors. Your skill at making necessary investigations and background enquiries, so useful during the campaign, will be even more positively required in reaching judicious decisions on some of the complex issues with which the governing body must deal.'

Greatly relieved, Louis smiled broadly. 'You can rely on me, dear Lotti,' he assured her, 'to check out issues and people as required. I still have useful contacts, in both high and low places, from whom I can discreetly obtain confidential information.'

Then she told them of the final person she intended to invite. They were very surprised and queried whether it was a good idea. However, after a brief discussion, they conceded that it probably would be.

Finally, a little before the meeting broke up, she informed them that, in order to get their programme off to a good and timely start, she intended to submit, for decision at the forthcoming meeting of the governing body, a motion granting all students, part-time and full-time, equal voting rights in all university matters on which they were entitled to vote. Her election committee endorsed this motion and its timing enthusiastically.

A little later, when the meeting had dispersed, she phoned Yves Leroy and invited him to dinner the following evening in a small Italian restaurant near her apartment. He accepted, with pleasure, both the invitation and the suggestion to come to her apartment beforehand for an aperitif.

He arrived there promptly at seven o'clock, bearing a bottle of Blanquette de Limoux, the famous Languedoc sparkling white wine, imitated subsequently by the more northerly beverage, champagne. She welcomed him and, as they sipped their aperitifs, she told him that besides enjoying the considerable pleasure of his company, she had something important to ask him.

'I want to invite you,' she said, 'to be one of the five student members who I am entitled to nominate to the governing body. I know we each have argued very different conceptions of the university. And we both know that mine prevailed in the election. However, now I would like to think that various views which you defended can be accommodated as, in some respects, complementary to my own overall programme. You represent over 40% of the students' first preference votes. It is better to have you representing them inside the governing body, working constructively on their behalf within the general parameters of my objectives, rather than having them wandering around outside complaining.'

Yves was genuinely astonished by the proposal. He enumerated various objections that might be made against it, not least the possible, if erroneous, perception by both groups of their supporters that each of them had betrayed their stated positions. Eventually, however, by the time the bottle was almost empty, he agreed that it was an excellent and generous, if somewhat hazardous, proposition, and he gladly accepted. To celebrate, they went to the restaurant nearby, which she had booked. They enjoyed an excellent meal and eagerly discussed their future professional co-operation. When he walked Lotti back to her apartment, he embraced her warmly and told her he hoped that their future friendship would be much more than a professional one.

As she slipped into bed a little later, she thought, *what a nice person he is.* She too hoped that their friendship might develop into something more than a professional relationship. As she dozed off, she imagined what form it might take. However, when she woke the next morning, the pleasant memories of the previous evening were replaced by a keen awareness that it was less than two weeks to the meeting of the governing body, at which she would have to initiate her attempt to implement her ambitious plans for the future of the University of St Chinian.

CHAPTER THIRTY-THREE
The Governing Body

This year's final ordinary meeting of the governing body of the university was scheduled to take place in the third week of May. This body was very different to the academic council, which was composed almost exclusively of academics and was devoted exclusively to academic affairs. The governing body made the final decision on broader issues of university administration and development, including appointments, financial arrangements, external relations, buildings, and infrastructure.

It has a very discrete composition of twenty-eight members. These included the president, the academic vice president, the secretary bursar, the deans of the four schools and five other elected academics. There are five student representatives, two representatives of the administrative staff, two national government representatives (usually a reward for local party faithful). Also, the mayor and a local councillor, a representative of the French Treasury, the chancellor of the Confrerie de Vignerons de Languedoc, one representative each of the local tourist board and the local Chamber of Commerce. Finally, (but certainly not least, in her estimation) the chairwoman of the Conmaternity of Concerned Mothers of St Chinian — if the vignerons could have a "confraternity" why not, she demanded, a "conmaternity" for concerned mothers?

The large chamber, decorated with portraits of notable or notorious former academics, gradually filled up with current members. Lotti and her "gang of four" waited at the back until the other members were seated, before taking what seats remained.

The president, opening the meeting, sought approval to sign the minutes of the previous meeting, and proceeded without delay to do so. Then, looking down to the end of the conference table, he said, 'Today we have the great pleasure of welcoming five new members to our governing body. They are the new president of the student union, Madame Lotti Beausang, and her four nominees whom, in a moment, I will ask her to introduce.

'But first of all, I wish to congratulate her warmly on her historic victory. She is the first mature, part-time student to hold this important office. She has obviously struck a resounding chord with a large majority of our students. I wish her great success and I know that I speak for all of you when I say that we look forward, Madame Beausang, to your constructive, imaginative, and effective contribution to the great work of this body.' His words provoked loud table-rapping and broad expressions of "Hear, hear".

Lotti stood up, thanked the president for his kind words and good wishes, and introduced her four companions. Then, looking around the room, she delivered a brief speech. 'President Boulanger and fellow governors,' she said, 'it is a great honour for me and my fellow students to be members of this august body. We are well aware that it has to address many matters of crucial importance to the university, matters which extend beyond student issues narrowly conceived. I can assure you that we are eager to work with you constructively, and solely in the interest of the university, in addressing all such issues.

'However, it would be disingenuous of me not to declare at the outset my own determined interest in matters affecting students and, in particular, the issue of the university's conception of itself with reference to its due recognition of its mature, part-time students who constitute the vast majority of its student body. This is neither the day nor the time to enter into detailed discussion of this important issue. However, I do want to put down a marker, even at this early stage, that it is a matter which I will be pursuing diligently at future meetings of this body. In so doing, dear President Boulanger, I believe I will only be seeking to bring to its logical, appropriate, and beneficial outcome, an inspiring and liberating vision of yours. This was your imaginative and enlightened decision to make the University of St Chinian a centre of excellence for the academic and social fulfilment of mature students, who have worked hard all their lives for the well-being of their community and their country. Perhaps in the course of the next couple of years, this governing body will realize the full potentiality of that momentous decision, a potentiality perhaps not initially appreciated or even intended.'

Lotti sat down to variously modulated applause. There was a rapturous reception of her remarks by Professor Didier Ritz and some of his allies. Others, who were comfortable with the *status quo,* recorded a more measured appreciation of her eloquence. The president smilingly acknowledged her somewhat qualified compliment and proceeded with discussion of the various items on the agenda. Henri Campion explained the salient points of the report of the finance committee which he chaired. Claire Macon outlined for discussion the various recommendations of the previous academic council. These were uncontroversial and were being nodded through until Madame Eveline Bombardier, the vigilantly concerned mother, queried the professor of social Anthropology's request for a year's paid leave of absence to renew his research about the relaxed sexual mores of the inhabitants of a distant and beautiful Polynesian island.

'Why can't the learned professor conduct his research here in St Chinian?' she demanded. 'It would be less expensive and surely more useful to us. I could certainly supply him with plenty of concrete information about the disgraceful immoral carry-on that is rife in this supposedly virtuous town.

'And if he wishes,' she continued, getting into her stride, 'to extend his research for comparative purposes, he need only go down the road to Capestang on the Canal du Midi. I have witnessed there, with my own eyes, the blatant promiscuity of German and Dutch libertines who, having sailed down from Amsterdam, high on marijuana from coffee shops there, dock their boats in Capestang to indulge in the most licentious orgies.'

This provocative intervention gave rise to lively and light-hearted discussion. It wavered between expressions of regret by those who had never witnessed the alleged lasciviousness in either St Chinian or Capestang and various suggestions about other locations from which the professor's research might benefit greatly. Eventually his request was approved with much appreciation of the hilarity it had occasioned.

The main item on the report of the buildings committee, also chaired by the secretary bursar when the president was unavailable, was the establishment of a subcommittee to process the recent munificent donation by former student, Jean Martin, to provide additional student residences and a new student centre and theatre. The mayor of St Chinian was included in this subcommittee to facilitate planning applications. Lotti's proposal to include mature student, Rudi Bruggerman, the retired business man and new partner of young Louise Amard, was also accepted. It was appreciated that his high-level commercial experience would be a valuable asset in addressing complex matters such as evaluating tenders.

Other items on the agenda were dealt with expeditiously. These included the proposal that the university confer an honorary degree on Jean Martin, which was enthusiastically agreed.

The final formal item was Lotti's motion that all students, part-time and full-time, have equal voting rights. She declared it was a key item in her election programme which was approved by a majority of students. 'Even apart from that consideration,' she declared, 'it is patently unjust to grant only diminished student rights to someone because of their age or limited academic involvement. Such behaviour can be viewed only as a throwback to the days when women or people of no property were denied a vote.'

Various members murmured support. Even those who broadly favoured the *status quo* thought this point could be conceded, and thereby give an impression of indulgent goodwill and tolerance, without much collateral damage. Only Marc Tavel, dean of the School of Viticulture, Oenology and Agriculture, objected. 'It seems clear to me,' he said, 'that a young full-time person studying for a serious professional university degree is more genuinely what is meant by the term "student" than some old dear who likes to attend a few talks about art or history between her games of bridge.'

'Outrageous,' declared Didier Ritz strategically. 'As somebody who has always admired the pure love of knowledge displayed by mature students, I find Madame Beausang's motion utterly compelling.'

After a few more conciliatory interjections, the president intervened and said, 'I think there is a broad consensus that this motion is accepted. Is that agreed?' Nobody objected further and the motion was recorded as passed by a large majority. Lotti had won the first round in her campaign. It would be greatly appreciated by the 8,000 mature students on whose behalf she had spoken.

As the only remaining item was "any other business", members began gathering up their papers. However, Guy tapped the table and said quietly but distinctly, 'There is one significant matter which I wish to bring to your attention under "any other business". It is a matter which concerns myself, but which you will have to address.

'I have been attending a cardiologist recently, with symptoms of chest pain and breathlessness. He informed me three weeks ago that my latest set of tests revealed serious deterioration and that I must undergo major surgery without delay. He assured me that the procedure is safe and effective and that good health will be restored. However, he advised me that I should consider relinquishing the stresses and demands which are an inevitable accompaniment of the office of president of a thriving university.

'Consequently, I have decided to relinquish the presidency of my beloved University of St Chinian from the beginning of next month when I will enter the clinic for my surgical procedure. It would be wrong of me to continue in the post if I am unable to give it the total and full-time dedication, which it requires and deserves.

'Having discussed the matter with her, I have decided to appoint the academic vice president, Professor Claire Macon, as acting president until you, members of the governing body, following the required procedure, appoint a new president. She will probably call a special meeting of the governing body to initiate that process. You have my very best wishes for a successful outcome to that important task. It has been a great pleasure working with you and I thank you warmly for your advice and help and for your dedication to our beloved university over the years. And now I think we can go next door, as usual after our meeting, for coffee and informal discussion.

'Please don't look so glum.' He smiled. 'I know you will make a splendid choice in the appointment of my successor. And don't think you have heard the last of me. I am already making plans to be back here again, hopefully next year, as a part-time, mature student. I am greatly attracted by many of the programmes, but my wife affirms that she may have to censor my choices.'

This last remark provoked a laugh which relieved the sense of shock and incredulity with which Guy's announcement had gripped the members of the governing body. They were profoundly saddened by it and wondered how the university, in which as professor and president he had played such a formative influence for many years, would fare without him.

The success of Lotti Beausang's programme for the reform of the profile and operation of the University of St Chinian would depend greatly upon the vision and goodwill of the new president, whoever he or she might be.

From the gleam in his eye, one could infer that, in the mind of Professor Didier Ritz at least, a very personal response had already formed about the identity of that person. He was already mentally factoring Lotti's five votes into his equation.

But perhaps Lotti's automatic compliance with his mathematical calculation was somewhat less assured than he presumed? Time would tell. However, one thing was sure; the University of St Chinian had certainly come of age.